FALLEN SNIPER

DAVID HEALEY

INTRACOASTAL

FALLEN SNIPER

By David Healey

Intracoastal Media digital edition published November 2020. Print edition ISBN 978-0-9674162-5-0

Cover image by Streetlight Graphics.

BISAC Subject Headings:

FIC014000 FICTION/Historical

FIC032000 FICTION/War & Military

"The world breaks everyone and afterward many are strong at the broken places."

— ERNEST HEMINGWAY

CHAPTER ONE

CAJE COLE HEARD movement on the trail ahead and signaled for the others behind him to halt. Abruptly, the sounds in front of him stopped and the surrounding woods and rocky terrain seemed to be holding its breath.

Whatever was out there knew that Cole's squad was here. It was too much to hope that it was a deer or wild boar. He hadn't seen much wildlife in Korea, even here in some of the more remote hills.

No, whatever was out there was likely Chinese, riled up, and well-armed.

He held himself very still, straining to hear something more. Mostly, he heard the permanent ringing that had developed in his ears, a consequence of firing a Springfield rifle through two wars.

At any moment, he half-expected gunfire to come ripping at him through the brush. He held his rifle with its scoped sight halfway to his shoulder, poised to fire—and just as ready to hit the deck.

But Cole wasn't one to turn tail and run. He sniffed the air like some prehistoric hunter—the rifle could have been his spear—and studied the brush ahead with his intense gray eyes.

Behind him, the kid asked, "What's the dope, Hillbilly?"

"Ya'll stay alert," Cole replied quietly in his soft Appalachian mountain drawl. "Might be some goons up ahead. I'll take a look. Stay put."

If they did run into trouble, the squad of four men was on its own out here. They had been sent to scout the surrounding countryside for enemy threats.

The army had air cover, but the pilots couldn't always see the enemy moving through the heavy brush. If there was one thing that the Chinese had figured out by now, it was how to slip through the landscape without being spotted by the planes that suddenly appeared on the horizon to deal death and destruction on the enemy troops below with bombs, Napalm, or their .50 caliber machine guns. The fact that the enemy couldn't always be seen from above necessitated the boots on the ground approach of patrols like Cole's.

As the senior veteran here and with his reputation as the unit's crack shot, he was in charge of the squad—although truth be told, Cole preferred not to be in charge of anything. He worked best alone, which suited him well as a sniper.

At least two miles behind them lay the bulk of United States and United Nations forces that had probed deep into the Taebaek Mountains. Before they advanced any further, they had to make sure that they weren't marching right into a trap set by the Chinese.

Cole crept forward, moving silently up the trail. The meandering nature of the narrow path through the brush and woods hinted at the fact that it had been cut by years—maybe centuries—of passing game and Korean peasants moving their small herds of livestock through the hills. The entire mountain range seemed to be crisscrossed by these paths, and the North Koreans who guided the Chinese forces knew the routes well. Cole was moving blindly forward, unsure of where the narrow trail was taking him.

One thing for sure was that whoever—or whatever—was waiting ahead of him must have heard the squad. He sensed that they were keeping still, hoping to hear more. They would also be expecting Cole to move right up the trail toward them, directly into the muzzles of their nasty little Soviet-made machine guns.

Time for a change in plans.

Cole slipped off the trail into the brush. His feet did not make a sound, moving as quietly as if the ground was covered with lush carpet instead of brush and pebbles. Growing up as a hunter had taught him how to move silently as the forest creatures that he had stalked.

Keeping low, he moved parallel to the trail, essentially flanking whoever was on it, waiting to ambush him. The one benefit to the narrow trail was that it forced whoever was on it to remain in single file, or at least, that's what Cole hoped. If the enemy was fanned out through the woods, then the squad was in trouble.

* * *

COLE SNIFFED. Finally, he could smell the enemy. The Chinese had a particular smell, like onions and garlic and maybe old fish worked in for good measure. When Cole explained that he could smell the enemy he didn't mean to be derogatory toward the Chinese, as some might think. The simple fact was that they smelled different from Americans.

According to the South Koreans, American troops also had their own smell, and not necessarily a good one—mostly like hamburgers and cigarettes. Being an American, of course, Cole couldn't detect that odor, but he could sure as hell smell the Chinese.

Through the brush, he saw a figure on the trail, and then more troops behind the leading man. The padded cotton uniforms of Chinese troops were instantly recognizable. The Chinese did not wear helmets, but favored caps or Russian-style *ushankas* in the colder months. Although the men were in single file, they gazed with singular purpose at the empty trail ahead of them, their weapons at the ready. It was clear that they intended to ambush the Americans headed toward them.

But not all of the enemy was facing forward. The Chinese weren't *that* dumb. One or two soldiers kept their weapons pointed into the brush. They couldn't see Cole, but their precaution marked them as experienced combat troops, prepared for an attack from any direction.

What are those goons up to? Cole wondered.

He could have opened fire and picked off the first couple of men, but he didn't like his chances with the bolt-action Springfield, which meant that he had to work the bolt each time he fired a shot. The slow rate of fire was a trade-off. It was a good rifle for a sniper—you couldn't find a more accurate weapon, in Cole's humble opinion—but a bolt action rifle wasn't the best weapon for taking on an enemy patrol in a firefight.

He reckoned his chances might be better if he could get behind these bastards and start picking them off. They wouldn't be expecting that.

Silently, he worked his way up through the brush. The enemy soldiers on the road appeared alert, but none the wiser to Cole's presence.

Up ahead, the brush seemed to open up, which was typical of this mountain landscape. It was a patchwork quilt of bounders, ravines, brushy swaths, and barren stretches similar to what the mountain people called *scald* land back home—too rocky for anything to grow except tufts of heather and lichen.

Cole was so intent on keeping an eye on the enemy troops who occupied the trail that he nearly made a fatal mistake. He emerged from the trees and froze. In the opening, he saw dozens of enemy soldiers. Some sat on the ground, drinking from canteens that they had picked up off various battlefields or smoking captured cigarettes. It was clear that the troops on the path were an advance party, probing ahead of this larger force.

Cole had run smack dab into a small army of Chinese.

Although the troops were not on high alert, he had emerged practically into their midst like a barn cat among the mice. The nearest soldier paused with a cigarette halfway to his mouth. The expression of surprise on his face likely mirrored Cole's own.

What have I got myself into? Cole wondered.

Somebody shouted. Soldiers dropped their canteens and cigarettes, reaching for their weapons, figuring that they were under attack.

Cole didn't disappoint them. He raised his rifle and shot the first soldier he saw who had leveled a submachine gun in Cole's direction. He ran the bolt, fired again.

Cole quickly lost the element of surprise. Bullets snicked into the brush at his back. He had gone and kicked the hornet's nest this time.

That's when he heard the roar approaching, like thunder that rolled on and on. What the hell was that? He was used to the sound of approaching Corsairs, but this was something louder, and faster. Just as the noise reached a shrieking crescendo, a shadow swept overhead and machine-gun fire blazed across the clearing, scattering the enemy troops. *Whoosh.* The plane swept over the clearing and was gone. Cole realized that he was seeing a jet in action. It was the first of these new, fast planes that he had seen up close.

But there was no time to stop and watch the action. Cole was forgotten in the frenzy caused by the plane, and he took the opportunity to plunge back into the woods. That plane had just saved his bacon. Although he was back into the cover of the thicket, he still had to run the gauntlet of the Chinese soldiers on the path to his left. Lucky for Cole, the roar of the plane masked the sound he made crashing through the brush.

Normally, Cole could move quietly, but stealth required time that he didn't have. He had to get back to his squad and warn them—hell, he had to get back to the whole damn American line with news that there was most of a Chinese army on their doorstep.

He dashed through the woods, grateful that the plane had swept back in for another go at the Chinese troops. Cole paused just long enough to pick off one of the soldiers who was watching the woods beside the trail—dead men tell no tales—then ran out on the other side of the thicket, where Tommy Wilson was staring at him, wide-eyed. Better-known as the kid, the two of them had been serving together in Korea since coming ashore at Pusan.

"We've got to vamoose, boys!" Cole shouted. "There's a whole mess of goons on the other side of those trees."

They didn't need to be told twice, not with the sound of firing coming from the other side of the thicket. The Chinese troops back there were firing at the plane that had come back to pester them for a third strafing run. The squad turned and hot-footed it out of there.

Cole lagged behind, covering them. Sure enough, the Chinese soldiers who had been on the path came running ahead. Cole picked off the first man, worked the bolt, then shot another. But the third man had a submachine gun, which he opened up with. Bullets churned the branches as the first burst went high. The Chinese soldier wouldn't miss again.

From just behind Cole came two quick rifle shots. The Chinese soldier with the submachine gun went down.

Cole glanced up to see the kid lowering his M-1. "Kid, what are you still doing here?"

"You don't have to fight the whole Chinese army yourself, you know."

"I don't plan on it, kid."

"You could've fooled me."

The dense brush on either side of the trail created a bottleneck, forcing the enemy to advance in single file. The kid fired a couple more shots at the path, forcing the oncoming Chinese to fall back.

They heard more roaring overhead. Cole looked up and was surprised to see several planes in the sky. Not all of the aircraft were American. There had been rumors that the enemy also had jet fighters, thanks to the Russians. He realized that they were seeing these enemy jet fighters for the first time.

As the aircraft soared higher, he spotted the flashes that indicated the planes were firing at one another. A rocket streaked across the sky and one of the fast-moving planes erupted in flames.

"Holy moly," the kid said, gazing up in wonder. It was an incredible spectacle, like watching the gods battle in the heavens. One thing for sure was that they weren't going to get any more help from the pilot, who now had problems of his own, with several enemy fighters on his tail. Cole wished him luck.

Even the Chinese on the trail had stopped firing to take in the aerial dogfight above. Cole thought it was the perfect chance to make a run for it.

"Let's go, kid," Cole said. "That pilot just saved my bacon again."

He and the kid ran until they had caught up with the others, who were waiting just ahead, crouched in a bend in the trail. Like everyone else, their eyes were on the dogfight happening above. One by one, planes burst into flame or streamed smoke as they cartwheeled from the sky and disappeared from sight. At least one of the planes shot down appeared to be American. To their amazement, it had become clear that there was just one American plane and several enemy jets. The American pilot looped and rolled, trying to shake off multiple opponents.

"That pilot is chewing them up," the kid said.

"He's a right good pilot, that's for damn sure, but he's outnumbered."

The pilot's luck didn't last. There was a plane behind him, and one coming up on his belly. Silver ribbons of sunlight flashed off his wings as he maneuvered, trying to shake off the enemy.

"C'mon, c'mon, watch out," the kid muttered, urging the pilot on.

Finally, a rocket etched a trail across the sky, faster than the U.S. plane could maneuver. The rocket caught a piece of the tail and exploded. It wasn't a direct hit, but it was enough for the jet to go into a death spiral, shedding a trail of black smoke tinged with flame. One of the enemy planes had finally clipped the eagle's wings.

"That poor bastard is done for," Cole muttered.

They watched the U.S. jet going down, saddened by the spectacle. But then, a parachute bloomed in the sky. The American pilot had managed to eject. The enemy jets roared past, letting him go rather than shooting him down. There seemed to be some element of decency that remained among pilots, enemies or not.

The white parachute drifted toward the north, in the direction from which the Chinese force had been marching. The kid seemed to read Cole's mind.

"He's going to land right in the middle of Indian Country," the kid said.

"Yeah," Cole agreed. He shook his head. "There's nothing but hills and enemy troops were that pilot was heading."

One of the other soldiers in the squad spoke up. "He's not our problem. Right now, we've got problems of our own. Those Chinese are right on our tail."

Cole thought about that. "All right, you guys go on back to warn the regiment."

"What about you?"

"I'm gonna see if I can find that pilot."

"What do you care? If you ask me, he's a goner."

"He's one of ours. That makes him our problem. The way I figure it, we owe him one. Like I said before, you guys vamoose."

Nobody moved.

"What are you waiting for? Get a move on, boys. Somebody had got to warn headquarters about the Chinese head their way."

The kid shook his head. "You still don't get it, do you, Hillbilly? You're forgetting that the rest of us are even here. We're not letting you do this alone."

"All right, kid, have it your way. You come with me. The rest of you go on back. The kid and I will have a better chance if we do this on our own. That's an order."

"All right," said Dowling, a squad veteran who looked clearly relieved that he would be heading in the opposite direction from the enemy. He and the other soldiers headed up the trail toward the relative safety of the main American line two miles away. With luck, they would arrive in just enough time to provide a warning about the approaching enemy force.

"Let's get a move on," Cole said to the kid. "The Chinese will be after that pilot, too, sure as flies on horse apples."

"Everyone for miles around saw that dogfight," the kid agreed.

"If we're lucky, we'll find this pilot before dark and skedaddle back to our lines. I don't want to be out here at night, not with the hills crawling with goons and God knows what else."

"But we can't use the trail. Not with all the enemy back there."

"Who said anything about a trail?" Cole produced a compass and took a bearing on the direction where they had last glimpsed the parachute descending. He put the compass in his pocket and nodded toward the nearest hill. "This way," he said.

In front of them, they heard shouts. The Chinese were approaching on the path. Cole fired off a couple of shots to give them something to think about and buy the rest of the squad some time to retreat. When the return fire got too hot, Cole slipped into the thicket with the kid right behind him, and they vanished into the underbrush.

CHAPTER TWO

HIGH ABOVE THE KOREAN LANDSCAPE, U.S. Navy pilot Lieutenant Commander Jake Miller had been guiding his Grumman Panther back toward their aircraft carrier in the Sea of Japan when they spotted the enemy bogeys. What had started as a milk run escorting a bomber squadron instantly turned into a deadly fight for survival in the mountain air.

He and his wingman, Lieutenant Jim Walsh, better known as "Guzzle" because of his propensity for sucking down beer bottles when off duty at the officer's club, had just finished babysitting the bombers on a mission deep into North Korea.

That was as far as they were allowed to strike. The limits imposed upon them were an endless source of frustration. God forbid that they should fly into China and cut off the head of the snake, because that was where all the enemy supplies originated.

Then again, Miller supposed that nobody wanted to start World War III. Hadn't Albert Einstein, the smartest man alive, said that he didn't know what weapons World War III would be fought with—but he knew that the next war after that would be fought with sticks and stones. President Harry S. Truman had tried to call the atomic bomb just another artillery weapon, but ol' "Give 'Em Hell Harry" couldn't have been more wrong about that. Even a Navy pilot knew that the stakes had changed.

With their bombing mission completed, the bombers had headed for their base while the fighter escort flown by Miller and Guzzle Walsh trailed behind before returning to their aircraft carrier. Miller glanced over at his wingman and said through the radio, "That was a cakewalk if I've ever seen one."

"Guess I owe you a beer," Guzzle replied.

Miller laughed. He had bet Guzzle the first round that they wouldn't so much as see another enemy aircraft on today's mission. There had been rumors and warnings about the Chinese getting more of their own jets into the fight, but so far, those had been rare as unicorns. "Glad I didn't have to remind you that you now owed me a beer. You ought to know better than to have taken that bet, anyhow."

"Yeah, but I thought it would change our luck."

"All we can do is hope for the best, my friend."

So far, in all their time in Korea, they had yet to tangle with any enemy fighters. Sure, there had been plenty of missions like this one, or strafing and bombing runs against enemy positions. They had been met with only highly ineffective anti-aircraft fire.

It was true that there were troops on the ground who might not have minded getting through the whole war without a glimpse of the enemy, but he and Guzzle were fighter pilots. They itched to do what they had been trained to do, which was to get into a dogfight with enemy planes. Soon enough, they might be rotating back home without ever mixing it up with the enemy. There would be little chance of air combat once they returned to the United States.

Off his shoulder, Guzzle's Panther glided along effortlessly as if on a cushion of air. Below, they saw the endless landscape of hills and mountains that comprised much of the Korean peninsula. It almost made him wonder why anyone was fighting over this place.

From the air, Miller had seen the Rocky Mountains and the Appalachians back home. The Taebaek Mountain range was somewhere in between, with peaks not as high and sharp as the Rockies, but not at all like gentle Appalachian peaks and valleys.

The Panther was a carrier-based aircraft that in some ways resembled a design out of a Buck Rogers comic book from the 1930s, about as different from a WWII plane as one could imagine. From its narrow wings with fuel pods on the tips to its sleek jet engine, Miller thought that the plane looked very futuristic. He was proud to fly it. Aircraft had certainly come a long way from the days of fighting the Imperial Japanese Navy Air Service in the Pacific.

Looks, however, could be deceiving. There were rumors that a much uglier plane being flown by the Communists was a match for the Panther, and then some. Miller had yet to see a MiG in person, but he had seen pictures as part of his aircraft identification briefings. The MiG looked less like something flown by Buck Rogers and more like a Buster Brown shoebox with swept wings. He would have been more inclined to bet that first beer on the Panther just based on looks, so go figure. But what did he know about aircraft design? He just flew them.

Guzzle's excited voice suddenly exploded over the headset. "Bogeys! I got bogeys eleven o'clock high!"

Instantly, Miller swiveled his head up and searched the sky. He was astonished to see a formation of planes at a much higher elevation. Surely, those planes had seen them. Miller felt foolish and a sudden frisson of fear. He felt like he'd been caught napping. If those planes had attacked, he and Guzzle would have been caught unawares.

Which gave him a thought. Why hadn't those planes pressed the advantage? They didn't seem to be looking for a fight.

"Who are those guys?" he wondered

"They sure as hell ain't Panthers or Corsairs," Guzzle replied in his Texas drawl. "Look at the wings. Those have got to be MiGs. I see one, two, three—holy moly, there's seven of 'em up there."

Intent on the planes now, Miller saw that Guzzle was absolutely right about these being MiGs. Their contrails dragged behind them like long fingers stretched across the sky. One thing for sure was that they had chosen to ignore the two Panthers below without engaging them. These planes were intent on going somewhere in a hurry. But where?

"I don't see any Chinese insignia," Guzzle said.

Miller looked more closely. "That's because those are Soviet planes."

"What are they doing over North Korea?" Guzzle asked.

It was a good question. He supposed that the planes must have been on their way to Vladivostok, where the Soviets had a base on the North Korean border. They seemed to be taking a shortcut through Korean airspace.

He and Guzzle flew along without changing course or reacting in any way. Miller sympathized with how ol' Brer Rabbit must feel, hoping that Brer Fox didn't spot him.

The difference was that this rabbit had teeth.

He heard Guzzle's voice again, the tone of his wingman's nervous excitement crackling through the airwaves. It was as if the two of them were deer hunting and had just spotted a big buck. "What do you think?"

"They're in our airspace. Engage and destroy," Miller said, all doubt disappearing as he decided to engage these Soviet fighters. He felt the excitement of the moment, tempered by the cold precision of his training.

"Aye, aye, Cap'n," Guzzle replied. With a decision made, he now sounded more certain of himself.

Miller worked the stick, bringing the Panther in a steep climb, directly toward the planes overhead.

The MiGs responded almost instantly by breaking into two groups, indicating that they had been well aware of the aircraft below and had initially chosen to ignore them. Miller's response had forced their hand.

Four planes were in the second group. They climbed higher and faster than Miller would have thought possible, directly toward the sun. It seemed apparent that the quartet was intent on continuing the journey to Vladivostok.

However, the trio of remaining MiGs had other plans. The MiGs went into a dive and began to circle around the two Panthers.

"They're trying to get behind us!" Guzzle shouted.

"Circle back, circle back!"

Miller turned his own aircraft sharply toward the attacking MiGs. With a shock, he saw their guns blazing as bright pinpricks along the wings. They were firing at him. He responded by unleashed a burst from his 20 mm guns.

The two groups swept through one another, no harm done. Miller directed his Panther into a hard left, gritting his teeth at the tremendous G forces. The bold maneuver caught one of the MiGs unawares and as it passed through his gunsights, he let loose with the Panther's 37 mm cannon. Bright flashes punched holes in the sky as the rounds struck the MiG dead center. Without warning, the enemy fighter erupted into a fireball.

He just had time to fire at another MiG, which began to trail smoke. He punched it again with the cannon and now the MiG broke apart with a shotgun burst of debris that the Panther had no choice but to fly right through. Miller caught a glimpse of the tumbling wings and a chunk of burning fuselage just a few feet from his fragile canopy. He breathed again when he saw open sky ahead.

Miller gave a cowboy whoop of satisfaction. He had just shot down two enemy planes.

"Guzzle, watch my tail." No response. "Guzzle, come in."

Anxiously, Miller swiveled his head in all directions, looking for that third MiG. Unless Guzzle had shot it down, the son of a bitch was still up here somewhere, but Miller didn't see it. He also didn't see his wingman.

He moved his eyes lower.

Off to his four o'clock he saw a plane on fire, plunging toward the earth.

It wasn't a MiG. There wasn't any parachute.

"Oh no, no, no!"

Miller tracked the tumbling, burning Panther, trailing smoke and debris as it fell. Before it could hit the earth, the plane disappeared with a final pop like a bottle rocket exploding.

Guzzle Walsh was gone.

But where the hell was that last MiG?

He got his answer when he spotted the plane rushing at him from below. Having finished off his wingman, the MiG was coming for him.

Not if he could help it.

Miller felt enraged and bent on revenge, but he tamped down those emotions, knowing that they wouldn't do him any good if he hoped not just to survive, but to win. He had to fight with his head.

He pulled hard on the controls, forcing the Panther into a hard left and rolling at the same time. It was a maneuver that he had practiced countless times, and all that practice paid off now as the plane responded by dropping like a stone, upside down.

Taken by surprise just as it was prepared to pounce, the MiG found itself in Miller's gunsights as he opened up with all three cannons, raining hellfire upon the enemy aircraft. The MiG responded by bursting into flame. Miller whooped.

"That's for Guzzle, you son of a bitch."

His sense of victory was short-lived. Something glinting high above caught his eye. There wasn't supposed to be anything up there. He had shot down all three enemy planes, right?

His heart hammering in his chest, he realized that the remaining four MiGs had not flown away. They had simply been biding their time. They came at him down, directly out of the sun.

His Panther didn't have a chance as cannon fire flayed the air. All at once, his aircraft was suddenly full of holes. On his instrument panel, gauges spun like roulette wheels. An alarm beeped insistently. Yeah, what do you want me to do about it?

The controls that had been so light to the touch a moment ago, almost an extension of himself, now felt as heavy as if he was trying to fly a barn through the sky.

Smoke appeared. Then fire. There wasn't any hope of getting this baby back to the carrier in one piece.

The Panther was going down. Incredulously, Miller realized that he had just been shot down.

He felt a strange sense of calm. If the aircraft exploded or if the MiGs returned and hit him with another burst of fire, he'd be dead instantly. But there was a chance, just a chance, that he might get out of this alive. Survival would take every ounce of skill that he possessed.

His training took over once again. He likely had just a few seconds to act. He reached for the eject switch.

Tiny explosive charges sent the canopy hurtling away, even as flames swept over him. An instant later, he felt himself ejected from the burning aircraft. His parachute blossomed above.

The enemy fighters swept past, one of them having the audacity to waggle its wings at him. But they didn't open fire. The MiGs raced away, bound for their destination, but with three fewer aircraft.

Miller watched his burning aircraft disintegrate. He felt relieved that he wasn't on it. He felt a strange sense of calm, even dangling beneath a parachute.

He looked below, seeing that the hills were coming up fast. Up in the plane, he had felt so disengaged from them, like he was looking down at a map or diorama. Now, individual trees began to take shape. As the Navy sailors liked to say, this shit was about to get real.

Hitting those trees was going to hurt. Those branches promised to pummel his body like a bitter old lady beating a rug. Desperately, he looked around for something resembling a clearing. But all he saw was trees.

Finally, he glimpsed what looked like a stone wall and a clearing and steered the chute in that direction. This parachute sure as hell didn't respond like a fighter jet. He tugged again at the stays, guiding out into the open.

He hit hard, rolling as he had been trained to do, but he still felt his ankle twist. No time to think about that now. He kept rolling.

When he came to a stop, he sat up. Thankfully, he had come down in a clearing—more like a gap in the trees, really—next to a tall stone wall that was covered in vines and vegetation. The damn thing looked ancient. If he'd smacked into that, he would have ended up with worse than a twisted ankle.

Miller gathered up his chute and shoved it out of sight, under some bushes.

He looked around, trying to figure out where he was. He knew that they had been flying over North Korea, just north of the 38th Parallel. It stood to reason that he had come down in enemy territory.

One thing for sure—he had a long walk ahead of him.

Miller tensed. He thought that he had seen something move among the trees at the edge of the clearing. His hand drifted toward the service weapon at his belt, but he didn't unbuckle the holster yet.

Worst case, it was a Chinese patrol. No point trying to shoot it out with enemy troops.

Best case, he had startled some kind of forest animal.

He saw the movement again.

Then several figures materialized from the brush. They wore old, mismatched clothes, like maybe they were farmers. But what really got Miller's attention was that one of the men was holding a rifle.

He'd never get to his pistol in time.

Slowly, Miller raised his hands into the air.

CHAPTER THREE

Don Hardy had never ridden in a helicopter before. The so-called "choppers" were usually just for flying the brass to wherever they needed to be, and they had to be highly polished brass, at that.

He tried not to think too much about the fact that he dangled from beneath a rapidly rotating blade—a giant eggbeater in the sky. With its bubble-like windshield, the front of the chopper resembled nothing so much as the bug-eyed face of a blue-bottle fly.

Ugly and ungainly, the chopper wasn't at all like the sleek U.S. fighters that streaked across the sky. The chopper also made a nice, fat, slow target for anyone on the ground.

Hardy settled himself into the tight space behind the pilot's and co-pilot's seats. It was more like a bench or a rumble seat than anything designed for transporting passengers in anything resembling comfort. The fact that Hardy was a big, strapping farm boy from Indiana made squeezing into the cramped space even harder.

The inside of the helicopter smelled like oil and more ominously, like an old electrical fire.

"You might want to sit on your helmet," the co-pilot had said back when they were still on the ground.

"My helmet?"

"Wouldn't want you to get shot in the ass. They don't give Purple Hearts for that."

He had thought that the co-pilot was ribbing him, but maybe not. Judging by the occasional muzzle flashes below, it was a rare enemy soldier who could resist taking a potshot at a chopper.

Hardy shook his head, thought about it, then removed his helmet and sat on it. Not exactly comfortable, but it was reassuring. Then again, if bullets started hitting this flimsy chopper, his helmet wasn't going to save him no matter where he wore it.

The co-pilot glanced back, gave him a thumbs up. Hardy flashed him a grin. The truth was, he found it pretty exciting to be riding in the helicopter. It sure as heck beat a bumpy Jeep ride to the front lines.

The thrill of the helicopter ride almost made up for the fact that he was on a PR mission.

Hardy was a reporter for the *Stars and Stripes*, the newspaper that covered all the news for the military forces and that was read mostly by servicemen. His dispatches from the Battle of Triangle Hill had earned him the grudging acceptance of the hard-bitten officers who served as the newspaper's editors. The editors had crossed out just about every adjective and adverb in his news stories, which had pained him. With a newly minted degree in English, he liked to work in a good literary allusion or a descriptive flourish wherever he could. The military editors did not share his enthusiasm for energetic prose.

"Let me explain something, Hornaday," the editor had begun.

"That's Hardy, sir."

"If you say so." The editor paused to gulp foul, burnt coffee, then inhaled deeply on a cigarette. He pointed at Hardy with a finger that was alternately stained black with ink and yellow with nicotine.

Despite all appearances and the stale fug that hung about his desk, the editor knew his craft. "You are not writing a novel. You are writing journalism. The five W questions. Do you know what those are?"

Hardy felt like a schoolboy put on the spot. He stammered, "Who, what, when, where, and why?"

"Are you asking me or telling me?" the editor wondered, sounding exasperated.

"Sorry, sir."

The editor waved his stained hand like Hardy was a fly annoying him. "Listen. You have thirty-five words to each column inch, and there are only so many inches of space. Stick with the who, what, when, where, why, and how. If you find yourself with the urge to use an adjective, go take a cold shower. Got it?"

"Yes, sir."

The editor had turned back to his typewriter, signaling that he had dismissed Hardy.

There was no saluting in the offices of *Stars and Stripes*, but the military pecking order was very much in place. The editor commanded his copy desk with all the confidence of an admiral on the bridge of a battleship.

In the end, Hardy wasn't sure if it was punishment or a reward of sorts that he had been sent to what was being called Outpost Kelly to write about the Puerto Rican troops helping to hold the section of the Main Line of Resistance known as the Jamestown Line against heavy Chinese incursions. He did know that if the chopper went down, he wouldn't be all that missed.

Before climbing aboard the chopper, Hardy had done his homework. His assignment to write about the Puerto Rican troops coincided with the fact that Puerto Rico had adopted a new Constitution as the Commonwealth of Puerto Rico, which some said brought the U.S. territory one step closer to statehood. The designation as a commonwealth also gave the island new clout and standing.

After all, it had been a territory since 1898 in the wake of the Spanish-American War. That had been the last gasp of the once-great Spanish empire before ceding its former colonies to the United States. The island was geographically about the size of the state of Rhode Island with double the population.

Hardy's assignment was to write about the 65th Infantry Regiment, made up mostly of volunteers from Puerto Rico. These troops fell into the strange situation of being neither fish nor fowl, although they were officially part of the United States military. As such, they had a great deal to prove on behalf of their island. The soldiers wanted to show the so-called "Continentals" that they were just as good as them. Also,

there was always the question of statehood. If the troops proved themselves worthy, the United States Congress might see its way to grant
statehood. The matter had been championed previously by Senator
Millard Tydings, but had been voted down.

The unit had also taken part in WWII, but had not seen much
fighting other than a few dust-ups with fragments of the Wehrmacht
in Italy. Korea was the first time that the unit had seen real combat.

Hardy's job was to write about it and show everyone what the
Puerto Rican troops were all about, doing their part to save the USA
from Communism.

Hardy's focus would be on the troops from Puerto Rico, but there
were other units out here, of course, making a stand against the
Chinese. He had written about one of these units making an attack on
a place called Sniper Ridge as part of the sprawling Battle of Triangle
Hill. If he ran into Lieutenant Ballard, he figured the officer owed him
a drink for making him and his platoon look good in print. Hardy's
photograph of the unit's sniper had gotten a lot of attention.

Below, he spotted more muzzle flashes, and the helicopter banked
sharply away. He had no idea whether or not rifle fire from the hills
could down the chopper, but the pilot evidently wasn't taking any
chances.

"Hold on," he heard the co-pilot said, the voice coming through the
headset. "We're going to change course. Those Chinese down there are
having a turkey shoot, and we're the turkey."

"Glad I took your advice about the helmet," Hardy replied.

"Last thing you want is a bullet up the tailpipe."

Hardy doubted that a helmet would stop a bullet, but it must be
some kind of insurance. Better than nothing.

Rumor had it that the Chinese were especially riled up because the
president of South Korea, Syngman Rhee, had announced that he
would not forcibly repatriate the 24,000 POWs that had been
captured during the war. Most of the Chinese and North Koreans had
made it known that they preferred to stay in South Korea, rather than
return to China or North Korea.

For the enemy, it was not exactly good public relations for the
Communist Party that their own troops wanted no part of returning to

the embrace of Chairman Mao. Maybe they just feared the conse-quences of having been captured rather than fighting to the death. Some of the poor POW bastards from the Soviet Union who had ended up in US hands during the last war had hanged themselves rather than be forcibly repatriated to Uncle Joe Stalin—who had them shot as traitors for not dying in battle.

Thinking about all of that, Hardy considered that he was very fortunate to have been born in the United States. It might not be perfect, but it was light-years beyond the dictatorships that its troops were fighting against.

The co-pilot's voice interrupted his thoughts, "There it is."

Hardy looked through the bug-eyed windshield. At first, all that he could see were more and more hills that seemed to stretch endlessly toward the Chinese border. All in all, the Korean landscape resembled a vast, rumpled bedsheet. And yet, wherever there was an open space, the industrious Koreans had planted crops. He could see these patches of cultivation among the wildness of the hills and mountains.

"Doesn't look like much," Hardy said.

"Somebody thinks it's worth fighting over," the co-pilot said.

"I don't see our position."

The co-pilot pointed. "Down there. That's Hill 199 where you can see our guys dug in. That's Outpost Kelly beyond the line."

Hardy squinted and on a hilltop was finally able to pick out a few foxholes and what looked like a command dugout. A handful of tanks appeared to be mired in the mud. "Doesn't look like much," he said.

"Blink and you'd miss it," the co-pilot agreed. "Good thing we didn't blink, huh? Nothing beyond here but mountains and Chinese."

From below, by way of greeting, they saw a few muzzle flashes and even some green tracer fire that indicated Chinese machine guns in the surrounding hills. If Hardy hadn't known better, he would have sworn that the tiny outpost was virtually surrounded by enemy troops. Nobody had said anything about the soldiers here taking on the whole damn Chinese army. As far as he knew, he was just supposed to be writing a fluff piece about the Puerto Rican troops.

"Still sitting on your helmet?" the co-pilot asked. "I would if I were you."

Still perched on his helmet, Hardy tucked himself into as small of a ball as possible, which wasn't easy, given his gangly frame. He held his breath, watching as the tracers stabbed skyward. At any moment, he expected the chopper to be riddled with bullets.

If he flew back on this thing, maybe he'd bring along something more useful, like the lid of a garbage can or better yet, some armor plating.

The chopper settled lower, the low hills themselves helping to screen the ungainly machine from incoming fire. There was just enough of an open, flat area at the base of the hill occupied by American troops for the helicopter to land.

"All right, let's move it," said the pilot, speaking for the first time. "This is as close as we can fly you. We're sitting ducks out here. You'll have to catch a ride the rest of the way."

The co-pilot got out, enabling Hardy to crawl between the two seats, then across the co-pilot's empty seat and out the door. If the chopper had crash-landed, he wondered how the hell he ever would have gotten out.

He dragged his pack behind him, careful because it contained his camera. He held his helmet in his other hand. It was only then that he realized that he had forgotten to bring along a weapon. From the looks of things, he might be needing it.

The co-pilot gave him a hand as he crawled awkwardly from the chopper. "You'll be back in two days, right?" Hardy asked.

"Sorry, Mac, all you've got is a one-way ticket unless someone tells us different. Besides, the weather forecast says there's a lot of rain coming. These birds don't like to get wet."

Hardy knew there was no point in arguing. He'd have to find a Jeep to take him back. Then again, he hadn't seen any Jeeps on the ground as they flew in.

"Thank you for flying the U.S. Army," the co-pilot said. "Now get the hell out of the way."

Hardy didn't need to be told twice. He ran from the chopper, keeping low as the blades whirred overhead.

Behind him, the chopper lifted back into the air and raced away. Hardy fought the urge to watch it out of sight. Even above the sound of the receding helicopter, he could hear the Chinese taking potshots at the unwieldy aircraft.

He suddenly found himself alone. Not another soldier in sight. Nervously, he glanced around at the rocks and scrub trees, half-expecting to see Chinese soldiers emerge. Never mind that he was technically behind the front line. What would he do if he suddenly saw the enemy? He didn't even have a weapon.

Fortunately, he didn't have to wait long for a ride. The driver of a supply truck saw him standing by the side of the road and came to a stop.

"Need a ride, Mac? Hop in. It's either me or the Chinese."

"That would be great," Hardy said, and climbed aboard the cab. He was a little surprised to find the driver alone in the cab.

"Don't you have anyone with you?"

"Sure, there's half a dozen South Koreans with me to load and unload the truck, but I make them ride in back. I don't want those slant-eyed bastards up here with me."

"OK," Hardy said, wondering, not for the first time, why so many of the American troops had nothing but disdain for the Koreans. He had found the people and the culture fascinating.

"What are you doing out here, anyhow?" the driver asked. "This isn't the best place to hitchhike."

"Believe it or not, I just got dropped off by helicopter."

"That was you? Huh. I saw that chopper. I thought only the brass and the wounded got to fly in choppers."

"I guess I was an exception."

"Lucky you," the driver said. He looked Hardy up and down. "You got a rifle?"

"No. I'm a reporter for *Stars and Stripes*. A rifle was too much to lug along, but I brought my camera instead."

The driver reached under the seat and took out an old-fashioned revolver, like something straight out of the Old West. He set it on the seat between them. "It's not regulation, but I brought it from home. I figure if it was good enough for Wyatt Earp, it's good enough for me. You see any Chinese, you start shooting."

"What are you doing to do?"

"If we see any Chinese, I'll be the one driving like hell in the opposite direction."

The driver went on to talk about the intricacies of hauling supplies and the difficulty of working with lazy Koreans. Hardy's mind wandered. He went back to observing the scenery.

They approached a large sign, nearly the size of a billboard. DANGER! YOU ARE UNDER ENEMY OBSERVATION FOR THE NEXT 500 YARDS. DANGER!

Beyond the sign, the road was overhung with camouflage netting. Hardy glimpsed the sky through it. Could the enemy see them?

"Should we be worried?" Hardy asked.

"What, that sign? You never know. Sometimes the Chinese shoot at us and sometimes they don't."

The driver shifted gears and the truck sped up, the motor straining as they began to climb a grade. Hardy held his breath, but no enemy shells came raining down on them.

Several tense minutes later, they had passed through the tunnel of netting and finally reached the top of the hill.

"Must have been your lucky day," the driver said, pulling to a stop.

Hardy wasn't so sure about that. He looked around at the outpost and wasn't encouraged by what he saw. The command dugout was more like a cave scooped from the side of the hill, fortified with a few logs that had been dragged into place to create a low wall at the entrance. In most encampments, there was at least some concertina wire strung around the perimeter to keep our Chinese infiltrators, but here there was no such barrier. A couple of tanks were the only reassuring sight.

He thanked the driver and climbed down from the truck.

Hardy was still looking around, trying to get his bearings, when a patrol materialized from the surrounding brush. He recognized the lieutenant leading the unit right away. The officer he'd been talking to walked away to the dugout.

"Lieutenant Ballard?" Hardy asked. "Sir?"

The lieutenant scowled, but then recognized the reporter. His face lit up.

"You're the *Stars and Stripes* reporter. Hardy, right? What are you doing out here?"

"I'm here to write a story about the troops from Puerto Rico, sir. I suppose you might say that it's an article to make them look good."

Ballard's smile faded. "Good luck with that."

"Sir?"

"Never mind. You'll see for yourself soon enough."

"I was hoping they would have someone here to meet me."

"There's a lot going on here, Hardy. But I'm glad to see you, even if nobody else has rolled out the welcome mat. You did a damn fine job writing about what happened at Triangle Hill."

"Thank you, sir. Is your sniper still here? The one I took a picture of?"

"Cole?" The lieutenant shook his head. "He's off on a wild goose chase, trying to find a pilot who bailed out."

Hardy perked up. "That would be a good story, sir."

"Would it? Maybe, if he finds him. Cole was on patrol with his squad when he saw the plane go down. Chances are that the pilot is already dead or captured, but you never know. Poor bastard. I sure as hell wouldn't want to parachute into countryside crawling with Chinese."

"If anyone can find that pilot, sir, I suppose it's Cole."

"You might be right about that. But I've got to tell you that not only did Cole send back word about the pilot, but also sent back news that the whole damn Chinese army is headed this way. You picked one hell of a time to visit Outpost Kelly."

"I saw the Chinese from the helicopter, sir. Lots of them. They were shooting at us."

"You should have turned around and gotten back on that helicopter," Ballard said. "You might have one hell of a story to write depending on what happens over the next few days, but I'm not so sure that it's going to have a happy ending."

CHAPTER FOUR

CROUCHED behind a large rock on the summit of a nearby hill, Major Wu scanned the American position for a target. He was far enough that, through his binoculars, the enemy soldiers appeared insect-like. Somewhat larger than ants ... more like locusts, perhaps? He thought that any insect analogy was fitting when it came to the enemy.

He pressed the binoculars tightly to his eyes and searched the lines for any soldier foolish enough to show himself. He knew from experience that it was only a matter of time before someone made himself a target. The Americans couldn't stay hidden forever.

Beside him was a soldier with a rifle equipped with a telescopic sight. This was Deng, Wu's new sniper and designated Hero of the People.

"Do you see that tank down there, off to the right?" Wu asked Deng, who acknowledged his superior with a grunt. Wiry but strong, he was a man of few words and simple tastes, which were qualities that Wu admired. So far, Deng did exactly what Wu told him to do without argument, which was a good arrangement.

The distinction even extended to their uniforms. Deng wore a drab, padded jacket and trousers that looked as if they had been sewn from a quilt, along with the *ushanka*-style hat typically worn by

Chinese troops. No Chinese soldiers possessed helmets. Wu wore a crisp officer's uniform with bright red hash marks and stars at his collar. He supposed that he stood out to any enemy snipers, much like a colorful bird in the surrounding brush, but Wu was too proud to think of not displaying his officer's rank.

"Keep your eyes on that tank," Wu said. "The hatch is open. Soon enough, you will see a head pop through that hatch. That will be your target. You should have no trouble reaching the target from here."

"Yes, sir," Deng said, his eye never wavering from the rifle scope. "Will it be an imperialist officer?"

"Of course," Wu said. "Don't you know by now that everyone you shoot is an officer?"

Wu wrote all of the reports and made a point of identifying most of Deng's targets as officers. It sounded better in the official reports.

It was unusual for someone of Wu's rank to be here in the field, directing one man. Most political officers would have been content to remain in camp until it was time for an attack. At that point, they would have taken up their position in the rear, pistols or submachine guns in hand, to encourage the heroes of the Chinese army by shooting anyone who dared to retreat.

Wu had no compunctions about shooting the cowards in the ranks, but he found that publicizing the achievements of outstanding snipers, artillery gunners, or other seemingly ordinary soldiers was a more constructive method of inspiring the troops. Also, with his eye always on personal advancement, Wu had learned that his ability to tell these stories was much admired by those in power. No one questioned the accuracy or truth of his stories, so long as they were motivational. As a result, Wu had created a special place for himself in the command structure of the People's Liberation Army.

Through the binoculars, he watched the tank. Wu thought of how he had once seen a fox waiting beside a gopher hole, patiently biding his time until the gopher raised its head. He and Deng were like that fox now, waiting behind this rock in the distance.

"Isn't there another target?" Deng asked, after several minutes had gone by.

"Shoot the tank officer. We must be patient," Wu said. Normally, it was Wu who felt that every minute not spent shooting at the enemy was a minute wasted.

Again, Deng answered with a grunt, but he obeyed the order.

Wu became aware of a strange sound, like thudding in the air. As he listened, the noise grew louder. He recognized the sound, but was surprised to hear it in this desolate place at the edge of the UN-held territory.

Deng took his eye away from the scope and asked, "What is that?"

"It is one of the American helicopters. Perhaps that will be a better target for us. Let's wait and see if it appears."

The sound grew yet louder. The thudding noise that the helicopter made was very distinctive. Although Wu thought that the flying machines looked ungainly, he knew that the helicopters generally carried the highest-ranking officers. The approach of this helicopter puzzled him somewhat because he was not sure why a helicopter would come all the way out here. What interest would a high-ranking officer have in this remote post?

The helicopter made him a bit nervous because at his back there was gathering a sizable Chinese force for yet one more push against the United Nations troops. The element of surprise was important if they hoped to overwhelm the enemy.

The fact that the helicopter had appeared might signal that the Americans knew something was happening. Why else would a high-ranking officer visit this remote outpost?

"Do you see it yet?" Deng asked. He was busy searching the sky with the telescopic sight, but the field of view was quite limited. The surrounding hills made the sound echo so that it was hard to tell where it was coming from.

"I will tell you when I do," Wu replied, using the binoculars, which had a much greater field of view. Binoculars remained rare in the Chinese military, and Wu guarded them closely as one of his most prized possessions.

He scanned the horizon, but there was still no sign of the helicopter, despite the fact that they heard it plainly. The rhythm of the rotors thumping in the mountain air vibrated throughout his body.

The problem here was that the hills were so low that they obscured much of the view across the more open territory that lay to the South. They could hear the helicopter, but they could not see it. Finally, he caught a glimpse of the flying machine, but it was moving quickly.

"It is off to your left, just above that middle hill," he said to Deng. "Do you see it?"

"Yes, sir."

Moments later, Deng squeezed the trigger. It was impossible to say whether or not he hit the flying target. He didn't have a chance for a second shot because the helicopter slipped behind a hill and disappeared.

"Did you hit him?"

"I don't know, sir. He was still in the air."

"You are too slow. You should have fired a second shot."

A long second went by before Deng replied, "Yes, sir."

This was Deng's way of showing that he thought the major was being unreasonable. Wu realized that he had hoped against hope that a single bullet from Deng would cause the helicopter to erupt into a massive fireball. He had seen that happening in his mind's eye. Could he get away with stating in his report that Deng had actually shot down the helicopter? Probably not.

"Never mind," Wu said. "It will take more than a bullet to bring down one of those helicopters."

"Yes, but maybe I shot the pilot."

"If you had shot the pilot, it is likely that the helicopter would have crashed."

"Yes, sir," said Deng sounding duly chastened.

"We have many other targets today."

Wu believed that snipers such as Deng were especially effective. Snipers could pick off the enemy unseen, thus demoralizing and terrorizing the American troops. Fighting against a hidden enemy served to frustrate and anger their adversary.

He had come to understand the power of snipers thanks to Li Chen. Wu had put Chen's talent to use at the Chosin Reservoir and then at the Battle of Triangle Hill. Ultimately, Chen had fallen to an American marksman, which was disappointing for Wu. At the time, Wu had believed that the Americans relied on their superior weaponry and he had been surprised to encounter the sniper with the Confederate flag painted on his helmet. That sniper was indeed a dangerous adversary, but if Wu encountered him again, he vowed that there would be a different outcome. Wu would eliminate the man, even if he needed to do it himself.

Although Chen had died, Wu had discovered that there was a kind of immortality to the fear of the Chinese snipers. As far as Wu was concerned, there would be a long line of snipers to replace Chen, like a line of dominoes. Hopefully, he would not need that many to chase the enemy from the Korean hills for good.

Deng was his latest sniper, with Wu having lost a less capable man in between Chen and Deng. Deng had the same small frame as Chen, but he was possessed of a wiry strength. Wu had witnessed Deng put much larger men in their place. When it came to a fight, Deng had the speed and killing instinct of a mongoose attacking a viper, qualities of which Wu approved.

"Major, what is that sound?" Deng asked.

Wu perked up his ears. Above the slow beat of the helicopter, he heard the roar of more aircraft. He looked up and spotted the contrails of seven airplanes streaking across the sky.

"Those are the new jet fighters," Wu said in surprise. It was unusual to see one of these jets because the American propeller planes known as Corsairs were more common. It was these planes that the Chinese troops feared more than anything because they could swoop in and wreak devastation with their bombs and napalm and machine guns in a way that the Chinese simply could not defend against because they lacked the antiaircraft weapons as well as an adequate air force of their own.

"I see them now, sir. I hope that they are not headed this way."

Wu pressed the binoculars to his eyes again and turned them skyward to study the planes. If this was a squadron of enemy planes, the Chinese would have just moments to seek shelter before the storm of bombs.

The aircraft had a stubby look about them, so different from the American Corsairs. As the planes approached, he picked out the red stars on the wings.

"Look, Deng, look! Those are our planes! These belong to us!"

With a sudden thrill of joy, he realized that these were not American planes coming to bomb and strafe them, but were instead the new MiG fighters that were being sent to bolster the Chinese defenses. Another present from their friends, the Soviets.

Wu was excited to see them because it was such an unusual sight. He scanned the sky with the binoculars, wondering where the aircraft were going in such a hurry. With a gasp, he saw that the Soviet planes were not alone. Just beneath them and off to the west, he picked out two more planes flying wingtip to wingtip. These other aircraft clearly had the appearance of American planes. As they grew closer, he could pick out the United States insignia on their wings.

"Look at that," Deng said. He had the eyesight of a marksman, much better than Wu's in any case, so that he didn't even need the binoculars to distinguish the planes against the clear blue sky. "Those are imperialist planes. I wonder if there's going to be an air battle, sir."

"That is a good question," Wu said, captivated by the sight of the two sets of combat aircraft. "If you put two hornets in a jar, they will fight. I would think that pilots in the same sky are much the same."

The question was soon answered. As Wu watched through the binoculars, the American planes suddenly shifted direction and swept upward toward the formation of MiGS. From the wings of the planes, he saw the flash of guns and cannon fire. As the Americans charged at the formation, it seemed foolhardy because they were so outnumbered. But when had the Americans ever had any sense? In their own minds, they thought of themselves as being invincible.

In response to the attack, the Soviet planes broke into two groups, four of the aircraft peeling off in another direction, and three sweeping down to meet the threat.

"Those others are running away," Deng said incredulously.

"Perhaps," Wu said. "Let us see what happens. Perhaps our comrades have a trick up their sleeve."

Flashes came from the MiGs as they attacked the American planes. Wu found himself mesmerized by the sight. He found it thrilling because he had never witnessed a dogfight before. It was almost like seeing the gods of old battle in the sky. He could hear the roar of the jet engines straining in the distance. However, the sound of the planes' guns did not reach them, although they could see the flashes of the guns.

Those distant flashes were more than a fireworks show. To their horror, one of the MiGs erupted into a fireball. Bits and pieces of the burning plane showered down from the sky.

"They have shot down one of ours!"

"I can see that," Wu snapped. "Perhaps the pilots are inexperienced."

Truly, the attack did not seem to be going well for the Soviet planes. Another MiG began to stream smoke and peeled away from the formation, headed back toward its base—most likely in Vladivostok. The remaining Soviet jet was now outnumbered, two against one.

But the four other jets had not simply disappeared. Instead, they suddenly reappeared out of the sun, diving toward the two American planes. One of these disappeared in a halo of fire, which left the lone plane badly outnumbered.

In an instant, the tables had turned.

The American wasn't about to give up the fight. He should have run away. Instead, he banked sharply and flew directly toward the oncoming planes.

Rapid fire flashed between the aircraft.

Madness, Wu thought, following the action through the binoculars as the single plane took on the entire squadron.

One of the MiGs exploded. The American jet plunged through the cloud of debris, but the pilot still had three enemy planes on his tail. And perhaps another waiting to pounce. By Wu's count, that still made it four against one. There was no way that the enemy pilot could survive this bout today.

Wu watched the enemy fighter plane dodge and dip, but he was unable to shake so many adversaries. Seconds later, another burst of cannon fire from the MiGs brought smoke pouring from the American fighter.

"He's done for," Deng said.

"Our forces have triumphed," Wu said, slipping into his political officer's role. "We should expect nothing less."

Wu was surprised that the American plane had done so well against such overwhelming odds. Their pilots must be well trained. Not for the first time, he realized that these Americans were not to be underestimated. Time and again, they had proven themselves to be highly motivated adversaries. Wu thought with a satisfied smile to himself that the Chinese had shown themselves to be capable as well.

Wu stared through the binoculars as a white parachute blossomed in the sky and began to drift downward, carried northwest by the wind.

"He is bailing out," Deng said.

"Why don't they shoot him down?" Wu demanded. "He destroyed three of our aircraft. "Shoot him down! What are they waiting for?"

Wu shouted as if the pilots high above could hear him. However, the MiGs did not open fire on the enemy pilot. There seemed to be some element of honor among pilots, even enemy pilots, because the Soviet fighters did not machine-gun the drifting parachute.

They were letting the enemy pilot go.

Wu had no such qualms. If he had been at the controls, he would had riddled the parachute with bullets and let the pilot plunge to his death.

"Can you hit him from here?" Wu demanded.

"It is very far, sir," Deng said.

"You must try!"

Deng raised the rifle, took aim, and fired.

Wu had hoped to see the body slump lifelessly, but there was no change in the tiny figure dangling from the parachute harness.

"You missed. Shoot him! Shoot him!"

The sniper worked the bolt action and fired again, but the distance was vast and the parachute seemed to pick up speed as it drifted farther away on the breeze.

"Here, give me that rifle!"

Wu grabbed the weapon away from the sniper. It was hard to pick the target out of the sky, and when he finally did, the parachute was even farther away. The crosshairs danced hopelessly as he tried to get them lined up on the speck that was the enemy pilot.

Cursing, Wu handed the rifle back.

"Come, get your things," Wu said. "We are going after him. We are going to capture that pilot."

"Yes, sir," said Deng. If he had any doubts, he knew better than to voice them with Wu so angry. Deng had grown up hunting and was a good tracker. With any luck, he would have a chance to redeem himself in Wu's eyes.

With Wu leading the way, they rushed back toward the Chinese encampment to gather a squad.

CHAPTER FIVE

As a political officer, Major Wu occupied a unique position in that despite his middling rank, in many ways he outranked even a Chinese general. It was true that a general could issue orders, but all that Wu had to do was whisper in the right ear, mention that the general was not patriotic, and the general would be spirited away. It might be Wu himself who would be doing the removing.

The general and every officer ranking below him were well aware of the situation.

Consequently, when Wu returned to camp and quickly gathered a dozen soldiers picked at random, there was no complaint from any of the officers or from the men. They knew that Wu was simply to be obeyed.

Wu's process was simple. If they saw a man holding a rifle and he looked competent, Wu tapped him for his makeshift patrol. Deng suggested one or two of the men and Wu accepted them readily. If they shared Deng's passion for petty cruelty while strictly following any order without question, then all the better.

Once Wu had assembled a handful of men, he left them in Deng's hands. "Tell them to bring enough food for a day or two, and tell them to bring some rope."

"Some of them want to know our purpose, sir."

Wu nodded and smiled, his face a picture of good cheer. "Tell them we are going after the American pilot who was shot down and when we catch him, we are going to truss him up like the imperialist pig that he is."

"Yes, sir."

As Deng dealt with organizing the patrol, the major turned to a man who stood nearby, patiently waiting to report to him. The man was dressed in civilian clothes, but he was actually a Chinese soldier who spoke Korean. Several days ago, the man had slipped into the Allied lines to work among the local Koreans who were carrying supplies and doing manual labor for the Americans, like coolies of old. His orders were simply to keep his ears and eyes open, observing anything of interest.

Wu motioned for the man to follow him until they were out of earshot of the others.

Once they were alone, Wu asked, "What did you find out?"

"The Americans will be rotating commands in two days," the spy said. "Several new units will be in the defenses. They will be unfamiliar with the terrain. Many of them are green troops as well, so there is some concern about that."

"Very well done," Wu said, smiling. "This is most useful. Go get yourself some real food, not that *Gǒu liáng* garbage they serve their Korean slaves. See me before you go back into the Allied lines because I may have something for you to watch for."

"Yes, sir."

Wu considered what to do with the information. He knew that the general was planning to attack one of the American outposts soon. In war, timing was everything. If the Chinese attacked when the Americans were confused and disorganized, they would have a higher chance of success. The waste of soldiers' lives was not a factor in his consideration. The question was, did Wu wish for the general to be successful in his attack? Perhaps. And if the general owed Wu a favor, so much the better.

With that thought in mind, he sought out the general. Several other officers were waiting to confer with their commander. Wu ignored the staff officer who informed him that he was third in line and walked into the general's tent. Wu's information had all but guaranteed that the attack on Outpost Kelly would come during the Americans' vulnerable transition period.

A few minutes later, he walked back out and smiled at the fuming staff officer.

"You did not follow protocol!" the officer said, clearly angry about the breach of his authority. The other officers who had been waiting occupied themselves by studying the clouds or distant hills. They knew better than to get on Wu's bad side.

"Do not worry," Wu said. "I made it clear to the general that you tried to stop me from bringing him this information. He was so impressed by your sense of duty that he said you will lead the first wave of the attack he is planning."

That stopped the officer in his tracks and left him silent. As everyone knew, Chinese doctrine accepted a great loss of life in trying to overwhelm the enemy with the first wave of an attack. Leading such an attack was akin to a suicide mission.

"I am to lead the attack?" the staff officer managed to stammer in disbelief.

"It will be a great honor to die in such a way," Wu said, smiling happily.

Leaving headquarters and the stunned staff officer in his wake, the major returned to where he had left Deng to organize things. The new squad looked squared away, if not entirely happy. Apparently, the prospect of chasing off into the hills did not appeal to them all.

Wu explained how it was going to be a great adventure, and then led the way into the hills with Deng at his side. No more than an hour had elapsed since they had seen the plane shot down.

"Sir, this is going to be like counting grains of rice," Deng ventured to say.

"It will be challenging," Wu agreed. "However, we will find him because that is what we must do. There is no alternative."

They were moving in the general direction of where they had last seen the parachute, using the hills themselves as landmarks.

"Did you bring a compass, sir?"

Wu shook his head and laughed. Deng should have known better. Even simple equipment such as a compass was hard to come by in Mao's ill-equipped army. "The hills have many eyes," he responded. Wu was thinking of the many North Korean villages that dotted the land-scape. "Someone will have seen something."

"These mountain people do not like us. They may not want to tell us anything," Deng said.

"Then we will make them tell us," Wu said. "That is what you are here for."

Now, it was Deng's turn to smile. "Yes, sir."

"Good. Let us hurry. We spent too much time getting organized."

Deng turned and barked at the soldiers to get moving.

One of the men made the mistake of lagging behind. When Deng shouted at him, the soldier said, "I have been marching for four days already. I didn't even get anything to eat."

Deng stepped back from the path and halted as the others went by. When the last soldier was even with him, Deng raised his rifle and swatted the man in the face with the butt of the weapon, knocking him down. Once the man had fallen to the ground, Deng kicked him several times.

"Are you still hungry?" Deng demanded. "Are you still tired?"

The soldier shook his head emphatically, spitting blood from his mouth.

"I did not think so. Get up and get moving. If you say another word, I will shoot you."

Up at the front of the patrol, Major Wu waved them on. "Hurry, hurry," he said, smiling.

* * *

COLE LED the way deeper into the thick brush and scrub trees, keeping well away from the Chinese patrol that they had encountered earlier. If they ran into more enemy troops, this mission was going to be ended before it even got started.

"Keep an eye open, kid," Cole said. "We won't be the only ones who saw that pilot's parachute."

"I guess that means we won't be the only ones looking for him."

"You catch on fast, kid."

Cole smiled to himself. He thought about what a greenbean Tommy Wilson had been when they first arrived in Korea. Their basic training had been cut short due to the desperate need for troops. The United States military had been caught by surprise and been totally unprepared for the well-coordinated invasion of Seoul and other cities by the North Korean Communists.

But since their arrival, the kid had learned more than a few hard lessons about being a soldier. His education had begun at the awful Chosin Reservoir campaign. Somehow, Cole, the kid, and their buddy Pomeroy had survived that icy disaster.

Since then, they had fought together across Korea, most recently in taking and holding Sniper Ridge at the Battle of Triangle Hill. Pomeroy had been badly wounded while serving as Cole's spotter—his extra eyes and ears as Cole took on a savage enemy sniper. Cole felt responsible for Pomeroy being hit. That wound had turned out to be Pomeroy's golden ticket back home. If Cole could help it, he wanted to make sure that the kid made it home in one piece. He wondered if maybe he should have ordered him back to camp with the others. Right now, their chances of success weren't looking all that good.

"How do you know which way to go?" the kid asked. "Look at all these hills and woods. Getting to that pilot is gonna be like finding a needle in a haystack."

"Nothing easy about it, and that's a fact," Cole said. "But we've got to try. Imagine how you would feel if you were that pilot."

"Yeah, he's probably not feeling all that great right about now. He's got to know that the Chinese will be after him, like you said. Hell, I'm nervous and there's not even anyone after me."

"We've got to hurry. I'm gonna move fast. Keep up now. Finding one lost soldier is bad enough."

Cole had seen the parachute drifting lower, and had a picture in his mind's eye of about where it would have gone down. Despite what the kid had said, it wasn't quite as bad as finding a needle in a haystack. It was maybe more like finding a pitchfork in a haystack.

He was using two of the distant hills as landmarks. As long as they kept lined up on them, they would be heading in the right direction. Cole only got occasional glimpses of those hills, however, as they fought their way through the thick cover. While the brush and scrub trees made the going tough, the cover also served to hide them from any curious eyes. He couldn't forget for an instant that they might stumble upon more Chinese troops at any moment.

Behind him, there was a sharp crack as the kid stepped on a fallen tree branch. Cole crouched, expecting at any moment for the woods to erupt in gunfire.

"Sorry," the kid muttered.

"Next time, why don't you send up a flare and make it even easier for the goons to find us. Watch where you put your feet."

"Got it."

They moved on. Above the trees, Cole spotted a trace of smoke. It was just enough for a cooking fire. The smoke meant one of two things. Either a Chinese patrol was out there, or a village. These hills were dotted with North Korean villages, some of them friendly and others not so much, especially if they had Communist sympathies.

One of the interesting things that Cole had found about the Koreans was that they rarely lived on individual plots, as Americans often did. Americans were very individualistic that way—Cole couldn't help but think of the tiny shack where he had grown up in the mountains near Gashey's Creek. Some might have found the family's ramshackle cabin lonely or isolated. Cole couldn't imagine living any other way and had built his own cabin in a remote location.

The Koreans preferred a village lifestyle, with dwellings grouped closely together. Many of the villagers were related somehow or had connections going back generations. The fields of rice and other crops that they cultivated surrounded the village and each day the farmers would head out to the fields, and then return at night. It was a more social way to live compared to the isolation of an American farmer.

If there was a village out there, maybe someone had seen something. He didn't speak a word of Korean, but he was prepared to draw a picture in the dirt of a parachute. Hopefully, the villagers could point him in the right direction.

Cole picked up the pace. Soon, he heard the kid panting heavily behind him. The kid had been a football player back in high school and he moved like one, bulldozing through the brush. Cole moved almost silently, finding gaps between the scrub trees and avoiding stepping on any of the dry bracken that littered the ground.

He winced as the kid stepped on another branch. To Cole's ears, the resulting crack sounded loud as a pistol shot.

"Keep up," he muttered. "And for God's sake, don't make so damn much noise."

They hadn't gone another fifty feet when Cole heard shots up ahead, coming from the direction that they were headed in.

"What's going on?" the kid asked.

"Sounds to me like maybe someone got there before us," Cole said. "Let's get a move on."

"I thought we were hurrying."

"That was just a slow hurry," Cole said. "Now we've got to hurry."

They heard two more quick shots, and then an eerie silence settled over the hills.

CHAPTER SIX

FACED with the Koreans pointed guns at him, Miller felt that he had no choice but to raise his hands in surrender. Shooting it out with the pistol didn't seem like an option against a handful of guerillas—or whatever these soldiers were.

"Lieutenant Commander Miller, United States Air Force," he said, his hands raised high. He wondered what else to say, such as *I surrender*. He settled on, "Don't shoot."

One of the Koreans stepped forward. Small and lithe, but unarmed, the Korean had Miller's full attention. He noticed long hair tucked under her billed cap and with a shock, realized that he was being confronted by a young woman.

"You are American?" she asked.

Miller's shock increased, owing to the fact that she had asked the question in English.

Dumbly, he nodded, then added, "Yes."

"Put your hands down," she said. Over her shoulder, she said something to the Koreans, who lowered their rifles.

Upon closer inspection, Miller could see that the weapons were antiques. If he wasn't mistaken, one of the rifles had a curved lock and a percussion cap, like a Civil War musket. He preferred not to be shot by it, all the same.

The soldiers didn't wear uniforms, but only dirty and ragged clothes, some of which appeared to be cast-offs from Chinese uniforms. How these fellows had obtained Chinese uniforms was a matter of open speculation.

Finally, he saw that these soldiers were mostly boys—not a one of them had a bit of facial hair—the exceptions being the young woman and an older man with a wispy, gray beard and a savage expression.

"We have to hurry," the young woman said. "The Chinese will be looking for you."

"Hold on. Who are you people?"

"There is no time to discuss this now. We must go!"

He saw that the young woman did, in fact, appear quite agitated as she scanned the trees surrounding the clearing. His eyes went to the top of the stone wall, as if there might be enemy marksman gathering there even now.

"What is this place?"

"An old fort. Now hurry, we must go."

The young woman and the other soldiers turned their backs on him and started toward the thicket. Miller had no choice but to follow.

After all, he didn't know where he was, and he had nothing more to guide him than a small compass that was just this side of something you might get from a bubblegum machine. Going down in the parachute had been a disorienting experience, but some part of his mind had remembered to look around and get his bearings. He knew that he had seen some sort of friendly defenses, but those could now be several miles distant, off to the south.

Right now, lost in the Korean hills with a guerilla patrol, the UN line seemed about as close as downtown New York City.

His only equipment consisted of a tube of water purification tablets, a Browning 1911 .45 caliber pistol with one clip, and a military-issue survival knife. He was grateful to have at least that much, but it was hardly enough to take on the Chinese army.

He soon found that he was struggling to keep up. Although none of them looked as if they could lift 50-pounds, they moved as if their legs were springs. Miller wrestled with the brush, forcing his way through, branches whipping at his face. Ahead of him, the others found their way without nearly as much trouble. If there was a path, however, Miller's eyes couldn't pick it out.

Soon, they came out on an old road—really just a cart track through the hills. Although weeds grew down the middle of the road, the ruts showed that the road had been used recently.

The road became more worn and less weedy. Off to the right, a tiny hamlet came into sight so suddenly that Miller was surprised by it.

Their arrival prompted a flurry of activity. Food and water containers were produced. Meanwhile, a knot of villagers gathered to look him over, like he was a monkey in a zoo.

"What's the matter, haven't you seen an American before?" he growled. "We're the ones over here fighting for you people."

Suddenly exhausted, Miller felt the need to sit down. The knot of villagers parted almost magically before him when he walked over to a section of log used as seating near a cooking fire and nearly collapsed onto it. The adrenalin from the dogfight, the grief at losing his pal and wingman Guzzle Walsh, the uncertainty of his situation, were all too much. He felt overwhelmed. Black dots swarmed in front of his vision and he felt shaky.

"We cannot stay," the young woman said.

Miller tried to focus on her without much success. Her voice seemed to be coming through a fog. "I need to rest."

"We are putting the entire village in danger."

"Don't you have something to drink?"

The young woman appeared exasperated, but her expression changed to concern when she looked at Miller's face. He supposed that he looked pale—he certainly felt like a ghost and that this whole experience wasn't real.

In rapid fire, she gave a string of commands in Korean. A cup of water was produced, and Miller drank it down greedily. A warm bowl was pressed into his hands. He looked down and saw that it was some kind of soup with some greenish leaves floating on top, like herbs. It smelled both sweet and pungent. There wasn't any spoon, but no matter. He gulped it down.

Immediately, he began to feel better. The black dots in his vision faded. His heart rate returned to normal. He also felt more confident.

"Thank you," he said and nodded, the tone of his voice conveying genuine gratitude, even if the villagers couldn't understand a word. He turned to the young woman, who was watching the road anxiously. "Have you got a name?"

"My name does not matter."

"You know mine. Lieutenant Commander Jake Miller."

She took her eyes off the road long enough to respond. "I am Jang-mi."

"Thank you for helping me, Jang-mi. Where are we?"

"This village is known as Kojang-ni." For the first time, a smile crossed her face. "However, you will not find it on many maps. It is much too small to be noticed."

"I'll bet. Look, how far do I need to go to hoof it back to my own lines?"

"It is only a few miles," she said.

"Just point me in the right direction and I'll be on my way."

She shook her head. "There is a problem."

"Yeah?"

"The Chinese are much closer."

"This is North Korea, sweetheart. There are always some Chinese around."

"These are not just patrols. There is an entire army moving in this direction."

That was news to Miller. He hadn't heard anything about that. He thought about those tiny UN outposts that he had seen from the air. It didn't seem like they knew anything about an entire army approaching, either.

"Doesn't sound good."

"No. That is why we must go now."

＊ ＊ ＊

Wu and his makeshift patrol raced in the direction where he had last seen the enemy pilot's parachute.

"Hurry, hurry!" he urged them, wishing that he'd had time to assemble a better team. He had simply grabbed any available man with a weapon in his hands. There had not been time for anything else.

Of course, Wu was no tracker, but he knew the general vicinity where the parachute had gone down. Deng was much better at such work, seeming to make his way almost effortlessly through the bushes that grabbed and clawed at Wu's legs and elbows. He recalled that Deng had grown up as a peasant, trapping rabbits and other game in the countryside. He was more than familiar with the outdoors.

Wu pushed Deng forward, indicating that he should lead the patrol. "Go!" he said.

Deng did not hesitate, but plunged ahead, leading the way. He found some sort of game trail, trotting down it, and the others fell into line behind him.

Wu was just behind Deng, but did not trust that the others would keep up. He waved his pistol at them in a threatening gesture, repeating, "Hurry!"

The game trail led to a larger path, and then to an old road with grass growing down the middle and deep cart ruts at the edges. Free of the brush, they continued to move at a trot.

Up ahead, Deng pointed. Wu spotted a trace of smoke in the sky. No Chinese soldier would have been foolish enough for that. Smoke brought the enemy planes with their bombs and Napalm down upon them, so any sort of campfires were expressly forbidden by the PLA officers. Could there be a village ahead? The hills were dotted with them.

Wu was too out of breath to question Deng about where he thought they were headed. They ran on.

Minutes later, the mountain road emerged into a clearing that revealed the small village that had been the source of the smoke. Deng pointed again, this time at group of figures scurrying through the fields beyond the village. The four figures disappeared into the wooded thicket, but not before Wu got a glimpse of a man who was clearly Caucasian and much larger than the slightly built villagers running beside him.

"This way," Wu urged, and ran toward the village.

* * *

FROM THE ROAD, Miller heard a distant shout.

"What was that?"

"Go!" Jang-mi grabbed his hand. "They are here!"

Some of the young men who had made up Jang-mi's patrol had shed their weapons and blended in with the other villagers. However, one young man and the old man with the wispy beard still held their rifles. They ran with Miller and Jang-mi out of the village, across a nearby field.

Miller realized that they had gotten out of Dodge not a moment too soon. He glanced back and saw a Chinese officer approaching the gathered villagers. Beside him was a soldier carrying a rifle with a telescopic sight. A sniper. He had not even been aware that the Chinese had snipers. That was just great. Miller kept his head down and two steps later he and the others were hidden by the dense thicket.

* * *

AS MAJOR WU APPROACHED, he saw that the villagers stood in a group, as if they had either been expecting company—or had just greeted a visitor. There were about twenty people, dressed in various homespun outfits and one or two of the older men wearing the peculiar flat-brimmed straw hats of traditional Koreans. Their dress and simple dwellings spoke of poverty and hardship, while their faces betrayed nothing as they greeted Wu and his men.

Wu smiled. It was not a welcoming smile. With him, it was a facial expression that conveyed the opposite of happiness.

"The American pilot, where are you hiding him?" Wu demanded in passable Korean, a language that was a close cousin of Chinese. He was still panting from the effort of racing down the old mountain road.

He did not feel like running off after the trio they had spotted, and there was no guarantee that he and his men would have caught them, anyhow. Not with that head start.

Wu was sure that if these peasants were anything like the ones in China, that they had a designated place where they went in times of trouble. It was how villagers survived centuries of constant invasion and warfare. It was where they would have hidden the pilot.

The villagers looked at Wu, and then at one another. No one spoke. Wu looked at Deng and nodded.

Deng raised his rifle and then seemed to hesitate, but he was only picking his victim. His muzzle settled on one of the old men wearing the ridiculous hats.

"You," Wu said to the old man. "Tell me where the American pilot was taken."

"Who?" the old man asked, his lined face like a mask of innocence.

Wu nodded at Deng, who pulled the trigger and shot the old man in the chest. He slumped down in the dirt, his silly hat rolling away.

"Where—" Wu started to shout his question again, but the villagers were not staying around to answer. Instead, they scattered. Some ran into their huts, while others snatched up children and ran for the woods.

Deng shot one of the fleeing villagers between the shoulder blades.

The soldiers accompanying Wu looked on in stunned silence but made no effort to join in the slaughter.

"Shoot them!" Wu ordered. "Shoot them all!"

When the soldiers did not act right away, Wu reached over and smacked one in the head with the muzzle of his pistol.

That got the soldiers' attention and they finally started shooting, but their hearts weren't in it. Some fired over the villagers' heads. Others fired directly into the air. They could not be ordered into being murderers.

Only Deng seemed intent on killing. He fired again, hitting a young teenage boy who had made the mistake of halting and staring back at the soldiers in defiance. He died clutching his chest in agony, then writhed on the ground.

The villagers had scattered like rabbits. In disgust, Wu ordered the shooting to stop. He would have liked to go from hut to hut, punishing the villagers for their insolence toward Chinese soldiers, but there was no time for that.

Wu walked over to the cooking fire, stepping over the body of the old man. He grabbed a burning stick from the fire and threw it into the thatch of the nearest hut. Tinder dry, the thatch smoldered for only a few moments before flames began to lick across the roof. From inside, he heard whimpers of fear. The flames spread, but no one came running out.

Wu had no patience for seeing how long the villagers could withstand the fire.

"Follow me," he shouted, then started across the field toward where they had last seen the American pilot.

* * *

COLE and the kid hurried toward the distant sound of shooting as fast as they could. *There I go again*, Cole thought. *Headed straight toward trouble.* Grinning to himself, he reckoned that he wouldn't have it any other way.

"What do you think is going on, Cole?"

"Sounds one-sided to me," he said. "The gunshots all sound the same, like nobody is shooting back."

"What do you suppose that means."

"I don't know, but we're gonna find out."

Lately, Cole had noticed that he didn't hear as well as he used to. Well, that wasn't quite true. He heard just as good, but there was a constant ringing in his ears whenever he was in a quiet place. An Army medic had told him it was tinnitus, caused by frequent exposure to loud noises like rifle shots, which was kind of hard to avoid as a soldier. Hell, half the artillerymen and tankers were just plain deaf, so he was way ahead of them.

They pushed their way through the brush, less worried now about the noise that they were making. Cole figured that any Chinese patrols in the area were doing the same thing that he and the kid were, which was to head toward the sound of gunfire ahead.

One thing about the Korean landscape was that it was just plain ugly. The hills and mountains were mostly barren, with the exception of scrub trees and brushy thickets. Back home, the Appalachian Mountains were lush with forests of chestnut, oak, and maple. God, he missed that, along with the smell of the fresh mountain air in summer or even the crackling leaves underfoot in the fall and winter. Down in the low places here, the air smelled mostly of the human excrement that the local farmers used to fertilize their crops of rice and cabbages.

A few more steps, and Cole emerged into a clearing. Signaling for the kid to stay put under cover, he crouched low and swept his rifle around, but they were alone. He waved the kid out.

"What is this place?" the kid asked.

Cole saw what appeared to be an ancient stone wall, half-covered in vines. The wall reached about ten feet high and it appeared to be several feet deep, with some sort of ruins hugging the top of the wall. In the shelter of the wall, a handful of actual trees had grown. They looked like hornbeams to Cole—a tree he hadn't seen much of in these parts. The smooth bark rippled as if with huge corded muscles.

To the left of the wall there was a narrow road that stretched off into the hills to the north. Tufts of grass grew down the center of the road, but the wagon ruts looked fresh.

"I've seen these places before. It's an old hill fort. People were fighting over Korea a long time before we got here."

"I don't know why."

Cole guffawed. "That makes two of us."

He moved into the clearing, his hunter's eyes noticing at once that someone had been here recently. Some of the rough grass was trampled. Above, a few branches hung down where they had been snapped off. At first glance, it was puzzling to say what could have reached that high.

He looked into some of the bushes at the edge of the clearing and found what he was looking for. Reaching in, he dragged out a handful of silken material.

"Looks like our friend was here."

"But where is he now?"

Cole nodded in the direction in which they had been moving. "I'd say he's in trouble. Time to leg it, boy."

They crossed the clearing and back into the endless thicket. The sound of gunfire had ended and the sudden quiet seemed ominous. When Cole looked up, he could see a column of thick smoke roiling into the sky. Not far now. In five more minutes of wrestling through the underbrush, they were close enough that Cole could smell the smoke. He heard someone sobbing, then a keening wail. The brush fell away and Cole found himself looking down on a village. What he saw down there made his jaw drop and his hands clench his rifle.

"God almighty," he said.

CHAPTER SEVEN

HELL HAD PAID a visit to this mountain village, Cole thought. One of the huts was in flames, threatening to spread to the other dwellings. Above the harsh crackling of the fire, Cole could hear the sound of crying and weeping.

Cole moved closer, rifle at the ready. He stepped over a dead dog, then passed a dead goat. Who the hell shot a goat?

He supposed that he shouldn't be surprised. He had seen just as much—and worse—in almost every Korean village touched by war. For that matter, he had seen similar scenes in the last war in Europe.

As if the dead animals weren't bad enough, he saw several bodies strewn on the ground, the dead surrounded by sobbing relatives. One of the dead was an old man, his wrinkled face and staring eyes serene in death. Nearby lay the body of a teenage boy, no more than fourteen or fifteen. He'd been shot in the chest. The way that his hands clutched his chest showed that he had not gone so peacefully. Cole shook his head at the thought. A woman and several girls who might have been the boy's mother and sisters knelt beside the body, sobbing. What a waste of life.

None of the dead held any weapons. What possible threat had an old man and an unarmed boy been to the Chinese soldiers? This was a massacre, pure and simple.

"What happened here?" the kid wondered. "This is awful."

"The Chinese happened, that's what."

"If we'd gotten here sooner, maybe we could have stopped them."

"Maybe, maybe not. In case you haven't noticed, there's just two of us, kid. We ain't the cavalry."

He supposed that he was trying to make the kid feel better. But deep down, Cole felt a rage begin to burn, every bit as hot as the fire that consumed one of the villagers' huts.

Not so long ago, this appeared to be a peaceful place. Even as remote and out of the way that the village was, it hadn't managed to escape the war.

He suspected that this was no random act of violence, however. More than likely, the villagers had brought the wrath of the Chinese soldiers down on their heads by helping the downed American pilot. They had known something or seen something.

The simple fact was that not all North Koreans were communists. The way they saw it, the Chinese were just more invaders, just as the Japanese had been during the last war—and in prior centuries. The North Koreans were just stuck in the middle, on the wrong side of the boundary being drawn up at the negotiating table in Kaesong.

He moved through this scene of brutality, keeping one wary eye out in case the Chinese returned.

Cole didn't need to ask any questions, not that there was anyone in the village who could have given him answers. He had heard the shooting and put two and two together. The villagers had helped the American pilot and the Chinese had found him—or had they?

The villagers had noticed their arrival and watched them warily, although there seemed to be some relief that he and the kid were not Chinese soldiers. Then again, what would it matter to these people which side he was on? He was another soldier with a gun and they were caught in the middle.

"American," Cole said. "Which way?"

All that he got was blank stares.

"*Eodi?*" the kid asked.

Some of the villagers pointed nervously toward the trees on the other side of the field beyond the village. Cole had turned his attention on the kid in surprise.

"Since when do you speak Korean?"

"I picked up a little here and there from the KSC," he said, using the abbreviation for the Korean Service Corps. These unarmed South Koreans provided the labor to support the military by doing everything from hauling supplies to building roads.

Cole could see the tracks where several men had passed. If the Chinese soldiers had captured the pilot, why had they rushed off into the thicket?

"We might still have a chance," Cole said. "I don't think they caught him. Not yet, anyhow. Come on."

The kid turned back to the villagers and said, "*Gamsa.*"

An irate old lady shouted something back and pointed again at the trees.

"What?" Cole asked.

"I have no idea. That's more Korean than I know."

"I've got a pretty good idea that she just said, 'What the hell are you waiting for? Go kick their ass.'"

"If you say so," the kid said. "Ready when you are."

Cole grunted, then headed across the field, following the tracks. The Chinese footprints were easy enough to pick out. He had seen enough of those in Korea. He also recognized a pair of U.S.-issue boots leaving their impression. He also saw two sets of tracks that appeared to have been made by the sandals that the locals wore. One set of these prints was quite small, as if made by a boy.

"I count six Chinese," Cole said. "They are definitely after our pilot friend. Looks like he has a couple of villagers helping him. They might be helping the Chinese, for that matter, but I doubt they would volunteer after that scene back at the village."

"Six against two," the kid muttered.

"With any luck, we'll catch them by surprise," Cole said, then plunged ahead into the thicket.

* * *

DENG LED the way into the thicket, hard on the trail of the pilot and villagers. His back was bent and scanned the ground as he ran, looking for any clue. Wu was impressed.

They soon came to a path, which Deng ran down.

"They went this way," Deng said, coming to a halt at a fork in the path through the thicket. "I can see tracks, and look, here's a broken branch."

"You had better be right," Wu said. He had no option but to trust Deng's judgment. "We must not let them escape!"

As they ran, the brush of the thicket seemed to press in on them from all sides. At least they were going downhill, which made the going easier. Instead of moving higher into the hills, their quarry seemed to be headed for the river. After another minute, he could hear the sound of the Imjin rushing over rocks below. He smiled. Where did the pilot think he was going? Unless they had a boat hidden somewhere, the Imjin was much too wide and swift to swim across. Then again, their quarry might be desperate enough to try. In that case, the pilot might be drowned in the currents, which was the last thing that Wu wanted.

"Faster!" he urged. It was all that he had breath to shout.

For Wu, the pilot would be an incredibly valuable prize, but the man must be taken alive. Dead, the American was of no use to Wu and this whole chase would have been pointless. The capture of the pilot would win Wu accolades, and also much valuable intelligence about the operations of the enemy aircraft.

The thicket ended at a rocky beach that marked the edge of the Imjin. Roughly one hundred meters ahead, he could see their quarry running along the shore.

Wu watched as the fleeing group splashed into the water. They did not attempt to cross the river, but ran parallel to the shore in the shallows.

"They are hoping to hide their tracks," Deng said. "But we have caught them."

"Get closer," Wu ordered. "Then shoot the others, but not the pilot. No harm must come to him!"

"Yes, sir."

The soldiers ran out onto the rocky beach and opened fire.

* * *

"Do not shoot the pilot!" Wu had ordered. "Kill the traitors!"

With the exception of Deng, the men in his patrol were not careful shots. Bullets sprayed the surface of the river and he feared that his prize would be lost.

"If anyone shoots the pilot, I will shoot him!" Wu shouted.

He saw one of the traitors, an older man, grab his arm and fall into the water. Smiling in satisfaction, he drew his pistol and began firing at the Korean who stopped to help him. To his surprise, Wu saw that it was a woman, and an attractive one at that. It seemed a shame to kill her, but a traitor was a traitor. Wu raised his pistol and fired, but his shot went wide.

No matter. There was nowhere for their quarry to escape, now that they were caught in the open. The jolt of the pistol had thrown off his aim, so he settled the sights on the woman again and held steady. He began to squeeze the trigger.

"I have you now," he said aloud, chuckling.

That's when they were attacked from the rear, well-placed shots tearing into his men. The man next to him threw his arms wide and collapsed face-first into the water's edge. Dead as a stone.

Within moments, two more of Wu's men fell. He swung his pistol to face the attackers.

* * *

Cole and the kid had arrived moments before, just in time to see the four figures struggling in the shallows of the river. Just as he had suspected from the footprints, he saw three Korean villagers and the American pilot wading through the current.

The edges of the river had wide sandbars that made the Imjin a favorite for cooling off. The Imjin was too wide and deep to cross easily, and the current was powerful in the middle of the river, but maybe crossing the river hadn't been their plan. Maybe they had simply been trying to throw the pursuers off their trail by wading in the river and emerging downstream, making their tracks hard to find.

At any rate, now they were caught out in the open. Their only choice was to try to swim the river and float downstream. There was no going back, because the Chinese pursuers stood on the riverbank, firing at them.

Bullets plucked at the surface of the water. One of the villagers suddenly clutched at his shoulder and went down, sinking beneath the surface. Another villager stopped to help him.

They were sitting ducks out in the open.

"Take the man on the left," Cole said to the kid. "After that, pick your targets and aim. Take your time. We won't have the element of surprise after the first couple of shots."

"If you say so."

Cole raised his rifle. Normally, he would have targeted the officer first, but the man appeared to be armed with only a pistol. Considering the range to the fleeing group in the river, it was an ineffectual weapon. Cole ignored the officer and aimed for one of the soldiers instead. He had a rifle against his shoulder and was banging away at the group in the water.

Cole put his crosshairs on the enemy soldier's mid-section. Nothing fancy at this range, he told himself, and not without any good rest for his rifle. His bullet might not kill the enemy soldier, but it would put him down.

He squeezed the trigger, and an instant later, the soldier fell down. Cole ran the bolt and fired again.

Beside him, the kid had followed Cole's instructions and taken his time with the first shot. Another enemy soldier fell.

"Got him!" the kid shouted.

That's two down, Cole thought, not looking up from his own rifle.

However, the kid hurried his next couple of shots, which did at least confuse the Chinese, who ran for cover.

Cole wasn't as hurried as the kid. He breathed in, breathed out, taking his time. When he finally fired, another one of the enemy fell.

Given a respite from the enemy attack, the pilot and his small band escaped the water and ran for the brush at the river's edge, where they scrambled out of sight.

The attack by Cole and the kid had managed to surprise and

scatter the Chinese. They didn't seem to know that it was just two soldiers attacking them. For all they knew, it could have been a regiment.

* * *

WITH HIS MEN dropping like flies, Wu had expected to find a squad of enemy soldiers at their backs. Instead, he saw just two men, crouched behind the driftwood debris on the riverbank. For a moment, he was so taken aback that he didn't even manage to fire his pistol at them.

The two men had been more than effective in rattling Wu's squad.

Caught by surprise, the others scrambled for the safety of the nearby thicket. Even Deng ran, leading the way to cover. Deng was fearless, but he wasn't a fool.

At the moment, the same could not be said of Wu. He stood alone like a deer frozen in the headlights, surprised by how close the Americans were. From this distance, he could even see their grimy faces under the brim of their GI helmets. The helmets made the men instantly recognizable as the enemy because Chinese and North Korean troops did not wear such cowardly headgear.

One of the men had something painted on his helmet. With a shock, Wu realized it as what the Americans called a Confederate flag. It seemed impossible, but this appeared to be the same sniper who had tangled with Wu's prize protege, Li Chen—and ultimately defeated Chen.

Angry now, Wu squeezed off several shots in the enemy sniper's direction. When the magazine was empty, it was all that he could do not to reach down and hurl rocks at the sniper. Instead, he started running after his men sheltering in the thicket.

* * *

COLE WATCHED the soldiers run off, leaving only one enemy officer by the river's edge. The officer seemed reluctant to abandon the chase. He stood for a moment, searching for his attackers. He refused to cut and run like the others.

Cole had to admire the man for having brass balls, or the Chinese equivalent. Jade balls? He lined up the crosshairs on the Chinaman.

Through the scope, he could see that the officer had spotted Cole and the kid, then seemed to stare at Cole. Does the son of a bitch recognize me? The officer shouted something and raised his pistol in Cole's direction. Cole was well out of accurate pistol range, but that didn't stop the Chinese officer from firing several shots in their direction.

Cole heard the *pop, pop, pop* of the pistol. Bullets whined around them and Cole hit the dirt.

When he raised the rifle again, the Chinese soldier was disappearing into the brush, following the lead of his men.

Three of the Chinese wouldn't be going anywhere. Their bodies lay on the sandy riverbank.

"If I didn't know better, I'd say that Chinaman knew me."

"Well, did you know him?"

"Can't say that we're on a first-name basis," Cole replied.

The only time when he had been up close and personal with any Chinese soldier had been during the Chosin Reservoir campaign, when he had briefly been captured. That officer hadn't been there, although the Chinese sniper that Cole had clashed with at Sniper Ridge had been. Things hadn't turned out so well for the enemy sniper.

"You know, that Confederate flag painted on your helmet kind of gives you away."

"Huh. I reckon I didn't think about that."

"Word gets around, Hillbilly," the kid said. "They must have figured out by now that there's an American sniper with a Confederate flag painted on his helmet. I'll bet those Chinese have a bounty on your head."

"Yeah?"

"I'll bet you're worth up to three, maybe four eggrolls by now."

"In that case, I'm glad that fella missed. Come on, let's go down and collect our pilot and his friends before them Chinese fellers regroup. That officer looks like he could be ornery."

As it turned out, the pilot hadn't gone far. Cole quickly tracked him down in the brush, hiding with the others. They were bunched together, their weapons ready for a last stand.

"Don't go shootin' us now," Cole said.

"You're Americans?" The pilot lowered his pistol. "Boy, am I glad to see you. The name's Jake Miller. My plane got shot down."

"I'm Cole and that there is the Kid. We saw the dogfight, Lieutenant," Cole said. "When we saw your parachute, we reckoned you might need a little help getting back to our lines."

Lieutenant Commander Miller's eyes quickly looked past Cole and the kid to the surrounding brush. "Where's the rest of your squad?"

"It's just us. I figured the two of us could move faster and have a better chance of finding you."

"I won't complain. Those Chinese had us cornered, that's for sure. They were following our tracks, so Jang-mi thought we could confuse them along the river, and then circle back. The villagers have a place where they hide in times of trouble, and they even have supplies there. Anyhow, those guys were regular bloodhounds. We couldn't shake them."

Cole looked around at the others. He saw an older Korean man and a Korean teenager, who was staring at Cole, wide-eyed. The third Korean was a woman, who was working to bandage the older man's arm, where one of the Chinese bullets had caught him. Cole took this woman to be Jang-mi. All in all, Cole thought that they had gotten off easy. Another half a minute and the Chinese would have chewed them to pieces.

The young woman met his eyes and said, "You are brave ... or a fool."

Cole raised his eyebrows. "Nice to meet you, too."

"She's direct like that," the Lieutenant said with a grin. "But I've got to say, I owe her my life."

"What happened at the village?" Jang-mi asked.

Cole shook his head.

"Sons of bitches," the young woman hissed.

"I like this one," Cole said. "Now let's get a move on and get back to the line before sunset. Trying to come back through our own lines after dark would be just as bad as having the Chinese after us."

CHAPTER EIGHT

As IT TURNED OUT, they hadn't moved fast enough. No sooner had the words left Cole's mouth, then a flurry of gunfire whistled overhead. Bit of branches flew as bullets chewed up the thicket.

"Damn it all, one of those boys has got himself a submachine gun," Cole muttered.

"And he's awfully trigger happy."

Cole cocked his head, listening to the rhythm of the firing. It sounded like a Thompson submachine gun to him, not one of the Chinese weapons. The Chinese had managed to arm themselves with a fair amount of weapons that were either captured or scavenged off the battlefield.

Considering that the Thompson spewed .45-caliber slugs, this wasn't good news.

Fortunately, they were all down in a gully, safely out of harm's way—for now. But Cole didn't want to press their luck.

More measured shots came between the bursts from the submachine gun. A bullet struck a branch just above the kid's head, and he ducked lower.

"Someone over there knows how to shoot, that's for damn sure,"

Cole muttered. "They want us to keep our heads down while he takes his time picking us off."

"When we were leaving the village, I got a glimpse at the Chinese hunting for us," the pilot said. "One of them was carrying a rifle with a scope. A sniper rifle."

"Yeah, I saw him when we jumped those guys," Cole said. "That must be him now."

Cole had to admit that keeping them pinned down was a good strategy on the part of the Chinese, but he was having none of it. Carefully, he worked his way higher in the gully, his face pressed into the gravel. He was sure that he probably shared the overgrown gully with snakes and other critters, which were the least of his worries now.

He chanced a peek over the rim of the gully. He didn't have a clear view of the enemy hidden in the thicket. Separating the two sides was a long stretch of sandy beach. Around the halfway point, he could see the bodies of the Chinese soldiers that he and the kid had shot. There was nothing in the way of cover out there.

He caught glimpses of their muzzle flashes, but for the most part, the Chinese were well hidden. One of the enemy soldiers could definitely shoot, which piqued his curiosity. It also caused Cole some uncertainly because his last encounter with a Chinese sniper had not gone well, until their rivalry finally ended on Sniper Ridge.

A bullet plucked at a stone near Cole's head and he slid deeper into the gully. The enemy marksman had picked him right out.

Keeping low, Cole made his way over to the others. They stayed huddled together as more fire turned the branches overhead into toothpicks.

"That submachine gun is keeping us pinned down," Cole said. "I'm going to see what I can do about it."

He crawled out of the gully, following the trunk of a fallen tree that provided some protection. The tree had washed up on the bank in some long-ago flood, its bark stripped away and the wood polished smooth so that it resembled nothing so much as a giant bone.

Cole moved to where he could get his rifle under the log without being seen. The Chinese had the gully pinned down, but they hadn't spotted Cole—not yet, anyhow. He saw the flashes indicating where the submachine gun was being fired from, and unleashed two quick shots in that direction.

The gunner fell silent. He was either reloading—or one of Cole's bullet had found its mark.

He belly-crawled back to the gully as fast as he could, keeping the log between him and the thicket.

No matter—a bullet still hit the top of the log near where Cole was crawling, showering him with splinters of driftwood.

"Go! Now's our chance."

Jang-mi cast nervous glances toward the Chinese position, but Lieutenant Commander Miller didn't give her time to consider her options. With an ignominious shove from behind, he propelled her out of the gully and into the thicket. The pilot was next, followed by the boy and the old man.

"Now what?" the pilot wondered.

"Now we run, Flyboy! That's what!"

Cole barreled through the thicket, wanting to put as many trees as possible between himself and that Chinese sniper, who had made some uncanny shots. He wasn't all that worried about making noise, although he was quieter than the others, whose progress was marked by the sound of snapping branches and loud curse from Lieutenant Commander Miller as he stumbled, fell flat, then picked himself up and kept going.

Still, a couple of shots pursued them, boring after them through the thicket. It was only by some miracle that no one was hit.

He was surprised by a blur of motion to his left as someone pushed past him. It was Jang-mi.

"You too slow," she said. "Follow me."

Cole didn't know whether to be amused or angry. "Lead the way then, missy. I just hope to hell you know where you're going."

To their benefit, Jang-mi did seem to know the way. She led them out of the thicket, where it was slow going, and to a path that led away from the river. Once on the path, they moved quickly now that branches and briars weren't constant clawing at them.

They paused long enough to catch their breath and take stock.

"Some rescue mission," the pilot said. "Don't you wish now that you had brought along some extra help?"

"How 'bout this, Flyboy. You wait here and I'll go bring back reinforcements."

"Here's a better idea. Why don't we all go with you?"

"Come along if you want to. I'm just gonna follow this girl."

"Sounds like a plan," the pilot said.

A few paces away, Jang-mi just shook her head and then started off down the path.

To hurry them along, a bullet snapped through the air just over their heads.

That was all the prompting they needed to follow Jang-mi, running full tilt down the narrow trail through the thicket along the riverbank.

* * *

WU CURSED as a bullet plucked at his sleeve, causing him to drop the submachine gun, which he had grabbed in frustration from one of the soldiers. He picked it up and threw it at the startled soldier. "What are you waiting for? Shoot back!"

The soldier did as ordered, firing wildly. Wu had to admit that it would be a miracle if the soldier hit anything, although he was doing a good job of trimming the tree branches. "Aim lower, you fool!"

Cursing, Wu wondered at the reversal of fortunes that had sent him cowering for cover among the stunted trees. Minutes before, he and his men had caught the American pilot and his helpers trying to escape along the river. He had sensed his great prize—the American pilot—almost within his grasp. But then, the enemy sniper had attacked.

Even so, his prize was still within reach, if Wu could only organize the tattered remains of his patrol to go after him.

Beside him, Deng sat crouched behind a fallen log, picking his shots carefully. His one bullet was more effective than a spray of fire from the submachine gun. If they were going to defeat this American sniper and capture the pilot, Wu had to admit that Deng was their best hope of doing so.

"Did you get him?"

As if in response, a single rifle shot cracked overhead, making Wu wince.

Deng fired, grunted in dissatisfaction, and worked the bolt. Wu wanted to ask more questions but refrained. He would let Deng do what he did best.

The submachine gunner had reloaded and he opened fire again at the hidden enemy. Seconds later, there came a shot from the enemy position, then another. The man wielding the submachine gun yelped in pain and the firing stopped.

Wu looked expectantly at Deng, hoping that he had seen where the enemy sniper was hidden. When Deng didn't shoot, Wu asked, "Don't you see him?"

Deng didn't answer for a long moment. "They are running," he announced.

Wu waved his remaining men to their feet. "Come on!" he urged, although he kept his voice to a harsh whisper. "After them!"

* * *

FOR COLE AND THE OTHERS, their path moved steadily south toward the Allied lines. Having been worn by animals and unhurried peasants, the path tended to wander, but at least it was taking them in the right direction.

They had given their pursuers the slip, but for how long? Cole recalled the angry look on the Chinese officer's face. That fella wasn't going to give up anytime soon, that was for sure. The thought encouraged Cole to keep up with Jang-Li, who moved swiftly and gracefully along the mountain path. The boy and even the wounded old man kept pace easily. It was the Americans who struggled to keep up.

Part of the problem was their boots. While the Koreans wore light, thin-soled shoes even in the rocky terrain, Cole and the kid wore heavy military-issue boots. The rugged boots were well-suited to the kind of duty that the soldiers faced, from digging foxholes to keeping their feet warm on the cold Korean nights, but they were not made for traveling light and fast.

The boots worn by the pilot weren't much better, although they were shinier. Pilots didn't spend much time digging foxholes or slogging through mud and dust, Cole reckoned.

Annoyed at the Americans' pace, Jang-Mi slowed just long enough to glance over her shoulder and wave at them to hurry it up.

"Go!" she whispered urgently.

"You go, we'll keep up," Cole replied, waving her forward. He realized that he was just this side of panting for breath.

They had gone another mile or close to it, when they heard a rifle shot behind them. A bullet ricocheted through the scrub trees. Something about the whine of a stray bullet always sent a strange tingle down Cole's spine.

The Chinese pursuers were sending them a message that they hadn't given up.

There were still a lot of miles back to the American lines. Cole didn't like their chances in a running battle all that way. But for now, they had no choice but to make a run for it. He was happy to let Jang-mi lead the way. He was second right behind her, but he dropped back to the back of their group. The Korean teen-ager had been bringing up the rear. If it came to a fight, Cole liked his own chances better of stopping the Chinese. But even that wasn't a sure thing, not with the enemy sniper on his tail, and not when they were packing at least one submachine gun.

The trail meandered until coming to a fork. One branch wandered off to the left, maybe following the river, while the right-hand branch headed upward into the rocky hills.

Jang-Mi hesitated for only a moment, as if debating which way might be faster, but then started up the steeper right-hand branch. Cole felt reassured that this woman seemed sure of which direction to take.

Behind them, he heard a shout and another rifle shot. Closer this time. The Chinese seemed to be gaining on them, although he wouldn't have thought it was possible. Those Chinamen must have wings on their feet.

Waiting for the others in front of him to follow Jang-Mi, he found himself staring at the fork in the trail a moment. An idea came to him.

"Hey!" he called. "Hold up."

Jang-mi had already started up the right-hand fork, and she looked back over her shoulder, clearly puzzled, as Cole waved her back.

"I know the way," she said defensively.

"I reckon you do," he said. "But these fellers are right behind us. Maybe we can throw them off our trail. Everybody follow me."

Cole started down the left-hand fork, the opposite of the one that Jang-mi had chosen.

"Wrong way!" she protested.

"Trust me on this," he said. "Come on."

They went about a hundred yards down the trail before Cole called a halt. The surface of the path had been dirt up to that point, making their footprint plainly visible, but now they had reached a rock-strewn patch. It was just the footing that Cole had in mind. He stepped off the trail, then unsheathed his big Bowie knife and easily chopped through the leafy branch of a nearby shrub.

"Everybody, go on back to that fork."

Again, Jang-mi led the way, moving confidently. She had figured out what Cole was up to and apparently approved. When they reached the fork again, she started up the right-hand branch that she had initially chosen.

Cole lingered behind.

"What are you up to?" Lieutenant Commander Miller asked.

"Hiding our tracks."

Deftly, Cole used the branch he had cut on the other trail to sweep the path behind him. Their footsteps were quickly erased from the dusty trail. Now, their footsteps clearly led up the left-hand trail.

Cole tossed the makeshift broom deep into the brush. "Let's go," he said.

The pilot needed no other prompting. Both men ran for all they were worth to catch up to the others.

* * *

SCANT MINUTES LATER, Deng arrived at the same fork. Without hesitation, he followed the left-hand branch with the footprints of the group they were chasing. It made sense that they would be heading down toward the river again, rather than up into the hills. There was nothing up there but rocks and ridges, whereas the river flowed directly toward the American encampment.

"We are close," Wu said behind him.

"Yes," Deng agree, keeping his rifle ready in case the Americans decided to ambush them and make a desperate last stand. If that happened, they would need some firepower. "Better get that fool with the submachine gun up here, sir."

Major Wu shoved the submachine gunner forward and they continued up the trail.

When they reached the rocky section of the path, Deng didn't give it much thought. Any footprints would not be visible on the rocky ground.

After another ten minutes of hard running, the ground grew soft and damp as they approached the river again. The path grew extremely narrow as the brush pressed in around them.

Deng was so worried about an ambush ahead that several more minutes passed before it dawned on him that there weren't any footprints on the path ahead. He stopped, puzzled.

Wu squeezed in beside him. "What is it? Why have you stopped?"

"I don't see any tracks, sir."

"They did not turn into birds and fly away," Wu said, annoyed. For once, he was not smiling. "What do you mean, there are no tracks?"

"I think it was a trick, sir. Back at the fork, I think they may have gone the other way."

"Nonsense. You saw the tracks as well as I did. They came this way." The political officer pointed at several marks in the damp earth of the path. "What do you call that?"

"Those are the hoofprints of a deer, sir."

Wu pushed past Deng to lead the way. The major hurried along the path, which grew narrower and hard to follow. They soon reached the sandy shore of the river. Whatever path they had been following had disappeared, along with their quarry.

The major realized that Deng was right, after all. The Americans had somehow tricked them.

Gazing out at the river, Major Wu shouted several curses that were not at all worthy of a political officer.

CHAPTER NINE

To Hardy's eyes, these godforsaken hills were the last place on earth that anybody would want to fight over. All that he saw were rocks, hills, and scrub trees. Beyond the outpost, he saw more rocks and more hills. He recalled the rich farmland of the Midwest, where he had grown up. The fields here were small by comparison, scratched out of the rock, and mostly smelled like excrement due to the human waste that was used for fertilizer.

The communists can have it if they want it so much, he thought.

Although Hardy was a recent college graduate with an English degree, his education in the great works of literature mostly failed him in trying to describe the view. The landscape was just plain uninspiring. Eventually, a few lines from a poem entitled "Ozymandias" by Percy Bysshe Shelley came to mind: *Look upon my works, ye mighty, and despair/Yet all around the empty sands stretch away.*

The Korean hills were not the desert, but the sentiment of futility was the same. What the hell was everybody fighting over?

"You look lost, soldier."

The voice behind Hardy gave him a start. He turned around to find a young lieutenant standing with hands on hips, an amused expression on his face. The officer was only a couple of years older than Hardy.

"Yes, sir. I mean, no sir."

"The billiards hall is just down this way, and ice cream parlor is just over the next hill."

Hardy realized that the young officer was kidding. He grinned. "Don't we wish, sir. But I am a little lost. I'm a reporter with the Stars and Stripes, and I'm supposed to write an article about the 65th Infantry."

"You mean the Borinqueneers? I hope you speak Spanish. Most of them don't know a word of English, and that includes the officers. We're supposed to be working together and we can't even understand each other." He frowned. "Don't put that in the article. Listen, the Borinqueneers aren't going anywhere. What you should write an article about would be my tanks."

"Tanks, sir?"

"Sure, that's where the real story is. Have you ever been up close and personal with an M-46 tank?"

"Can't say that I have, sir."

"Then follow me, Private. I'm Lieutenant Dunbar, by the way."

Lieutenant Dunbar led the way forward. Hardy wasn't sure if he was being ordered to write about tanks or not, but he was curious now. With a shrug, he followed the lieutenant.

They climbed higher on the hill. Officially, this was designated as Hill 122. From up here, Hardy had an impressive view of the valley below with the Imjin River cutting through it. More hills marched away to the horizon.

The lieutenant pointed out one of the largest hills, front and center. "The Chinese hold that one right there. Hill 377. The boys call it the Rice Mound. Every now and then the Chinese get a hair up their ass and fire some artillery at us, and we shoot back."

Hardy squinted at the Rice Mound, hoping for a glimpse of the Chinese fortifications, but didn't see a thing.

The lieutenant seemed to read his mind. "They don't show themselves during the day because our planes will knock the hell out of them. But they're dug in on that hill, believe me."

One of those hills was occupied by Outpost Kelly, the lieutenant explained, a forward position meant to provide warning of any attack.

"Who is Kelly?" Hardy asked. There was often a good story behind a name, but maybe not in this case, it turned out.

"Beats me," the lieutenant said. "Just to the south of us there are three outposts named after cities in Nevada, so go figure. I guess somebody was homesick."

Climbing a little higher, they passed a solid-looking dugout or bunker, its flat roof and sides heavily sandbagged. However, the front of the bunker was big as a garage. Hardy wasn't far off about that. As he watched, a crew backed a quarter-ton truck fully laden with boxes of ammunition into the bunker. This must be a support vehicle for the tank unit.

Finally, they reached the tank battery itself. It was not what Hardy had expected. Instead of the tanks sitting out in the open along the ridge, each tank was pulled into its own dugout or revetment so that only the turret and gun sat above ground level. There was a lookout in the open turret, his head just visible above the hatch. The rest of the crew lounged on the ground at the back end of the tank, smoking cigarettes. They tossed them away and stood up as the lieutenant approached.

"How's it going?" the lieutenant asked. "Anything?"

"No, sir," one of the tank crew said.

"All right, I want you to make sure all the ammunition is squared away. When the supply comes around today, make sure you stack a dozen rounds right here."

"Will do, sir."

His orders given, the lieutenant turned back to Hardy. "Climb aboard."

They scrambled onto the tank. Once he was standing on the back or deck of the tank, his perspective changed. Even dug into the revetment, the tank was much bigger and higher than Hardy had expected.

"Got a notebook?"

"Yes, sir." Hardy was beginning to realize that not much got past this officer.

"Here are a few facts about the M-46 for you. This tank weighs forty-eight tons. It is twenty-eight feet long, twelve feet wide, and nine feet high. The steel on the front and the turret is four inches thick.

The tank is powered by a twelve-cylinder engine that generates eight hundred and ten horsepower, which makes her a little thirsty. Three gallons of gas to the mile."

"Glad I don't have to fill her up, sir." Hardy scribbled frantically in his notebook as the officer spouted facts. "That could get expensive. Back home, it was a big Saturday night if I could put two gallons of gas in my old man's Buick."

"You've got that right. Lucky for us, Uncle Sam foots the bill," the lieutenant said, laughing. He moved forward, nodded at the man in the turret, then slapped the big gun. The easy way that he moved around the tank showed that he was right at home aboard this beast. "This is a 90 mm gun. You can see that we've also got a .50 caliber machine gun and two .30 caliber machine guns."

Hardy whistled. "That's a lot of firepower."

"This is the finest tank in the world," the lieutenant said. "A truly formidable machine of war, if there ever was one. There's only one problem."

"What's that, sir?"

"A tank is meant to be mobile. We're the modern cavalry, for God's sake! Do you see a problem with our current situation, Private?"

Hardy ventured a guess. "Well, you're not very mobile at the moment."

"Not hardly. This isn't France or Belgium, where Patton could race across Europe, chasing the Germans. The Chinese are dug in. We are dug in. So here we sit."

Hardy thought about that. "Seems like a shame, sir."

The lieutenant laughed. "You've got that right."

From their vantage point atop the tank, Hardy watched as a group of soldiers passed by along the line of defense in front of the tanks, which had been situated to fire over the heads of the defenders. To Hardy's surprise, the men wore U.S. uniforms but appeared dark-complected. All of them wore mustaches, which stood out because soldiers were required to be clean-shaven. None of them carried weapons, which was unusual on the front lines. The men strolled along in group of three and four, talking as if they didn't have a care in the world—never mind that the Chinese were almost within hearing distance. Hardy didn't know whether to be appalled or reassured.

A couple of the men smoked cigars, thick clouds of smoke swirling about their heads.

"Those are the Borinqueneers that you're here to write about," the lieutenant said. He started to say more, then hesitated. "The jury is still out on them."

"What do you mean, sir?"

"If there is an attack on this outpost, those are the men who will be defending my tanks."

"In that case, they might want to pick up their rifles, sir."

"Military training seems to be a little lackadaisical in Puerto Rico," the lieutenant said, then seemed to realize that he was saying too much. "Don't quote me on that."

"No worries, sir."

They made their way back to the ground. There was something pleasurable about climbing around on the tank, as if it were a jungle gym for soldiers.

Looking up at the monstrosity that was the M-46 tank, Hardy was glad that he did not have to face anything like that on the battlefield.

Hardy had to admit that he had been so focused on his assignment to write about the 65th Infantry that he might easily have overlooked this other, interesting story about a tank unit deployed to Outpost Kelly. Maybe the lieutenant was somewhat self-serving in that regard, but Hardy was appreciative all the same.

He took out his camera and took several photographs of the tank crew stacking ammunition, and got the lieutenant to climb back up on the tank and pose with the Chinese-held Hill 377 in the background. He also interviewed several of the crew members, getting their names, ages, and where they were from. To his surprise, none of the crew was a day older than 19. The lieutenant was 28 and had served in the last war as an enlisted man, though he looked younger.

The lieutenant seemed pleased by Hardy's efforts, and they chatted for a while. Once the lieutenant found out that Hardy was a recent college graduate, he appeared to relax even more. He seemed to feel that could let his guard down a bit considering that Hardy wasn't under his command.

"Listen, where are you bunking while you're up here at sharp end of the spear?"

"I have no idea," Hardy admitted. "I think the last thing the CO is worried about is where a reporter should lay his head for the night."

"We've got room in our bunker," the lieutenant said. "I'm in there with my sergeant and the tank crew, but we can squeeze in one more."

"That would be swell, Lieutenant."

"Good, that's settled then. Say, how are you at catching rats?"

AS IT TURNED OUT, Lieutenant Dunbar wasn't kidding about the rats. They had moved into the bunker almost as soon as it was built, attracted by the relative warmth and the promise of food scraps. It was a strange thing, considering that they were nowhere near any cities, which were the sort of places Hardy usually associated with rats. Then again, when he thought about it, there had been plenty of rats hanging around the chickens and barns even in rural Indiana, where he had grown up.

Of course, the soldiers did everything they could to reduce the appeal of the bunker, being sure not to leave any open food around, but the rats hadn't gotten the memo.

"Do they bite?" he asked Dunbar.

"Not as long as you keep moving," the lieutenant said. "When you go to sleep, make sure that you wrap everything up tight. I wouldn't sleep commando, if you know what I mean."

Hardy winced at the notion. "Some of these rats are the size of cats."

"You must have seen some puny cats in your life," Dunbar said. "These rats are bigger than most cats."

He ended up sleeping fully clothed, except for his boots. As it turned out, that was a good thing.

A tank crew of five men, along with Lieutenant Dunbar and Hardy, shared the cramped bunker. He would have thought the bunker would be warm, but it felt cold and damp. The nights were chilly here in the Korean hills. To take the chill off, a gasoline-fueled heater burned inside, vented through a pipe through the roof.

Hardy viewed the heater with some skepticism. He had grown up around kerosene heaters, and those were dangerous enough. Left untended, the fumes could kill and they were a fire hazard. But a gasoline heater? It seemed to him that they might as well be sleeping with a potential firebomb in the room.

Judging by the sounds of snoring around him, the takers didn't seem worried. Hardy was so tired that he puts aside his fears of rats and rickety heaters, and went to sleep.

It was around midnight when a crescendo of small arms fire woke him up. He rolled out of the bunk and onto the dirt floor. The fire seemed to be coming from inside and outside their own lines.

Dunbar and his tank driver were already on their feet, shoving on their Mickey Mouse boots and running out the door. Dunbar had his gun belt in hand and he shouted back at Hardy, all business now, "Better grab a weapon, soldier!"

There was no doubt that their position was under some kind of attack. But by the volume of fire, it was clear that this was not a full-on assault. Hardy was glad for that much.

From the lead tank, a soldier was shouting that he'd lost his weapon. "They shot my rifle right out of my hands! Where are my grenades, dammit!"

Hardy had grabbed an M-2 carbine that was leaning against the wall of the bunker. He had no ideas whose weapon it was, or even if the thing was loaded. He followed Dunbar and the sergeant, who ran for the tank. None of the other tanks seemed to be under attack. Without hesitation, Dunbar and the sergeant leaped up onto the tank, which was still parked in its enfiladed position.

The two men ran forward to the front of the tank and angled their weapons down. If the tank was still under attack, then this was where the attackers would be found. The lookout in the turret might have lost his rifle, but he held a pistol in one hand and a grenade in the other. Hardy moved forward, his carbine at the ready.

"Nobody there," Dunbar said in a low voice, looking out at the darkness. If the Chinse attackers had gotten this close, they had either breached the defensive line ahead or somehow slipped through it.

"They were there a minute ago," the lookout insisted. "I saw some guys and called out to them thinking that they were from the 65th, and the next thing I knew, they're shooting at me. I started shooting back, but they shot the rifle right out of my hands!"

As if to prove the lookout's point, gunfire erupted, stitching the darkness with tracer fire.

"Take cover in the tank!" Dunbar shouted.

One after another, they slid down the turret. Hardy banged up his knees and elbows in the process, but it was still a hell of a lot better than being shot. They had been sitting ducks up there around the tank. The others were more than a little familiar with tanks and easily slipped inside. Dunbar was the last man, and no sooner was he inside than he slammed down the hatch and secured it. They were now buttoned up tight.

From behind four inches of armor plating, they could barely hear the bullets splashing against the metal. To Hardy, it sounded a bit like rain falling on a tin roof. Of course, that was a peaceful sound. There was nothing peaceful about bullets hitting the tank.

"I'd shoot back if I knew what to shoot at," the sergeant muttered.

"All dressed up and no place to go," Lieutenant Dunbar agreed. "We've got all this firepower and we can't even use it."

Once the firing had subsided, the crew emerged.

Now that the excitement was over, the night seemed very quiet.

After an hour with nothing doing, Lieutenant Dunbar doubled the guard and returned to the bunker with Hardy. "You may as well try to get some sleep," he said. "Besides, the rats are getting lonely."

"What about you?"

Dunbar shook his head. "I'm going to make the rounds to the other tanks and make sure they've got both eyes open," he said.

"You think the Chinese will be back?"

"It's hard to say, but they've lost the element of surprise. If I were them, I'd wait a couple of nights and try again."

Hardy curled himself tight in a blanket to keep out the rats, and much to his surprise, fell into a dreamless sleep.

He was awakened early to find Dunbar and his crew making coffee on the gasoline-fueled heater.

"Anything else happen last night?"

"All quiet on the western front. But now that it's daylight, we're going to walk out and see if we can figure out where that patrol came from and what they were up to."

After a quick cup of coffee, he joined the tank crews on the line.

By light of day, they were able to inspect the damage to the tanks. The hail of Chinese gunfire had still caused its fair share of damage.

The radio antenna used to communicate between tanks drooped, having nearly been severed by a bullet. A second antenna for the radio to the command post had been shot clean off. Bullet splashes were spread across the flat surfaces of the tank. The bullet-proof glass of the viewing port was chipped and cracked from bullet strikes. Even the inside of the turret hatch had a bullet splash from when it had been flipped open. If the sentry hadn't dropped inside to radio for help at that moment, he would likely have been killed.

Inspecting the damage, all that Lieutenant Dunbar could do was shake his head.

"I'll bet you thought that we were giving you a quiet place to rest lay your head," he said to the reporter. "Instead, it turned out to be one hell of a night here on Outpost Kelly. How's that for a story?"

Lieutenant Dunbar formed the men into a skirmish line, just in case any of the enemy was still lurking in the tall grass and brush, and they moved forward from the tank position.

One of the first things they found was the sentry's shattered carbine.

"I'll be damned." Dunbar picked it up and stared dumbfounded at the pieces. It really had been shot right out of his hands, the bullet smashing the stock to kindling. The man had been lucky that the wooden rifle stock had been there to stop the bullet, or he would have been the one to be mangled.

"Sir!" a soldier called.

Dunbar ran over and looked down at what the man had found. It was a Chinese soldier, shot through the chest. It looked as if he had died instantly, his eyes open and staring. He wore the familiar padded uniform, the once bright fabric gone grayish from hard campaigning. On his feet were a pair of thin-soled sneakers that wouldn't have done much to keep the soldier's feet warm. He wasn't even wearing socks.

The dead combatant had been carrying a captured M-1 rifle, still slung over one shoulder. The sight of the rifle rankled them. Knowing the awesome firepower of that weapon, nobody wanted to see them used against their own troops.

"Our sentry managed to fire a few shots before that bullet wrecked his carbine, and I suppose he must have hit this guy."

"Looks like the bullet drilled him right through the breastbone. He was dead before he hit the ground."

"Poor bastard," Dunbar said, shaking his head. "I'll never get used to the sight of a dead man or feel good about it, either, whether he's the enemy or not. Then again, I guess it was either him or us."

As it turned out, the lieutenant wasn't far wrong about that. Near the Chinese soldier's body lay not one, but two, Bangalore torpedoes. These were essentially shaped charges on a stick, designed to destroy vehicles or even penetrate tank armor. Wielding them was basically a suicide mission.

The small arms fire had done enough damage to the behemoth tank. The blast from a Bangalore torpedo would have had a far worse outcome and probably killed most of the tank crew.

Oddly, scattered around the dead soldier's body they could also see several leaflets in English. Dunbar picked one up, read for a moment, then snorted in disbelief. "Get a load of this. The Chinese want us to surrender and come over to their side. They're asking us to abandon our imperialist ways and join our Communist brothers."

"Do you think that ever works?" Hardy wondered.

"Hell, the Germans tried the same tactic in the last war," Dunbar said. "We know how well that worked. Let's just say that when they weren't dropping leaflets, the Germans with any sense were busy surrendering."

It did seem unlikely that any American soldiers would join the Chinese Communists, but Hardy supposed that stranger things had happened. Maybe one in a million switched sides just because he was crazy.

On the other hand, it wasn't nearly as unusual for the Chinese or North Koreans to abandon Communism. One ploy that had worked was the U.S. Government offering a reward for a Soviet-made MiG. A North Korean pilot had taken them up on the offer, earning himself a hundred thousand dollars and amnesty for delivering a MiG that could be taken apart and studied by the military.

Unfortunately, the rumor was that MiGs were outflying U.S. planes due to a superior design. The design came from German engineers snatched up by Stalin at the end of the last war. This was all part of the on-going chess game known as the Cold War.

But here on Hill 122 overlooking Outpost Kelly, there were more immediate concerns.

"If that Chinaman had gotten through with his Bangalore torpedo, we might have lost the tank, not to mention the crew." Dunbar shook his head. "We need to be on the lookout in case they try this stunt again. Knowing the Chinese, you can bet they will."

CHAPTER TEN

COLE RETURNED to the main line, having outfoxed the pursuing Chinese and delivering the downed pilot and three civilians to safety—not to mentioned himself and the kid. Considering what they had been up against, it was no small feat. But if Cole had expected praise, he was sadly mistaken.

"Don't ever pull a stunt like that again, Cole, you got that?" demanded Lieutenant Ballard, hands on hips, as he glared down at the sniper using all the advantage of his six-foot-three height.

"Yes, sir."

Ballard always seemed to have it in for him. Even after all that they had been through, the lieutenant did not seem to trust him entirely or much like him. It probably had something to do with the fact that Ballard was a college-educated officer and Cole was a nobody hillbilly —but deep-down, Ballard likely knew which of them was the more capable man.

For his own part, Cole didn't give a damn what Ballard thought. He considered the lieutenant to be a decent officer, just as Ballard would have reluctantly admitted that Cole was a capable soldier. As for being a hillbilly, no arguments there—that had been Cole's nickname for years now.

The lieutenant could dress him down all that he wanted, but to Cole, the words were only like so much water off a duck's back.

However, the pilot was having none of it. After all, he had just been rescued by Cole and seen him in action. He didn't give a damn if the man talked like a peckerwood and had a Confederate flag painted on his helmet. As far as he was concerned, Cole was the real deal.

"Now hold on a minute," Lieutenant Commander Miller said, stepping forward to address Ballard. "I owe this man my life. Without him, I'd be a Chinese prisoner and halfway to Beijing by now."

"You're the pilot who got shot down," Ballard remarked.

"Lieutenant Commander Jake Miller," he said. "And yes, I did get shot down—along with my wingman. But not before we took out a few of those MiGs. We were fighting Soviets up there, not Chinese or sorry-assed North Korean pilots. Hell, I don't think those people fly anything more than kites."

"Soviets?" Ballard seemed surprised.

"Sure, they're mixed up in this war, although they're trying not to get their hands dirty. I think they would have left us alone, but we weren't going to stand for that."

Ballard didn't seem to know what to say. Instead, he turned his attention to the three civilians. The older man and the boy kept their eyes on the ground. However, Jang-mi glared defiantly at the officer.

"The last thing we need is more gooks around here. Who are these people, anyhow?" Ballard asked, clearly bewildered. He was even more surprised when it was the Korean woman who answered him.

"We helped save your pilot," she said. "I am not a gook. I am Korean. You can call me Jang-mi."

"You speak English?"

"When I must," she said. "Many people in our village died when the Chinese soldiers came looking for your pilot."

"Your village?"

"Many miles from here, between the Imjin-gang and the Lǒngmo Sanseong. You would call it Fortress Lǒgnmo."

"Fortress?" To his surprise, every response from the woman seemed only to prompt more questions and leave him more confused. He was not aware of any fortifications beyond Outpost Kelly. From the corner of his eyes, Ballard noticed a grin play over Cole's thin lips.

"Yes, it is where my ancestors stood against the Japanese and the Chinese. You see, my people are used to fighting invaders."

"It was Jang-mi and these two who found me after my parachute came down," Miller explained. "There were some others, but they didn't make it."

"We ran into some Chinese," Cole explained. "Just a patrol, but they were determined cusses, I'll give 'em that. The thing is, sir, there's a whole lot more Chinese out there. A lot more than we thought. Hell, I'd say there's a whole army out there in the hills."

"That's nonsense," Ballard said. "We've seen some enemy activity, but there is no evidence of a large army."

"I have seen them," Jang-mi spoke up. "Many Chinese soldiers."

"She's right," Miller said. "When I was coming down in my chute, the hills looked like they were crawling with Chinese."

Ballard looked at Cole. He didn't know these other two, even if one was a fellow officer, and so he did not trust their observations. Even if he didn't like Cole, he knew that his designated sniper wasn't one to exaggerate.

Cole nodded curtly. "It's true. If the Chinese are headed our way, I reckon we're in trouble."

"Nuts," Ballard said.

* * *

TO ADD TO THE SITUATION, it seemed that there was a lot of rain coming. It was what the Koreans called a monsoon. Korea's weather wasn't all that different from that of the United States, with a few notable exceptions. The summers could be hot and humid, with temperatures getting into the nineties. Winters tended to be cold and dry, although the mountainous regions received their fair share of snow —just ask any survivors of the Chosin Reservoir campaign about that.

What made Korean weather a bit different was monsoon season, generally a couple of weeks each summer and winter. This occurred when moist air swept in from the Pacific and brought with it deluging rains—or snow in the winter monsoon season. The weather pattern was a little like what Americans would call "El Nino" in decades to come.

While the South Koreans were well-familiar with the monsoon season, this was something new for many of the U.S. troops.

"Gonna rain," Cole announced, sniffing the air like a caveman. As someone who had lived his whole life mostly outdoors, he was attuned to the weather and the seasons.

"If you say so," the kid replied, looking doubtfully at the Korean sky. He saw a few clouds, but it didn't look like rain to him.

Cole took out his trenching tool and dug the ditch deeper around their pup tent, which was comprised of two canvas shelter halves buttoned together along the ridge.

The kid watched him for a moment, then joined in with his own trenching tool. He knew that not much got by Cole. If the hillbilly said it was going to rain, then you had better dig a deeper ditch around your tent.

The tent didn't provide more than basic shelter. Two short poles raised the roof just enough for them to sit upright as long as they were directly under the highest part of the tent. There wasn't any floor.

Their tent was not the Ritz, but after the mission to rescue the pilot, they had some welcome down time. Nobody was shooting at them, at last.

The pilot along with Jang-mi and her companions were staying at the MLR for now. With the hills crawling with Chinese, it would be dangerous for Jang-mi and her companions to try to get back to her village. Besides, how much of the village was even left after what the Chinese had done to it?

As for the pilot, he was cooling his heels until he could get a Jeep ride out of here. Again, the Chinese hadn't been making that an easy proposition.

For Cole and kid, some extra time without much to do was welcome for a change. It helped that they had plenty of rations and actual choices—the canned franks and beans were the most popular among the men, with Hershey bars for dessert. They could make fires to heat up their rations and boil coffee. Unlike the Chinese, they didn't need to hide their cooking fires from enemy planes or from the Chinese, who knew they were there and were watching them from the heights of the Rice Mound, about a mile distant from the outpost.

During the night, there had been a hot little fight to repel a small raid against the line of tanks defending the crest of the hill that anchored this section of the line, but it had not been a full-fledged attack. One thing about the Chinese was that they loved their raids and they were excellent night fighters.

"I heard those guys let the Chinese through," the kid said, nodding at several soldiers from the Puerto Rican regiment who were walking by at the moment. Even by the standards of troops who had been in the field a while, these fellows looked sloppy—some not wearing helmets, uniforms a mess, and none of them carrying weapons in a combat zone as required.

"If Lieutenant Ballard sees them, he'll have a fit and give them hell."

"For all the good it will do," Cole said. "I understand that most of them don't speak English."

"No wonder the Chinese got through our lines and hit those tanks."

"One thing about the Chinese is that if they want to get through, they usually do," Cole said. "They must have been after those tanks to knock 'em out. They may be planning a larger attack."

"I sure hope not," the kid said. "I'm no general, but now would be a good time for the Chinese to catch us with our pants down."

Cole grunted. "You got that right, kid. Let's hope the goons don't figure that out."

One of the units assigned to the outpost was rotating out and new troops were coming in. This meant that for a few days at least, there would be new soldiers and new officers who didn't yet have their bearings. If the Chinese had any inkling of that situation, it would indeed be a good time to attack.

Mail call came around. It was a testament to the efficiency of the military that letters and packages reached them even out here, but then again, mail from home was considered almost sacred. The kid went down to collect his mail. He almost always got a letter from home or from a girl he was sweet on back home.

Cole didn't bother. Instead, he spread out his rifle on a blanket and began to clean it meticulously. He did this daily, whether or not the rifle had been fired or dragged through the mud and dust.

The kid came back all smiles. "Cleaning your rifle again. Why don't you just wait until before we go on patrol?"

"If you're always ready, you ain't got to get ready."

"Maybe you can tear yourself away from that rifle long enough to take a look at your mail."

"What?"

He looked up in surprise at the envelope the kid was waving at him. Cole had received exactly two letters while in Korea, both from Norma Jean Elwood.

"It's your girlfriend again," the kid said. Because he had read Cole's two previous letters to him, this could only mean that this was another letter from Norma Jean.

Truth be told, she was the reason why Cole was in Korea in the first place. He had been hunting on a fall morning back home when he came across two men about to attack the young woman after her old car had broken down. Those two lowlifes had ended up dying of lead poisoning, and Cole had been left with the choice of prison or Korea. He didn't regret those events at all and would do it all over again in a heartbeat rather than choosing to leave Norman Jean to the wolves.

Cole shook his head at the proffered envelope.

"Go on and read it to me," he said. "I've got gun oil all over my hands."

The kid tore open the envelope. Although Cole hadn't come out and said it, the kid had figured out by now that the hillbilly couldn't read. The kid had even written back to Norma Jean on Cole's behalf.

He knew that he could josh Cole about spending all that time cleaning his rifle, but he left the topic of illiteracy alone. He thought it would be a bad idea to embarrass Cole about not being able to read—

not if you wanted to live to tell the tale. If Cole liked you, you could consider yourself lucky. If you got on his bad side, you were just a step away from getting flensed by that big Bowie knife he carried. When Cole got mad, he had the coldest, hardest eyes that the kid had ever seen.

Without further comment, he cleared his throat and read:

* * *

DEAR CAJE,

Another season has gone and went, so I reckoned I should write. I do appreciate your letter. It was real nice to get that.

The mountains have changed a lot because many of the younger people who left for jobs during the war never came home. That's the way of things, I suppose, but I never plan to leave home. I want to stay here and raise a family someday. What do you think of that?

I hope you don't mind that I went by your workshop and swept out the cobwebs and mice. Mrs. Bailey said that was all right to do. I figured it was the least I could do so that is ready when you come back.

Maybe that won't be so long from now. President Truman says this war won't last much longer, and who don't believe what they say in Washington?

Your friend,
Norma Jean Elwood

* * *

"WELL HOW ABOUT THAT," Cole said. He was a man who mostly kept his emotions in check—except for the angry ones—but he had to admit that the letter made him feel an unexpected warmth inside. It wasn't the words so much as the fact that someone on the other side of the world gave a damn about Caje Cole. She was even looking after the workshop that Hollis Bailey had given him.

"You want to write her back?" the kid asked.

"No," Cole said.

"What? Why not? She's got it bad for you, you know."

"The next time I say something to Norma Jean, it's going to be in person, not in a damn letter."

Cole went back to cleaning his rifle, his lips tight, but he was grinning to himself.

CHAPTER ELEVEN

THE NEXT MORNING, Hardy reluctantly left the company of the tankers and went down to complete his primary mission, which was to interview the soldiers from Puerto Rico.

At his arrival, a few soldiers had emerged from their foxholes. While it wasn't unusual for discipline to be relaxed on the front line, this was the most motley crew of soldiers that he had seen by far. Their uniforms were new enough, but the troops had a disheveled look that ranged from untucked shirts and ragged, muddy trouser cuffs to several men wearing wide-brimmed hats rather than helmets. Compared to the rest of the U.S. Army, their appearance was certainly unique.

Hardy had seen a few Aussies wearing similar hats, but no Americans. Anyhow, who wouldn't prefer a steel helmet on his head?

These Puerto Ricans were in stark contrast to the well-disciplined tank unit that he had just left. Under Lieutenant Dunbar, the tankers were not necessarily spit and polish, but they were battle ready. They drilled relentlessly, followed a strict schedule, and maintained everything from their rifle and uniforms to the tanks themselves religiously. Could the same be said of these men?

Hardy didn't think so.

While Hardy sized up these soldiers, they were busy staring curiously back at him, mainly because he carried a notepad and a camera.

There was something else different about these soldiers and he stared back, not quite able to put his finger on it.

Before Hardy could figure out what had caught his attention, an officer appeared from the dugout. The man was not as dark-complected as the men, but like them, he wore a carefully trimmed mustache.

That's when it dawned on Hardy that all of these men wore mustaches—the ones who were old enough to shave, at least. In an army where most men were required to be cleanshaven, this instantly set them apart.

During a few days in the field or under combat conditions, soldiers weren't expected to shave. A few days of stubble was the norm. But once they were back in camp, out came the razors as the soldiers cleaned up their appearance.

"Who the hell are you?" the officer with the mustache demanded. To Hardy's surprise, the officer did not look or sound Puerto Rican.

"Private Hardy, sir. I've been sent by *Stars and Stripes* to write about the 65th Infantry. I flew in yesterday. Didn't anyone tell you I was coming to do a story?"

"Hell, no," the officer said, looking Hardy up and down skeptically. "That was you who flew in? When we saw the chopper, we were expecting General Ridgeway. Or somebody important, at least. Not a reporter."

"No sir, just me. I hope that I can have a few minutes of your time, sir."

"Here we are facing the Chinese, and this is what division sends. A guy with a notebook and a camera? It figures. We could use some ammo. Better yet, why not ship us a crate of steaks on that chopper?"

"I'm not sure, sir."

The officer muttered something in Spanish. "*Que desastre. Qué idiota.*"

"Sir?"

"That's Spanish for hello and welcome."

Having caught the word idiot mixed in there, Hardy thought that he wasn't getting the full story. However, he wasn't here to antagonize the officer. Just the opposite—he needed this officer's blessing to write the story. If he didn't get it, it was going to be a long trip back and a chewing out by the editor out once he returned to *Stars and Stripes*.

"Do you have a few minutes to talk to me, sir?"

"All right, all right. What do you want to know?"

"If you would, sir, please tell me a little about the unit."

Up until then, the officer had seemed annoyed. Now, he threw back his head and belted out some good-natured laughter. "Private, this is one of the most unique units in the whole army. Where should I start?"

"It's best to start most stories at the beginning, sir."

The officer scowled at him and said, "I can't tell if you're serious or a smartass, Private, but I will give you the benefit of the doubt. Walk with me. I'm Captain McDaniel by the way, and as you have probably deduced, I am not Puerto Rican. That's a whole different part of the story, believe me."

* * *

THE CAPTAIN GAVE him a run-down of the unit's background, which Hardy appreciated. He knew some of it, but McDaniel gave him more details.

"Here in Korea, the Puerto Ricans feel that they have something to prove," McDaniel said. "They want themselves and their island to be seen as the equals of the rest of the United States. Their actions on the battlefield might even prompt a first step toward statehood."

"They don't have any representation in Congress," Hardy said. "It's like the colonies back in the days of King George."

"More than that, the Puerto Ricans intend to prove that their soldiers were very much the equal of their mainland military counterparts," McDaniel said.

"Are they, sir?"

McDaniel did not answer the question directly. "There are three things that you need to know about the 65th Infantry," Captain McDaniel said, leading the way along a narrow path that ran behind

the unit's placement along the MLR. "First, we're known as the Borinqueneers."

"What's that mean?" asked Hardy, who was busy scribbling in his
notebook while simultaneously trying to watch where he was walking.

"Well, it doesn't really have a translation," the captain said. "It
comes from the name of an Indian tribe, like the Cheyenne or the
Cherokee. You see, the Borinque were one of the main Indian tribes
on Puerto Rico before the Spanish came, and a lot of the men trace
their ancestry back to the tribe. Hence the nickname, Borinqueneers."

"Got it."

"The second thing is that we wear mustaches," he said, touching
the impressive stash on his upper lip. "We're the only unit in the
United States military allowed to skip the razor on a regular basis."

"What's the third thing?"

"I saved the best for last. You see, as Borinqueneers our rations
officially include rice and beans. It's what most Puerto Ricans live off,
you see. It seems our boys can't fight without a belly full of rice and
beans."

Hardy smiled. "No offense, sir, but I think you should have told the
army that you couldn't fight without a belly full of prime rib."

The captain laughed. "The army got off cheap, wouldn't you say?
Don't put that in the article."

"Again, no offense sir, but you don't look Puerto Rican."

"I'm not," Captain McDaniel admitted. "I got assigned to the unit
because I'm from Texas and picked up a little Spanish over the years.
Most of these boys don't speak a word of English. They were short on
officers, so here I am."

"I can't think of any other unit that doesn't speak English. You'd
have to go back to the Civil War, when there were units made up
mostly of immigrants who only spoke German or Gaelic."

"You know your history," McDaniel said. "Of course, the fact that
most of the men don't speak English has caused more than a little
confusion at times, believe me."

"I can imagine, sir."

"I've got to tell you that I wasn't thrilled at first about being
assigned to this unit, but since then, I've seen how the Borinqueneers

got the short end of the stick over the years. For starters, up until this war, the dark-skinned Puerto Ricans were sent to serve in colored units. Never mind the fact that they were every bit the equal of the other men who signed up to serve. The Puerto Ricans don't judge people by their skin color, the way that we do. In that regard, you might say that they are more advanced than mainland Americans."

"It doesn't seem right, sir."

"It's not. It's an attitude that's changing slowly. If these fellas do a good job, minds may change faster."

It was all a lot for Hardy to absorb. He reassured himself that his editor didn't want a piece on the sweeping history of Puerto Rico. *Stars and Stripes* wasn't looking for a unit history, either. Hardy found it all very interesting because he had a natural affinity for soaking up stories and information, but he knew those paragraphs would have been deleted with a few strokes of the editor's sharp pencil.

He would try to sum the unit's history in a few sentences and focus on the present, instead. McDaniel was giving him plenty. He was here to write about the contributions that the Borinqueneers were making to holding the line against the enemy.

In other words, he had been sent to write a puff piece. Being a budding wordsmith, Hardy knew that the term came from "puffery," which was when male birds puffed out their feathers to make themselves look bigger to scare off rivals and impress females. He couldn't help but wonder if the Borinqueneers' mustaches were a similar form of puffery. Or did they have the stuff to be good soldiers?

Up ahead, someone waved at Captain McDaniel and shouted something in Spanish.

He turned to Hardy. "Look, I've got to go. I'm sure that I talked your ear off enough as it is. Why don't you go talk to some of the men? There's a handful that speak English, but you might have to look."

"I'll do that, sir."

"Here's a tip. Start with, '*Hola.*' At least you'll be speaking their language."

* * *

LEAVING THE CAPTAIN, Hardy approached a group of men sitting in a rough circle, heating water for coffee over a fire. They looked up at him with questioning expressions that were not entirely friendly.

"Hello, uh, *hola*."

For someone like Hardy, who had grown up in the Midwest of the 1940s, the Spanish language was something exotic. In America, it was accepted that most people spoke English, just like the Pilgrims did. Spanish was the language of brown-skinned foreigners. Thus, it wasn't much of a surprise that the Puerto Ricans were seen as second-class citizens by everyone from the U.S. command structure to other troops.

His hope was to find at least one soldier who spoke enough English that he could get the common soldier's perspective to include in his article. Considering the blank looks that he was getting, maybe that was too much to expect. He wondered on earth these men were supposed to understand orders if they were not spoken in Spanish. And then the answer came to him that they would not.

He shook his head and was just about to move on the try elsewhere when one young soldier spoke up. "Yes?"

The soldier had been sitting, but now he stood. Hardy looked him up and down. He was shorter and slighter than the reporter, whose hefty build betrayed his roots as an Indiana farm boy. The Puerto Rican soldier was barely more than a teenager, by all appearances. Like the other Puerto Ricans, he wore a mustache, but it was struggling to get itself established, like spindly corn stalks in a drought. Some of the other men were much older, with hard, lined faces and mustaches shot through with gray. They might have been veterans of the last war. Their dark eyes were cold and appraising.

"You speak English?" Hardy asked hopefully.

"A little," the soldier said. "My grandmother was American and she taught me."

"Excellent," Hardy said. The soldier's accent was thick, but the meaning was clear enough to Hardy's ears. "What's your name?"

"Francisco Vasquez." The youngster grinned. "*Mis amigos* call me Cisco."

"Thanks for talking with me, Cisco. My name's Don Hardy." Cisco seemed momentarily taken aback, and Hardy remembered something about "don" being an honorific like "lord" in the old Spanish empire. He hurried to explain. "Don as is Donald, not Don Quixote. How long have you been with the 65th infantry?"

"Just a few weeks."

Hardy was surprised. "Didn't you have basic training in Puerto Rico?"

Cisco shook his head. "They gave me a uniform and put me on a boat for Korea," he said. "Once I got here, they gave me a rifle and *estos soldados viejos* taught me how to shoot. A lot of us here are like that."

Hardy stopped writing. "That's it for training?"

"*Si. Esa es la verdad.*"

Hardy shook his head. If that truly was the extent of the training Private Vasquez—and possibly the others had received—it explained a lot about their less-than-military appearance. At least this young soldier spoke some English. For those Puerto Ricans who only knew Spanish, Hardy couldn't imagine what it must be like not to understand what the officers were saying.

Hardy felt sympathy for these men. He could see that they had drawn the short straw in more ways than one, both as second-rate soldiers and citizens. The trouble was that many officers expressed only disgust for these men who were fighting for their country. Hardy thought it wasn't right and was glad for a chance to write about it.

"I'm not all that surprised by what you just told me," Hardy responded. "I wasn't here then, but I heard that there were a lot of guys rushed through basic training so that they had troops over here, especially last year when it looked like the Chinese and North Koreans were going to overrun the peninsula. Sometimes, basic training was shortened to two weeks."

Cisco held up two fingers and grinned. "*Dos semanas?* Wow! More like *dos dias por mio!*"

* * *

WHAT CISCO VASQUEZ didn't add was that life as a Borinqueneer wasn't so bad, once you got used to it. So far, he had come through the limited fighting unscathed. There was enough to eat, including the daily beans and rice, and plenty of camaraderie among the enlisted men. Many tended to treat Cisco like their little brother and took him under their wing. The fact that he spoke English gave him a small measure of importance because he could communicate with the officers and mainland soldiers.

He had come from a large family of eight brothers and sisters in Puerto Rico. That was a lot of mouths to feed, and so it was with some relief that his parents received the news that he had enlisted. There were a few middle-class Puerto Rican families—doctors and business owners or higher-ranking officials of the government. For everyone else, life was mostly a struggle. Many young people left for places like New York City or joined the military like Cisco because it was their best option for a better life.

He wasn't even eighteen yet, but that didn't stop the recruiter. The United States needed soldiers to fight the war in Korea, and Puerto Rico was eager to do its part.

Always, there was the carrot that the United States held out that Puerto Rico might someday become a state if the island did its part in the Korean War.

"You will grow to be a man," the recruiter had said, giving Cisco's thin biceps a squeeze. "When you return, you will need to beat the girls off with a stick!"

That had sounded good to Cisco. But in his first skirmish, Cisco had quickly realized that he would be lucky to get home to his island again. War proved deadly and terrifying. Everything had been so confusing, with explosions and bullets whistling overhead. He had struggled to load and fire his unfamiliar rifle, but he did the best he could. He was a Borinqueneer now, and the Borinqueneers did not run from a fight.

But when one of the officers shouted an order in English, the men around him had not known what to do. "*Que? Que?*" they asked. The noise of battle added to the confusion and uncertainly.

Cisco had found himself translating the orders as best he could. He soon found himself assigned to be a runner, carrying messages from the officers to the Spanish-speaking squads in the field. It was a dangerous task, but Cisco had never shirked from danger. It was also an assignment of some importance. The others depended on him now, never mind the fact that he was young and inexperienced. He was glad that his *abuela* had made him practice English.

Of course, he did not share any of this with the reporter. It was more than the reporter wanted to know.

"How's the food?" the reporter asked. "I hear that you guys prefer rice and beans over C rations."

Cisco smiled and nodded. Here was a question that he could answer.

"A Puerto Rican soldier fights on rice and beans. What good will canned food do him? Canned food feeds the belly but not the soul."

The reporter wrote it all down.

CHAPTER TWELVE

LIKE A FAUCET TURNED ON, the monsoon rains came down. To Cole, the volume of water coming down reminded him of a summer downpour in the mountains, but whereas those thunderstorms unleashed their fury and rolled on through, these monsoon rains fell unrelenting.

"Better build an ark," Cole said to the kid. "We might be needing one, from the looks of things."

"At least the rain will keep the Chinese quiet," the kid responded.

"Don't be so sure about that."

In Cole's experience, the Chinese chose to attack in the dark of night and in the bitter cold. Why should the rain be any different? The enemy took every advantage of the weather and terrain. Grudgingly, he had to admire that, because it was just the way Cole himself chose to fight.

They sat in their tent and watched it rain, glad that they had dug the ditch around their tent deeper. Even so, the ditch threatened to overflow and flood their blankets. From time to time, others in the squad shouted through the storm to one another. Some stripped off and took a shower under the streaming sky, taking advantage of the fact that the cool nights had been replaced by warm and humid conditions riding the coattails of the monsoon.

Jang-mi and the two Korean villagers who had helped them rescue the pilot were bivouacked with the South Koreans. Briefly, Cole wondered how they were faring in all this rain. He was sure that Jang-mi just shrugged it off. The monsoon season was something that the people here had learned to take in stride. Not much seemed to bother her, anyhow. In Cole's opinion, she was one tough customer.

They heard the squishing footsteps of someone approaching through the rain.

"Hello? I'm looking for Cole and Wilson. Anybody home?"

To their surprise, it was Lieutenant Commander Miller, slogging through the rain in a sodden poncho. He had been billeted with the company officers near the command post. He was carrying some sort of package.

"Over here, sir," the kid shouted into the rain.

"Scooch over," the pilot said.

Moments later, he came barreling in through the tent flap, wet poncho and all. The three of them were suddenly like sardines in the confines of the tiny tent. The pilot also seemed to bring the monsoon inside with him. He flipped back the dripping hood of the poncho and took off his helmet, further managing to drench the interior of the tent.

"I like what you've done with the place," he said, pulling his legs under him and sitting awkwardly at one end of the tent.

"I'm sure it's not what you're used to, coming from officer country."

"There is a little more room in the officer's quarters," the pilot agreed. "However, you have to share the space with the rats. Big buggers, they are."

He lifted the package. "Anyhow, that's why I brought this over. Can't let the rats have it."

"What is it?" the kid asked.

"Open it and see."

Like a kid on Christmas morning, Tommy tore into the package. To his pleasant surprise, he found a box filled with snacks from the United States: Crackerjacks, chewing gum, Oreo cookies, and some Slim Jims.

"What in the world? Look at all this stuff."

"It's some sort of Red Cross package. I swiped it when nobody was looking. You can share it around with your squad. I figured it was the least I could do for you guys, to say thanks for saving my bacon."

"We saw what you did up there," Cole said. "You shot down those other planes. We saved your bacon so you can get yourself another plane and do it all over again."

"That's the plan, but I won't be going anywhere in this rain. Everything is bogged down." The pilot rearranged his poncho, pulling it back over his helmet. "I ought to be getting back. I think three is a crowd in this little tent."

The kid was grinning. "Thanks for the snacks, sir."

Lieutenant Commander Miller gave a wave, then disappeared into the heavy rain.

"That was awful decent of him," the kid said.

"Glad we didn't let the Chinese get him, after all," Cole had to agree. "Now pass them Crackerjacks over here."

* * *

A SHORT DISTANCE AWAY, Hardy and the tankers of the 7th Tank Company were also contending with the heavy rain. The road up Hill 199 that had been so dry and dusty for weeks now resembled a muddy river. Across the Imjin River valley, the heavy rain also obscured the hills held by the Chinese and hid the U.N. outpost positions forward of the MLR. Those poor bastards on Outpost Kelly were truly on their own in this weather, Hardy thought.

Right now, there were more immediate problems caused by the rain. One of the tanks was trying to come back up the hill after refueling and repairs.

Lieutenant Dunbar was aghast. "What the hell do those guys think they're doing? I told them to stay put!"

"They must not have gotten the order, sir."

"No kidding."

Dunbar waded across the deep ditch beside the road that was now a torrent, then reached the muddy road, hoping to get the tank turned around before it became mired down. Already, water ran downhill across the surface of the road in a stream several inches deep. The running water met the tracks of the tank and pooled deeper. Soon, the tracks were spinning hopelessly in the muck, digging itself in deeper.

The lieutenant gestured for the tank to reverse, but nobody could see him through the rain. He tried to run toward the tank, but the running water swept his feet out from under him and the officer sprawled in the wet road.

Hardy helped him back to his feet.

"I can't believe this," he spluttered. He shouted into the rain and wind. "Turn around, dammit!"

Finally, the poncho-covered man in the turret waved an acknowledgment. The tank started to back up, but it was a case of too little, too late.

The sodden road under the tank could no longer support the weight of the tank and began to give way, collapsing into the ditch along the roadside. The sheer weight of the tank worsened the avalanche of mud, carrying the great armored beast into the ditch. The tank slid backwards and sideways before finally lodging in the ditch, stuck fast.

"Dammit!" the lieutenant cried. He waded toward the tank, and after the crew had crawled out, gave them a memorable ass-chewing. There was nothing to be done with the tank until the rain stopped and the road dried out, so Dunbar headed back to the bunker to wait out the storm, with Hardy in tow.

"What are you going to do about the tank?" Hardy asked.

"Frankly, there's not much we can do in this rain and mud. This is lousy country for tanks." The lieutenant shook his head. "Don't put that in your article."

* * *

THE MONSOON LASTED THREE DAYS. While the rain seemed endless, they were lucky that the deluge hadn't gone on longer. According to the South Koreans, the unrelenting rain sometimes lasted for a week or more, but this monsoon had come late in the season.

When it finally stopped raining, it was hard to know whether to measure the rainfall in inches or feet. Every ditch and stream overflowed with muddy water. Even the snakes had sought refuge in the scrub trees—or the bunkers, much to the horror of the soldiers. Some of the men took to going everywhere they went with a trenching tool, which made a handy weapon for beheading snakes. Suddenly, the threat of a Chinese attack took a backseat to their common misery of mud, water, and reptiles.

Hardy soaked it all in, having become a keen observer. He doubted that the *Stars and Stripes* would be interested in a story about waterlogged soldiers, but he found it all fascinating. The cool weather before the monsoon had temporarily disappeared. The sun returned and superheated the steamy air, making everyone and everything drip with humidity. Hanging out wet bedding or clothing to dry seemed pointless in the damp, still air, but everybody did it anyway. The machine-gun emplacements and trenches of the Main Line of Resistance appeared to have been replaced by an endless laundry line.

Maybe that sight would intimidate the enemy where all that weaponry and barbed wire had not, he thought.

Hardy started toward the bunker where he was staying with the tank crew, thinking that he might as well try to hang his damp blanket out to dry. There was a chance that it would smell better, at least.

As he started toward the garage-like entryway, a shout stopped him in his tracks.

"Don't go in there!" He looked around and spotted Lieutenant Dunbar waving at him. "The whole damn thing is about to give way!"

Hardy thought at first that the lieutenant had lost his mind. The bunker was sturdy enough to withstand mortar fire and machine guns. There was nothing more threatening than the blue, humid sky.

But looking more closely, he could see that the bunker was sliding sideways, ever so slowly. The sandbagged roof appeared to be going in one direction, while the walls were going in another. The bunker had become so waterlogged that the saturated ground was literally oozing out from beneath it.

Hardy thought about his notes and his precious camera within. "Sir, all my gear is in there."

"Private, that bunker is about to fall down."

Hardy glanced at the teetering structure. All that he needed with thirty seconds to get in there, grab his camera and notebooks, and run back out.

Without waiting for the lieutenant to tell him otherwise, Hardy dashed inside.

The dark interior looked and felt like what being inside the belly of a whale must feel like. Going from the bright daylight to the dark bunker meant that he had to feel his way toward his bunk. All around him, he heard the structure creak and groan. Even the rats had abandoned the place. As for any snakes, he tried not to think about them.

He grabbed his camera bag and the stack of notebooks shoved under his blanket for safekeeping, then turned to go.

He saw the bottle of bourbon on an upended crate that had served as the lieutenant's desk, and on a whim, he grabbed it.

Overhead, something gave way with a shuddering pop, and he was showered with mud and debris, the force of it knocking him to his knees. He looked toward the bright portal of the doorway and was horrified to see the rectangular shape being pulled and stretched into something more like a trapezoid.

More pops and groans filled the space. Scrambling to his feet, Hardy made a run for the door and twisted sideways to get through it, clutching his gear to him.

As soon as he was out on the muddy road, he turned and watched as the bunker finally collapsed. Another few seconds inside and he would have been buried under tons of mud, timbers, and sandbags.

"That was a bonehead thing to do," the lieutenant said, coming up beside him and staring at the wreckage. "I hope that was worth it for a bunch of notebooks."

"I think so. If I had gone back to *Stars and Stripes* without anything to show for this trip, the editor would have buried me for sure." Hardy held up his reporter's tools. Then he brandished the bottle of bourbon that he had retrieved and presented it to the lieutenant with a grin.

"Huh," the lieutenant said, taking the bottle. "You know what? I was about to chew you out for your sheer stupidity, but now I might just put you in for a medal."

While the Chinese had remained quiet in the wake of the rain, the tankers were soon put to work in new and unexpected ways. Hardy tagged along to watch.

A couple of tanks had been at the bottom of the hill undergoing servicing before the monsoon began, and now there was little hope of getting them up the muddy road to occupy an enfilade position. It turned out to be a lucky thing.

The days of rain had left the Imjin River badly swollen. In places, the river overran its banks and flooded the river valley. That didn't much concern the troops occupying the hills. However, the supply road to the MLR and the string of outposts ran through the valley and relied upon a low, narrow bridge to span the Imjin. The brown, turbulent water was now even with the bottom of the bridge, even washing across the floorboards in places. Even so, the bridge still held.

But for how long? Bridge crossings had been limited to one vehicle at a time, so that if the bridge suddenly gave way, an entire convoy wouldn't be lost. To be sure, every driver held his breath and prayed when it was his turn to make the crossing.

To make matters worse, clumps of debris that included trees and even parts of peasant houses swept down the current and collided with the bridge.

That's where the tanks came in.

"All right, boys, time for some target practice," Lieutenant Dunbar announced.

The two spare tanks were maneuvered into position on the river-bank. The two crews were tasked with shooting the larger debris before it could reach the bridge.

Soon, the humid air was filled with the sound of tank fire, the rounds turning the debris into splinters. From time to time, the trajectory caused a round to bounce across the water like a skipping stone. The rounds then went flying off into the valley to explode, terrifying the truck drivers and South Koreans who found themselves on the winding road through that valley. The danger posed by the friendly fire was outweighed by the necessity of saving the bridge.

Watching the tanks unleash their firepower, Lieutenant Dunbar just laughed. "This must be the most unusual duty I've seen yet for a tank. Is this the craziest damn war, or what?"

Nearby, a tank fired, resulting in a burst of flame and a gout of water that transformed a drifting tree threatening the bridge into splinters. Hardy clicked his camera shutter at just the right moment to capture the scene on film.

"Crazy," he agreed.

Still, it was a hell of a lot of fun to watch.

The tanks kept at it well into the night, when a big searchlight was brought in to illuminate targets on the river. Hitting the debris was more challenging at night, but the tank gunners still did an impressive job.

Gradually, Hardy and the lieutenant became aware of the sound of more distant firing. They turned around and saw the flashes of artillery and mortar fire in the hills.

"What's going on?" Hardy wondered. "That doesn't sound like our own artillery."

"So much for it being quiet around here. It looks to me like Outpost Kelly is under attack," the lieutenant said.

CHAPTER THIRTEEN

WHEN THE ATTACK on the outpost began, Cole and the rest of his squad were called from their sodden tents to bolster the defensive line. There was always the possibility that the Chinese attack on Outpost Kelly was just a ruse and that their real intent was to punch through the Main Line of Resistance.

"Don't this beat all. I've seen hog troughs that looked better," Cole muttered, slogging with the others into trenches half-filled with muddy water. They used their helmets to bail out the trenches as if they were on a sinking boat. Most of the men found themselves crouching in the muddy water as the occasional Chinese shell whistled overhead. Keeping dry was hopeless. Keeping the actions and muzzles of their weapons free of mud was challenging.

"Do you think we have anything to worry about from the Chinese?" the kid asked nervously.

"It's hard to say, kid. They are sneaky bastards."

"That's for sure."

"Whatever you do, keep your weapon clear of the mud. If the Chinese do show up, you'll need it to shoot more than spitballs."

The monsoon had been like a respite from the war, the heavy rain shutting things down, but now the war had returned.

Watching from a distance, Cole saw the explosions of mortars pounding their boys on the hill. The crackle of small arms fire and the chatter of machine guns carried clearly to them on the humid air. The damn Chinese blew their bugles and whistles. When you weren't in the middle of a battle, getting shot at, Cole reckoned that war was indeed a grand spectacle.

He settled back, Cole's boots squelching as he tried to get comfortable. He put the rifle to his shoulder, using the scope to scan for any targets. However, Outpost Kelly was just too far to do any good against the Chinese, who were mostly keeping out of sight.

Briefly, he considered working his way forward so that he could lend a hand against the Chinese, but just as quickly decided against it. If an attack on the main line did come, he would be stranded in no-man's land.

It was best just to wait. He was sure their time to fight would come soon enough.

Until then, Cole would do what soldiers always had done. He would wait.

"Seems like a lot of fuss over nothing, don't it?" Cole mused, watching the fighting from the sidelines.

"Sure does," the kid agreed. "It's just another hill. If you don't like that one, pick another. There are plenty to choose from."

Cole grunted. "You'd be right about that."

There was nothing special about Outpost Kelly. It was just another outpost beyond the MLR that Cole and the others occupied.

The earlier days of the Korean conflict, with both sides moving over vast distances and fighting for control of huge territories, had long since devolved into something more akin to trench warfare. And yet, the lines remained somewhat fluid, with both sides pushing and pulling for every advantage.

The outposts set up by the United Nations forces were a way to lay claim to more territory beyond the MLR. The outposts also functioned as a canary in the coal mine to warn of enemy attack.

The problem was that the Chinese also wanted that territory—which explained the fight over Outpost Kelly, which otherwise occupied a useless hill among the many that filled the landscape.

It was no secret that the war had become like a game of musical chairs. When the music stopped, both sides wanted to make sure they had grabbed as much territory as possible, which explained why neither side was content to sit in their defenses and wait. Seizing the advantage of pushing a few miles one way or another could mean being able to lay claim to huge swaths of territory when the final lines were drawn between North and South Korea.

These lines on the map had real meaning, however. The entire futures of generations of Koreans would be decided by these final battles, depending upon which side of the boundaries their villages ended up. For Jang-mi and her village, it was looking more and more as if they would be on the wrong side of the fence.

Cole thought about that. Maybe he could talk her into staying? But for all he knew, she had already returned to her village in the hills.

The attack had come near dusk, and as full darkness arrived, the night came alive with explosions and tracer fire.

"Hey, that's the best Fourth of July fireworks I've ever seen!" somebody shouted.

"Shut up, you damn greenbean. See how you like it when you're in the middle of it."

That comment silenced the soldier, who surely had been one of the replacement troops who had just rotated in. Even the damn officers were all new for the most part in this section of the MLR. If the Chinese and North Koreans attacked now, they would have every advantage against the green troops and officers.

Cole watched the attack with the others, his sense of apprehension growing. "Those boys are catching hell," he said. "How much longer can they hold out?"

"The Chinese are throwing everything at 'em but the kitchen sink, that's for sure," the kid responded.

Cole had to agree, and before long, they had their answer. The fire on Outpost Kelly began to slacken, but not because the U.S. troops were winning the fight.

A pair of figures loomed out of the darkness.

Nervous fingers soon found triggers, a shot or two was fired, and the figures threw themselves to the ground.

"Hold your fire!" Lieutenant Ballard shouted. "Those are our guys!"

Ballard ordered the squad out to help them, and they half-dragged, half-carried the men back to the lines. These were the survivors of the fight for Outpost Kelly, which had been completely overrun.

A dozen more stragglers came in, battered and bloodied by the fight.

"Where's the rest of them?" somebody asked. The outpost had been in company strength. But as hard as the men in the trenches peered into the darkness, they couldn't see any additional survivors.

"The Chinese wiped them out," the kid said.

"So they did," Cole agreed.

"The whole company," the kid said in disbelief, a catch in his throat. "Just gone."

The kid was expressing how everybody felt, thinking about so many men being lost on that hillside. The Chinese would have used their bayonets to finish off any wounded left behind. Those poor, unlucky bastards. More than a few of the men around Cole had friends or acquaintances in the decimated company.

Soldiers shouted out names to the survivors. "Did Jameson make it?"

"What about Bowlegs Johnson?" another asked. "He still owes me ten bucks from a poker game."

The survivors just shook their heads before moving off toward the rear. In the darkness, a gloomy silence fell over the muddy ditches and trenches.

"Better get some sleep if you can, kid. Sure as a cow chews a cud, they're gonna send us to take back that hill in the morning."

* * *

"ALL RIGHT, men, here's the plan," explained the battalion commander at the bunker. "We cannot allow those Chinese to occupy Outpost Kelly permanently. If they establish artillery on that hill, they will be within easy range of our lines. Hell, they can just throw rocks at us if they want. It will also give them a base from which to constantly attack and harass our MLR."

In the crowded bunker, there were only grunts of assent. "Damn straight," someone muttered. "Shouldn't have lost Outpost Kelly in the first place."

"All right, that's enough of that," Lieutenant Colonel Switalski said impatiently. "We're just going to have to get that hill back."

The lieutenant colonel waited until everyone settled down. During the monsoon rains, the CP had been spared the same fate at the tankers' bunker and remained standing. Several officers and NCOs were packed into the cramped bunker, along with a few company clerks to serve as errand boys. The air was thick with cigarette smoke and the smell of bitter coffee, along with the dank odor of unwashed men and damp uniforms. It was clear that this was not a party at the 500 Club.

Don Hardy glanced at his Timex, blinking at the fact that it was two o'clock in the morning. For the men and officers in this section of the MLR, there was going to be precious little sleep tonight. Maybe not the next night, either.

Hardy stood in the back of the jammed bunker, trying to blend in. At over six feet tall, he stood out from the crowd, so he slouched down a bit.

"You may as well come along," Dunbar had said. "That way, you'll get the lay of the land for the attack."

"Are you sure it's all right, Lieutenant?"

Although Hardy was an enlisted man, he and the lieutenant had hit it off because they were nearly the same age and both college graduates. They had also turned out to have a similar enjoyment of reading western novels. They had even ended up swapping the paperbacks they had just finished. In the pages of a good western, the good guys always won and the bad guys always lost, which was not the case in Korea.

In one on one conversation, they were on a first-name basis. In front of anyone else, Hardy was careful to address the lieutenant as "sir." He was an officer, after all.

Unlike some officers, the lieutenant seemed to respect the fact that Hardy was doing his best to cover a war that was largely being forgotten. Americans back home had lost their taste for the war. Fighting Hitler and Emperor Hirohito in the last war had been a necessity that anyone could grasp, but defending a place most Americans couldn't pick out on a map felt pointless.

Although the *Stars and Stripes* was mainly a military publication, a lot of people back home read it—mainly the families of those in the military or retired military. Nonetheless, it remained an influential publication.

"If anyone asks, I'll just say that you're my aide de camp," the lieutenant had said. "But believe me, nobody is going to ask."

"All right, then. I'll come along and bring my notebook."

Hardy was just as happy to remain with the tankers during any counter-attack against Outpost Kelly. At the battle of Triangle Hill, he had found himself as part of the squad assaulting Chinese positions. While it had given him a great story, it was not an experience he was eager to repeat anytime soon.

Hardy didn't feel any need to prove himself again, nor did he feel any sense of cowardice at not being part of the attack. Instead, he felt a strong desire to survive the war and get on with his career as a journalist, preferably somewhere like the *Indianapolis Star*—where nobody would be shooting at him.

Lieutenant Colonel Switalski went on with the battle plan. "After the artillery and tanks firing in support soften them up, our assault will begin. The boys from the 65th will lead the advance, here and here." The officer tapped at a map that had been hung on the wall. "Charlie Company will attack here. Your orders, gentlemen, are to occupy and hold all positions. We need to take back that outpost."

"Yes, sir."

Looking closely at the map, Hardy could see that it was rudimentary—almost like something the coach would have drawn to illustrate plays back in his high school football days. And yet, the map effectively showed the hilltop, on which was a single command bunker and several mortar and machine-gun emplacements fortified with sandbags. About two thirds of the way up, a deep trench encircled the crown of the hill itself, reminding Hardy of a monk's tonsure. Basically, for the defense of Outpost Kelly, the United States Army had reconstructed an ancient hill fort.

Even from the back of the room, the plan seemed clear to Hardy.

But he had been in the Army long enough to know that plans were one thing, and what actually came about once the shooting started could be something totally different.

* * *

THE COUNTERATTACK BEGAN before first light. A remnant of the monsoon had moved in, resulting in a light drizzle adding to the misery of the already damp troops. After the gathering at the command post, the officers had returned to their units to prepare for the attack. For the men of the tank unit, this preparation had meant stacking rounds both on the ground and high on the back deck of their tanks for easy access.

Normally, ammunition was stored within the tank itself. But with the tanks stationary and acting as artillery, the idea was to enable a high rate of fire. Lieutenant Dunbar's plan was to essentially create a bucket brigade passing shells into the tank turrets. Hardy could have sat out the fight as an observer, but he volunteered to help with passing the shells.

"Much appreciated," Dunbar said, clearly pleased because the tankers were going to be shorthanded, even with the mechanics pressed into service. "This is going to be harder than pushing a pencil, you know."

"No worries there," Hardy said, flexing his big shoulders. He had stuck his reporter's notebook in his back pocket. "I grew up tossing hay bales, so this is nothing."

"One bit of advice," the lieutenant said. "Stuff some cotton in your ears."

When the firing began, Hardy was glad for that cotton. The four tanks on the hill opened up on the outpost with a deafening cacophony amplified and echoed by the hills and valleys.

Soon enough, Hardy realized that tossing hay bales into the loft of a barn had been good preparation for tank duty. Each 90 mm high explosive round weighed forty pounds and required wrestling it up from the ground to the tank turret. The first few shells weren't so bad, but then the work became grueling. It was taking two smaller men working in pairs to lift the shells, while the bigger men like Hardy insisted as a matter of pride that they didn't need help. They soon swallowed their pride and worked in pairs. The surface of the tank itself became slick with mud and rain. Hardy slipped and banged his knee hard against the tank. He felt his trousers rip and blood trickle, but there was no slowing down.

"Keep 'em coming!" one the tank crewmen shouted, popping his head out of the turret. If this was hard work out in the open, Hardy couldn't imagine what it must be like handling the heavy shells inside the cramped, stifling interior of the tank. The tankers' knees, elbows, and shins paid a heavy price with all of the jutting metal configurations of the tank interior that they navigated in semi-darkness.

It didn't help that the monsoon had left steamy summer-like temperatures in its wake. The sun hadn't even made an appearance, but the young men stripped off their shirts and let the sweat run off them in the humid pre-dawn stillness.

Hardy barely had time to look up and notice the fireworks show taking place on Outpost Kelly. Not only were four tanks hammering the Chinese-occupied position, but also the artillery. One white-hot explosion followed another on the hilltop. A dense pall of smoke hung over the hill, lit an angry red from below. The scene reminded Hardy not of a bombardment so much as a volcanic eruption.

It was almost possible to feel sorry for the enemy troops up there. How could they possibly survive?

However, the Chinese were not defenseless. Mortars returned fire from Outpost Kelly, along with Chinese artillery from Hill 377—the Rice Mound. Lucky for the tankers, they were well dug-in and protected.

A head popped out of the turret again. "Where's the lieutenant? We've got a problem. We can't see a thing. The barrel keeps steaming up."

The tanks were delivering such a high rate of fire that the light rain instantly turned to steam when it hit the hot steel of the barrel, obscuring their aim.

Expecting just such a problem, Lieutenant Dunbar had already worked out a solution earlier by plotting an azimuth and gunner's quadrant elevation to deliver fire to the hill. "Forget aiming by sight," he said. "We're going to aim by the numbers."

The tanks continued firing, adding to the hell on the hilltop.

CHAPTER FOURTEEN

COLE MOVED FORWARD, rifle at the ready, trying to see into the gloom. He was the first man in the squad, on point, leading them in the attack to retake Outpost Kelly.

Behind him, he heard a soldier fall out of line and retch, overcome by nerves. The squad was forced to halt and wait for him.

Cole held his breath, worried that the sound would give them away.

"Sorry, Hillbilly," the soldier muttered, wiping his mouth with the back of his hand and getting back into line. The man was no green-bean, but a veteran of more than one fight.

"Ain't nothin' to be sorry about," Cole replied quietly. Cole himself had lain awake much of the night, using the time to hone the Damascus steel of his Bowie knife to a razor's edge. "It's just the jitters. Hits everybody different."

"You think the Chinese are up there?" the kid asked, right behind Cole. "It's really quiet. Maybe they pulled out. Maybe they're all dead."

"Keep hoping, kid."

"I don't know how anyone could have survived that bombardment. That was a real pounding."

"You know these Chinese as well as I do, kid. They're damn hard to kill no matter how many bombs you drop on them."

"You've got a point, Hillbilly."

"Keep your eyes sharp. I want intervals, ya'll. Spread out now."

Cole resisted being in charge, but giving orders to the squad felt natural, like these men were an extension of himself.

Right now, their lives were in his hands.

It was also fair to say that his life was in their hands as well. They were counting on one another. That was the thing about combat. You knew the other guy had your back. He knew that you had his back. You might not like the other guy much; you might not even know him very well. But you sure as hell would fight for each other.

The kid was right about it being quiet. The bombardment by the tanks and artillery had been a real fireworks show. Now, the quiet was spooky.

The only sound was the scampering of rats, unseen in the gloaming. Humans and rats, he thought. Where you found one, you were likely to find the other.

But even the rats seemed to tread lightly, trying not to disrupt the quiet.

What made it worse was that Cole knew for damn sure that they weren't alone. Off to their left and right, more troops were converging on the hill. Behind them, yet more soldiers waited to move in and hold the defenses as the advance squads cleared them.

The troops around them were a given. But it was hard to say how many Chinese awaited the attack that they surely knew was coming. They had attacked in force, so there was at least one company dug in like ticks.

Outlined against the growing daylight, he could see the hump of the hill ahead. He had visited the outpost once or twice and was somewhat familiar with the layout. The crest of the hill contained defensive positions—or what was left of them after that hellish bombardment. He guessed that any Chinese who had survived would be waiting for the attack in the defensive ring of trenches that surrounded the crest of the hill. Several slit trenches stretched outward from the ring, resembling the fingers of a groping hand, extending down the face of the hill. It was one of these slit trenches that Cole and the squad moved through now.

Suddenly, he came to a stop. He could smell the Chinese just ahead. It was a foreign odor of garlic and raw onions, maybe with some fish mixed in.

He raised his rifle to his shoulder and pointed it down the trench.

Something shifted in the darkness ahead.

Cole fired.

The muzzle flash was like a stab to the eyeballs.

Up head, somebody cried out. Cole worked the bolt, fired again. Again, another stab of flame in the dark. He heard another body fall.

Cole felt pleased that they had taken the Chinese by surprise, slipping up on them in the darkness.

But any element of surprise on the main body of defenders had now been lost. Cole knew that these enemy soldiers in the trench had likely been in forward positions intended to detect the enemy advance. They had served their purpose. Higher on the hill, the Chinese would have heard the gunshots and known that the enemy attack was coming.

The next round of the fight over Outpost Kelly had begun.

He turned to look behind him. "All right now, don't bunch up. We've got to get through this trench up to the main defenses as fast as possible. They know we're comin' for 'em, and they'll be ready."

He started forward, but didn't get far. As it turned out, the Chinese had a few tricks up their sleeves.

What Cole hadn't suspected was that some of the enemy lurked outside the trench, hidden in the jumble of debris. They had the advantage of surprise and of height in that they were attacking the soldiers in the trench from above. They had been waiting for just this moment. And now, they pounced.

A screaming shape launched itself at Cole from above.

He was fast, but not fast enough. An instant later, he found himself knocked into the muddy bottom of the trench. A Chinese soldier stood over him, shouting and stabbing down at Cole with a bayonet on the end of a rifle.

Cole rolled just in time. The blade sank into the mud. His rifle had been knocked out of his hands. There was no time to go looking for it.

With his left hand, he grabbed the end of the rifle that the Chinese soldier was about drag free of the mud. With his right hand, he drew his Bowie knife and slashed it at the Chinese soldier's leg.

The enemy went down, his angry shouts now turned to screams of pain. Cole's knife slashed again and the screaming stopped.

Behind him, similar fights were taking place. Cole turned back to do what he could to help. The kid was grappling with a soldier and with another quick swipe of the knife, he ended the fight in the kid's favor.

He reached down and dragged the kid to his feet.

"Holy cow, where did they come from?" the kid wanted to know.

"They done got the jump on us, that's for sure."

The rest of the squad had made quick work on the attackers. Lucky for them, there had only been four Chinese. If they had only dropped a grenade into the trench, or fired their weapons instead of using bayonets, the outcome would have been different.

The kid must have had the same thought. "Why didn't they just shoot at us?"

"Maybe they're low on ammo," Cole said. "Maybe they just hate us. A bullet is one thing, but a bayonet is personal. Let's just count ourselves lucky. One thing for sure, it ain't even sunup and it's been an interesting day."

"Yeah, I just hope we live to see sundown," the kid replied.

"Me too, kid. Me too."

* * *

THEY SURGED FORWARD, no longer worried about being quiet. The sounds of battle erupted all around them, with the stillness shattered by mortar fire, grenades, and machine guns. Red and green tracers etched patterns up and down the hill.

"Hot enough for you?" somebody shouted.

"Just you wait."

The Chinese must have been spread thin, because after their encounter with the enemy, they ran into no one else in the outlying trenches. The trouble was that the only way forward was straight up the hill, following the line of the narrow trench.

While the trench gave some cover, Cole worried that one well-placed machine-gun burst would knock out the whole squad like so many dominoes lined up one behind the other. He ordered the men out of the trench as they approached the main defenses that circled the hilltop. Better to take their chances out in the open.

"Find whatever cover you can," he said. "Try to pick the bastards off."

Fortunately, there was no shortage of rocks and even clumps of scrub brush. With the others, Cole scrambled out of the trench and got behind a rock. As enemy tracers streaked overhead, he just wished that the rock was bigger. It was just like Korea to be stingy with its rocks when you needed one.

Finally, he was in range to do some good with Old Betsy. The Chinese were close enough that he could make them out clearly. Cole put the sights on the machine gunners and pulled the trigger. The stream of machine-gun bullets stopped like a faucet being shut off.

A soldier stood to throw a stick grenade at the Americans, but Cole put him down. The soldier fell back into his own trench and the grenade detonated, resulting in cries of agony.

In the respite from the machine-gun fire, the Americans crept closer, keeping up a steady fire.

"You've got a good arm, kid," Cole shouted. "See if you can get a couple of grenades into that trench."

"I'll have to get closer," the kid said.

Without further explanation, he sprang up and ran at a crouch toward the enemy position.

Cole swore. Though brave, a move like that was going to get that stupid kid killed. He raised his rifle and fired just as a Chinese soldier rose up and took aim at the kid.

He worked the bolt and scanned the trench to pick off anyone else who tried to get the kid. By now, the kid wasn't more than fifty feet from the trench. In rapid succession, he threw two grenades that dropped neatly into the trench. Seconds later came the flashes and bangs. The firing from the enemy line directly ahead of them stopped.

Up ahead, the kid was already plunging ahead toward the trench. "Wait a minute, kid," Cole muttered. He waved the others forward.

It was now or never. Had they gotten all the Chinese? There was only one way to find out.

Panting with the effort of charging forward up the steep hill, the men of the squad covered the distance to the trench and leaped inside. Some had fixed bayonets, ready for hand-to-hand fighting.

But the enemy was wiped out. A handful of bodies lay in the trench, taken out by the grenade. One soldier was trying to crawl away, and someone slipped a bayonet into him.

"All right," Cole said. "We hold here."

To their right and left, similar battles were taking place as the Chinese defenses were attacked from several directions. To defeat the attack, the Chinese were sending more defenders from higher on the hilltop down toward the trenches.

Cole saw them coming.

"Swing that machine gun around," he ordered.

Two men scrambled for the abandoned Chinese machine gun, a nasty bit of weaponry supplied to the Communists by their Soviet allies. There was nothing like it for turning Americans into mincemeat. Now, the Americans returned the favor, opening up on the enemy soldiers running downhill toward them. By the time the magazine was empty, the wind had gone out of that attack.

Things weren't going as well in other sections of the trench. Off to their left, the boys there were having a hot time as the Chinese attackers spilled into the trench. Cole could see men grappling with one another. He raised his rifle and shot an enemy soldier who was about to bayonet an American.

Off to their right, the situation looked better. The soldiers had made it into the trench and were occupying it without any intervention from the Chinese. Cole was glad to see it because the trench was like a chain and any weak link was going to mean trouble for the other attackers.

"Now what?"

"Now we wait for word from the lieutenant. Once this trench is secure, we'll push on up toward the top of the hill. Our job will be to take one of the bunkers."

"Hold on. Where the hell are those guys going?"

Cole turned away from the struggle on their left to look to where the kid was pointing to their right. In disbelief, he watched as the American soldiers there started climbing back out of the trench and returning down the hill. What was even more surprising was that they seemed to be taking their time, retreating at a leisurely pace in groups of two and three. It reminded Cole of watching a baseball game breaking up.

"They're abandoning their position. What the hell?"

"But those guys aren't even under attack!"

"Who are those guys?"

"See their mustaches? It's the Borinqueneers. The Puerto Ricans."

Farther down the hill, an officer moved to intercept the retreating men. He was screaming at them, then drew his pistol and gestured at the men with it, but they ignored him and continued their retreat.

Cole couldn't believe it. No sooner had the troops pulled out than Chinese soldiers ran in behind them to occupy the position.

The enemy had found their weak link.

* * *

CISCO VASQUEZ WAS among the Borinqueneers taking part in the attack to reclaim Outpost Kelly. An officer had come by before the attack to explain what was expected, but most of the men who spoke Spanish could not understand him. They relied on one of the noncommissioned officers to translate for them, along with Cisco.

But some things needed no translation. As the men advanced, they fired at the enemy awaiting them. They could see the bright muzzle flashes up ahead as they moved closer to the enemy.

"*Dios mio!*" a soldier cried, stumbling as he was hit. He fell into the mud and did not rise again.

Cisco felt his legs turn rubbery with fear, but he had no choice but to press forward with the others.

In one sense, they were lucky. This section of the trench did not seem that well-defended. With a final cry and scramble, the Borinqueneers pressed forward and leaped into the trench.

But their luck didn't last. A sudden burst of fire killed Captain McDaniel. The sergeant ran to help him and was killed as well.

The captain's death stunned the soldiers because he had been a good officer. Suddenly, the company had no leadership. And nobody who could speak a word of English, other than Cisco.

A runner approached, bearing a message, but he had such a thick accent that Cisco had a hard time understanding him. Americans spoke in many confusing ways and this soldier was from Boston. Finally, the runner patted Cisco on the shoulder as if he was satisfied that he had understood, even though Cisco had only absorbed about half of what the runner had said. The runner ran off through a hail of fire.

"*Que?*" someone asked Cisco.

Cisco shrugged. "*No se.*"

What was so confusing was that they seemed to have reached their objective. They had captured the trench. Now what?

From the hill above them, a single rifle shot rang out. One of the soldiers fell, a bullet having drilled right through his helmet.

Another shot stabbed down and another soldier went down. Cisco thought there must be a Chinese sniper up there.

A couple of the men decided that they'd had enough. They climbed out of the trench and started back down the hill. Others soon followed. There was no discussion. At first, the men abandoned their positions in twos and threes, and then by entire squads.

Cisco stayed until there were just a handful of others in the trench. They looked at one another, not sure what to do. Had they been forgotten out here? If they stayed, surely they would all be killed if the Chinese counter-attacked, now that the others had abandoned them.

The remaining soldiers reached a consensus without speaking. One climbed out and the others followed, started down the hill.

Cisco was the last to go, but he soon followed the rest of the Borinqueneers down the hillside.

Behind them, Chinese troops poured into the gap.

* * *

MAJOR WU KNEW that a wise man takes opportunity where it is given, which is why he volunteered himself and Deng for the attack on Outpost Kelly.

Not only that, but he felt as if he needed to save face after allowing the American pilot to slip through his fingers. They had been so close! However, between the interference of the villagers and the American sniper, the pilot had managed to get away.

"This is close enough," Wu had said, leading Deng to a ridge some distance away from the outpost.

"Sir?"

Major Wu smiled. "You see, the Americans are going to bombard the hill now. This is what they always do. They have plenty of shells to expend. Would you prefer to be here or there?"

Deng looked around, then replied, "Here, sir."

"Good."

They settled down to wait. As Wu had promised, artillery and tank fire plowed the hilltop. Watching the explosions pound the hilltop, they were both glad not to be on it. When the bombardment stopped, Wu and Deng slipped through the defenses and joined the defenders on the hill.

As the light grew in the east, the attack on the outpost commenced. With his binoculars pressed to his eyes, Wu called shot after shot out to Deng. He watched with satisfaction as his sniper killed one soldier after another.

Nonetheless, the Americans still managed to reach the trenches ringing the hilltop. From their sniper's nest, Deng was able to pick off several of the soldiers in the trench.

"Look, sir, they are leaving!"

"So they are," Wu said, unable to hide his surprise. "You have driven them off."

As the American soldiers abandoned their hard-won position, Chinese troops moved back in, giving them a position of strength from which to attack the trenches once again.

"Keep shooting," Wu encouraged him. "Every soldier you kill is one less imperialist for our men to face."

Deng kept firing. Through the binoculars, Wu watched, the grin never leaving his face.

* * *

TO COLE, the thought came to him that they were teetering on the edge of a knife. The attack now felt like that moment when you struggled to keep your balance on an icy trail, but knew you were going to fall no matter what. The best you could do was brace yourself for when you hit the ground.

His squad was holding the platoon's left flank. Lieutenant Ballard was somewhere off to Cole's right. He didn't envy the thoughts that must be going through the lieutenant's head.

"Dammit all," Cole said. "There's not enough of us now to hold this trench."

It didn't take the Chinese long to come to the same conclusion. Enemy reinforcements ran down the hill and flowed into the trench, then spread out to attack the troops on either side.

Cole's squad was soon overwhelmed as a tide of screaming Chinese flowed toward them from the right. More soldiers attacked from the hilltop above.

"Where are they all coming from? Holy cow!"

"They must have been dug in deep on the hill, where the artillery couldn't reach 'em. Here they come, for sure."

This time, the enemy didn't even bother with their drums and bugles. They just ran down the hill, screaming and firing, bayonets gleaming in the flashes from explosions. They got so close that he could see their eyes, their teeth, their twisted expressions of hatred.

He fired at the nearest enemy soldier and the man went down, but there were many more behind him.

"Kid!" Cole shouted. "Grenade!"

"I'm out!"

Off to his right, Lieutenant Ballard was scrambling out of the trench. He turned and fired a couple of shots up the hill, then shouted, "Let's go!"

"Sir?"

"We're pulling out, Cole. There's no way in hell we can stay here. We'll fall back and try again."

Obeying the officer, the soldiers in the squad climbed out of the trench and began to make their way back across the hard-fought ground.

Cole was the last one to leave. He fired a couple more shots at the attackers surging toward him, but the bolt-action Springfield wasn't enough to turn the tide. Maybe if he'd had a Thompson—or a bazooka.

With bullets pelting the mud around him, Cole crawled over the top of the trench and down the hillside after the others.

It went against his grain to turn tail and run, but sometimes you needed to have the good sense to live and fight another day.

His squad and the rest of the platoon had fought hard and bled for that damn hill, all for nothing. The counterattack on Outpost Kelly had failed because of those damn Borinqueneers.

Cole wouldn't mind finding those boys who had retreated and giving them a piece of his mind.

As it turned out, he was going to have to wait his turn.

CHAPTER FIFTEEN

"IT'S TOO bad we can't just shoot them for desertion," Lieutenant Colonel Switalski announced, looking over the Puerto Rican troops. The unit sat dejectedly before him, stripped of their weapons, and not understanding a word of what was happening to them. "That would sure save everyone a lot of trouble."

"What have they got to say for themselves?"

"I guess we would know if any of them spoke English," the colonel said, clearly disgusted.

The object of his disdain was Company B of the 65th Infantry, who had managed to attain the defensive trench on Outpost Kelly, but had then abandoned it. They had not been under direct attack at that time, but had clearly lost their nerve. When an officer had confronted the retreating troops and ordered them back into position, they had ignored him.

They had been lined up against a wall of sandbags that delineated the MLR. Their weapons had been taken away and they were under guard. As far as anyone was concerned, they were now prisoners.

For their own part, the Puerto Rican troops did not seem to understand what was happening to them. Several had been wounded in the ill-fated counterattack and wore blood-stained bandages. Almost all of them were covered in mud or had uniforms in tatters from crawling through the barbed wire defenses on the hill. These men looked tired, hungry, and thirsty—pretty much how all soldiers looked after a fight. But a coward was a coward, and these troops wouldn't be getting any sympathy from the commanding officer.

They returned the lieutenant colonel's glare sullenly, which only made him madder.

"Shooting them is too good, now that I think about it," the lieutenant colonel added as an afterthought. "Let's see how they like eighteen years of hard labor at Fort Leavenworth. That's the standard sentence for desertion. Of course, the Chinese or the Soviets or even the Germans in the last war wouldn't have gone to all that trouble. No sir. A firing squad would be the end of it."

"What do you want me to do with them, sir?"

"I'm thinking about it. Damn it all, lord knows I've got enough problems as it is. We need every soldier on the line so these Borinqueneers are letting us down. What the hell is a Borinqueneer, anyhow?"

"Must be Spanish for fleet of foot."

"You got that right. Don't they have any officers?"

"They were all killed in the attack, along with most of the noncommissioned officers. There was a great deal of sniper activity in that sector. The sniper seemed to be targeting the officers, at any rate."

The lieutenant colonel's mind was churning. He was well-versed in how the Army worked, and he hadn't received the insignia on his collar by being a fool. The failure of the attack on Outpost Kelly did not reflect well on him, not to mention that the outpost had been captured in the first place. Normally, blame would fall squarely on his shoulders. He might even expect to be relieved of command and sent back to Japan to shuffle papers, his upward rise in the Army having ended on the muddy hillside in the distance.

But the cowardice of the Borinqueneers might just save his career. Somebody would need to be blamed for the failed attack. If not him, then who? These Borinqueneers would make a good scapegoat.

He intended to court martial the whole damn unit, but there wasn't time for that at the moment.

"I suppose we shouldn't be surprised that they ran. Look at them. They're just this side of coloreds, aren't they?"

"Sir?"

"Never mind. Here's the thing. I can't shoot 'em, much as I'd like to. Hell, Puerto Rico would probably secede if I did that. I can't afford to keep them under guard because we need every available man in case of a Chinese attack. Now with those goons dug in on our outpost, you know that's coming. As for these deserters, I'm not about to give them back their weapons, but I need these men doing something useful until we can begin court martial proceedings. In the meantime, they will need a decent officer to keep an eye on them."

"Might I suggest Lieutenant Ballard, sir? If anyone can whip them back into shape, it's him."

"Good idea. He can start by ordering them to shave off those damn mustaches."

* * *

WATCHING THE ANGRY COMMANDING OFFICER, Cisco did his best to translate for his confused fellow soldiers. It was true that they had not stayed in the fight, but all of their officers and sergeants had been killed. No one had sent them orders. It was as if they had been left on that hilltop to die, and so they had made the decision to abandon their position and survive.

Cisco was likely the only one who could have explained their viewpoint to the lieutenant colonel, but he knew that he wouldn't get the chance. A lieutenant colonel didn't want to hear from a private, especially not one who spoke broken English.

"When will we get some food and water?" asked one of the men, an old campaigner who had been with the Borinqueneers since the last war. "We have many wounded men who need help."

Cisco shook his head. "They are talking about shooting us as deserters, so I don't think we will get water any time soon."

"Deserters!" The older soldier shook his head in disgust and spat into the mud. "We are Borinqueneers! We are fighters!"

Cisco agreed that the soldiers didn't lack courage. They had helped take that hill like everyone else. But even he could see that his unit lacked training. There were a few experienced veterans like this old soldier, but most of the men were relatively new recruits like Cisco who had been rushed from the recruiting station to Korea.

They settled down to wait. Other soldiers passed by, casting dirty looks at the Puerto Rican troops. Word had gotten out they had run and handed Outpost Kelly over to the Chinese.

The sun came out, baking the muddy road dry and adding to the misery of the thirsty men. It was typical fall weather with hot days and chilly nights. They would be shivering after dark. Noon came and went, and still they'd had nothing to eat or drink. Those who could, closed their eyes and slept.

In mid-afternoon, a younger officer appeared. Tall and haughty, there was nothing kind or understanding in his gaze. He looked down at the Borinqueneers and scowled.

"My name is Lieutenant Ballard," he said. "I'm your new CO for now. Let's get a few things straight. First of all, you are no longer Borinqueneers. Unit nicknames are earned in this Army, and believe me, you don't even want to hear some of your current nicknames."

Speaking softly so as not to draw the attention of the lieutenant, Cisco translated the lieutenant's words into Spanish. The men kept quiet, but Cisco could still sense their outrage.

However, the sharp-eyed lieutenant had seen Cisco's efforts at translation. "You there, stand up and tell them what I'm saying."

"Yes, sir." Cisco took a moment to explain the lieutenant's orders so far.

The lieutenant went on, "Next, I want all of you cleanshaven. Those mustaches must go."

Cisco hesitated before relaying the order to the Borinqueneers. He knew that the order would be devastating to the troops. He looked at the lieutenant, just to make sure that he had heard correctly. "Sir?"

"Go on, Private!" the officer said impatiently. "Those are my orders."

Again, Cisco translated. This time, there were grumbles of disbelief, but the lieutenant did not seem to hear them, or if he did, he didn't much care.

The lieutenant was not done. "There will be no more rations of rice and beans. You can eat C rations like everyone else. The special treatment of this unit ends today. Under normal circumstances, there would be serious re-training of this unit for combat readiness, but we cannot afford the time or effort right now."

Prodded by his fellow soldiers, Cisco finally raised his hand. "Sir, *estos soldados* want to know if they will get their rifles back."

The lieutenant glared at him a long time before answering. Cisco felt himself shrinking smaller and wished that he had kept quiet. Finally, the lieutenant seemed to lose patience.

"If I could, I'd take away your damn uniforms, let alone your rifles," Ballard said. "If you ask me, you don't deserve to wear them."

Cisco struggled to keep his voice even. They deserved better treatment than this, but he didn't dare say anything to the officer. "Yes, sir."

"No weapons, but you'll all get shovels," the lieutenant said. "Instead of being soldiers, you can expect to be put back to work as laborers, digging ditches and so forth. It seems to suit your people. Once we've dealt with this latest threat from the Chinese, we'll start the court-martial process for all of you cowards."

* * *

HAVING ADDRESSED THE FORMER BORINQUENEERS, Lieutenant Ballard stood some distance away and surveyed the dejected soldiers, shaking his head. Sergeant Weber and Cole stood beside him, along with the pilot, Lieutenant Commander Miller. Although no love was lost between Lieutenant Ballard and his hillbilly sniper, the lieutenant respected Cole's skills as a scout and marksman. Ballard knew that if anyone could take the measure of these men and do something with them, it was Cole and the sergeant.

"Sergeant, is there any hope for these men?" the lieutenant asked.

"I do not know, sir," said the old German sergeant, who had served in the Wehrmacht in the last war in Europe. He had seen his share of both the worst and the best troops. "To be fair, it is clear that they have had little training and with the loss of their officers and sergeants, no leadership."

"Cole?"

"Sir, I don't believe half them boys could find the pointy end of a bayonet."

Ballard nodded. "Gentlemen, your assessment matches my own conclusions."

Cole and the sergeant exchanged a look. Ballard had a knack for talking like a college boy, which he was. Someday, he'd likely go far in the officer corps if he survived Korea.

"I'll tell you one thing," Cole added. "They've got plenty of fight. Look in their eyes. Those could be some mean sons of bitches if somebody taught 'em the ass end of a rifle from the muzzle."

"Fortunately, that's not our job," the lieutenant said. "We've just got to teach them to use a shovel, which shouldn't take long. They're basically wetbacks, after all."

The Army had only integrated in July 1948, and old attitudes prevailed. Many officers were not very accepting of the idea of all soldiers being equal. In Ballard's mind, there were white troops—and then there was everybody else. His assessment of "others" failed to take into account the heroism of blacks, Hispanics, and Asians—Koreans in particular.

While there were South Korean troops, and many had fought with distinction, there was a much larger number of South Korean laborers, or KSC. These men were given all the dirty work from digging latrines to building roads. The prevalent thought was that it was their country, so they could work for it.

"Yes, sir," the sergeant said. "I will find shovels."

"They can work alongside the KSC," the lieutenant said. "They will fit right in with the gooks."

Lieutenant Commander Miller had kept quiet until then, but he now spoke up. "Hey now, don't call them that. If it wasn't for the Koreans, I wouldn't be here. Those people are a lot braver than you think. They've been fighting for their country for centuries, and we've been here for a couple of years."

Lieutenant Ballard was not impressed by the pilot's speech. "I'm sure things have a way of looking different from the air," Ballard said. "Here on the ground, you'll find out how things really are."

* * *

WITH THE LOSS of Outpost Kelly—not once, but twice—the problems
for the troops defending the MLR were just beginning. The outposts
were meant as a buffer. In a game of chess, the hilltop outposts would
have been the pawns. The Chinese were maneuvering for a checkmate,
but short of that, they'd be happy to clear the board of as many other
pieces as possible.

Now, the Chinese had a foothold within easy striking distance of
the main line. Up until then, the Chinese had been content with raids
such as the one against the tanks, in which they had tried to disable
the tanks using their Bangalore torpedoes. Fortunately, that attack had
failed thanks to an alert sentry. However, it was only a matter of time
before a larger force attacked the line.

Much to Lieutenant Commander Miller's disappointment, Jang-mi
had left with her two fellow villagers, intending to return home.

Cole had been present when she came to make her goodbyes. The
pilot had taken her by the shoulders and thanked her again for
rescuing him and saving his life. But Cole could see that the pilot's
emotions went deeper than that. The poor son of a bitch was smitten.

Cole grinned at the thought. The pilot had known the Korean
woman for just a few days. Was there such a thing as love at first sight?
He didn't spend much time pondering such things. In Cole's view,
emotions were an annoyance, along the lines of rain or a bitter wind.
You had to ignore them and keep going.

What he did know was that he himself had experienced an intense
wartime romance with a French freedom fighter named Jolie
Molyneux. That romance had been cut short in a field outside Bienville
in Normandy, when she had been badly wounded. They had reunited
months later at the Battle of the Bulge, but things hadn't lasted. The
cold and snow of the battlefield had smothered the spark between
them.

Sometimes in war, Cole knew, you just needed a human touch as a
reminder that you were still alive. With the pilot having survived a
dogfight in which he lost his plane and wingman, and then being the
object of a manhunt by the Chinese, Cole could understand the pilot's

connection with Jang-mi. She was also the softest and prettiest thing around and despite her mannish clothing, she had received more than a few second looks from the young soldiers.

"In a different time and place," the pilot had muttered, watching her go. "Well, who knows?"

Jang-mi had looked back once over her shoulder, and then slipped into no-man's land.

Much to their surprise, Jang-mi had returned several hours later. The pilot was pleased to see her, but Jang-mi's face was troubled. She explained that a large Chinese force was marching through the hills toward the MLR. This was far worse than a few attacks based out of Outpost Kelly. It was clear that the Chinese planned a massive push to overwhelm the line and perhaps change the boundaries being discussed at the negotiating table.

The news was passed up the chain of command. Within an hour of Jang-mi's return, Lieutenant Colonel Switalski had called a staff meeting to discuss the situation. In a highly unusual move, he had included Jang-mi in the meeting. Lieutenant Commander Miller stood beside her for moral support.

"There has been some prior intelligence that the Chinese were up to something big," he said. "But nobody knew what."

"You'd think someone would have spotted them from the air."

"You know how well they move when they don't want to be seen. They keep to the brush by day and move at night."

"Sir, we don't have enough men to hold the line against a massive attack. We are spread too thin."

The officer had spoken the truth. The line was stretched thin by the necessity of defending a long boundary. The recent monsoon rains had left the supply roads a mess, putting them behind on receiving reinforcements and supplies.

Still, someone had to ask. "What about reinforcements?"

"Not a chance. First of all, everybody is stretched out like a rubber band. China is right there and can march in all the troops they want. We have to get troops here from half a world away. There are no extra divisions just waiting for our phone call. Second of all, they'd never get here in time. Not with these muddy roads and flooded rivers to contend with. No, if the Chinese come, we will have to deal with them on our own."

Several officers who had lived through the Chinese attacks at the Chosin Reservoir or Triangle Hill remembered the crazed nighttime attacks with thousands of enemy troops pouring down on them under the intense glare of flares overhead. It was not an experience anyone was eager to repeat.

Lieutenant Commander Miller spoke up. "Sir, if I may. It was Jang-mi here who spotted the Chinese moving toward us. She comes from a village in the hills. She knows that territory like the back of her hand."

"All right. What about it?"

"Sir, she said the bulk of their army will have to go through the pass at Lŏngmo Samseong. That's the name of the old hill fort that guards the pass. If we're going to stop the Chinese or at least hold them up, that's our best chance of doing so."

The colonel shook his head. "We don't have men to spare for what sounds like a suicide mission."

Lieutenant Ballard spoke next. "Sir, what Jang-mi has suggested makes sense. I've seen the maps. With your permission, I could lead my platoon out there. It sounds as if a small force could hold back the enemy and buy us some time."

"We can't afford to spare a platoon of good men."

Ballard wasn't ready to give up. "How about a squad, sir?" He paused. "Also, I could take the Puerto Ricans with me. It would be a chance for them to redeem themselves."

The CO thought it over, then nodded. "I won't order you to do this, Lieutenant. But if you're saying you want to volunteer, that's a different story. Make sure your men are all volunteers as well. This might very well be a one-way trip. As for the Borinqueneers, they won't be especially missed."

* * *

NOT LONG AFTER the staff meeting, Ballard had gathered his platoon. He announced the mission and soon had twenty volunteers, with Sergeant Weber, Cole, and Tommy Wilson among them. Lieutenant

Commander Miller, Jang-mi, and the two Korean villagers, Seo-jun and Chul, added to their number.

Lieutenant Ballard had taken Cole aside and explained about the Borinqueneers coming along.

"Hell now, Lieutenant, what are they going to do, hit the Chinese with shovels? They don't even have weapons."

"They'll be getting their rifles back, Cole. They had better know how to use them this time around. That's where you come in."

"Sir?"

"Once we get to this hill fort, with any luck, we'll have a day or two to whip them into shape. I should say, *you* will have a day or two to whip them into shape."

"I ain't a drill sergeant, sir."

"No, you're not. But hear me out, soldier. I know we've had our differences, Cole, but I'll admit that you're the best damn shot in the company, the regiment, maybe the whole damn United States Army. If anyone can teach those sorry cases how to use a rifle, it's you."

"That's just swell," Cole said.

CHAPTER SIXTEEN

COLE MOVED SWIFTLY down the line of men that was preparing to move out.

By mid-morning, the task force had been assembled. It was being called Task Force Ballard, in keeping with the tradition of naming similar units after their commanding officer. Whether Ballard's name was about to become famous or infamous remained to be seen. Cole couldn't help but recall that it was Task Force Faith that had been involved in the Chosin Reservoir campaign that he remembered all too well.

He'd heard something about how back in the old days, a group of soldiers asked to carry out an impossible task, a suicide mission, really, were called Forlorn Hopes. For Forlorn Hopes, their reward was often promotion or redemption. Right now, that seemed just about right.

At the front of the column were members of his own squad. Other than giving a nod to the kid, he barely gave these battle-hardened veterans a glance. They could be counted on to do whatever needed to be done.

He was surprised to see Lieutenant Commander Miller at the front of the group, along with Jang-mi and the two Korean villagers.

"You're not coming with us, are you?"

"Sure I am," Miller said. "My wings are clipped for now, so I might as well make myself useful."

Miller wasn't wearing a helmet, but had somewhere found a broad-brimmed bush hat like the Puerto Rican troops sometimes wore. On anyone else, the hat would have looked ridiculous, but it matched the pilot's jaunty personality. The pilot noticed Cole's stare.

"Like the hat? I got it from one of the Borinqueneers."

Cole shook his head. "I've yet to meet an officer with a lick of horse sense. Sir. I do see you have a weapon and not just that Browning."

Miller held up a 12-gauge combat shotgun. At close range and loaded with buckshot, the shotgun was a formidable weapon. "I'm not much of a shot," he admitted sheepishly. "I figured it would be hard to miss with this."

Cole grinned. He was well aware of the damage that a shotgun could do. "Sir, any Chinese who get close to the business end of that scattergun will be on their way to Commie heaven."

Nearby, Jang-mi stood watching the exchange quietly. Though small, she looked far more capable than the pilot. A carbine was slung over her shoulder and a large knife hung at her belt. Her hair was hidden under one of the *ushanka* hats similar to what the Chinese wore. Her face betrayed no emotion, but dark eyes assessed Cole in a calculating manner, as if sizing him up. Jang-mi was one tough customer. Cole liked that in a woman. He gave her an approving nod. Her assessment of Cole completed, she nodded back.

"Ya'll ready?"

"Yes," she replied grimly. To his surprise, she then turned to the pilot and smiled. "Jake said he would carry my pack, but I think I may have to carry him."

"Ha, we'll see about that," Miller fired back.

Cole looked between the two, more than a bit surprised. So it was Jake, was it? Miller was smiling back at Jang-mi with something like puppy dog eyes. Cole would have figured that Miller's interest in Jang-mi would make as much of a dent in that tough exterior as rain beating on a rock, but he'd been wrong. There was definitely two-way traffic happening on this street.

He just hoped it wouldn't mean that Miller or Jang-mi did anything stupid if one of them got in hot water. That would usually get both people killed.

Both the old villager and the teenager stood off to one side. They had improved upon their worn old clothes by donning some cast-offs from the American troops. The boy now wore a helmet and a jacket that looked far too big for him. The sleeves were rolled up. But his hands gripped a carbine easily enough. Cole didn't have any worries about the Korean villagers holding their own.

He moved on. Checking to make sure that the men were ready to move out was Sergeant Weber's job, but the sergeant was busy distributing a last-minute supply of ammo.

Besides, Cole wanted to see for himself what Task Force Ballard looked like.

He wasn't impressed. Discounting the squad members, Lieutenant Commander Miller, and Jang-mi and the two villagers, the bulk of the task force was made up of the disgraced platoon of Borinqueneers. Technically, they remained former Borinqueneers, having been stripped of their old sobriquet.

To Cole's eyes, they looked like men who had lost something—their self-respect. They were all fresh-shaven, having been ordered to shave off their mustaches, but instead of making them look more soldierly, their stark faces added to the overall impression of loss. They looked naked and exposed.

Many of them wore muddy uniforms and a few still sported bandages from the minor wounds they had received during the fight on Outpost Kelly. Cole wondered about that. Typically, even slightly wounded men would not be rotated right back into duty. Maybe they had volunteered? If that was the case, maybe Cole and the others had misjudged these boys.

As part of their assignment to Task Force Ballard, the Puerto Ricans had been reissued weapons.

Cole stopped in front of one soldier holding a rifle.

"When was the last time you cleaned this weapon?" Cole demanded.

The Borinqueneer stared at him blankly. "*Que?*"

Looking more closely at the rifle, Cole could see that part of the stock was caked with dried mud. Spots of rust bloomed on the action. In the wet, humid conditions of the last few days, metal needed to be kept oiled to keep corrosion at bay.

"I said, when was the last time this weapon was cleaned?" In frustration, Cole had repeated his question, much louder this time, as if the problem was that the soldier hadn't heard him, rather than not being able to understand him.

Again, the soldier replied, also louder this time, "*Que?*"

Cole shook his head in disgust.

One of the Puerto Ricans stepped forward. "He can't understand you, sir. He speaks no English."

"Too damn bad for him," Cole said. "Anyhow, a rusty rifle don't need no explanation in English or any other language. Any soldier ought to know better."

The Puerto Rican soldier turned and barked something in Spanish to the men around him. Word spread to those who had been farther away. Within a couple of minutes, the entire platoon was busy cleaning their rifles.

They were doing a lousy job of it, though.

"You've got to get some oil on there," Cole said in irritation, reaching to help a soldier who was just wiping down the outside of the rifle with a dry rag.

The Puerto Rican soldier who had given the original order now repeated what Cole had just said. The men turned to their rifles with fresh attention. "I told them to make sure there was no rust, sir."

"I ain't an officer or a sergeant, in case you ain't noticed."

"Yes, sir."

"Oh, to hell with it. You can call me a general as long as these boys clean their rifles."

Cole and the other man moved among the Borinqueneers, showing them how to clean the worst of the mud and rust off their weapons. There wasn't time to field strip the rifles and give them a real cleaning, but at least the weapons now had a better chance of functioning if they ran into any Chinese.

"Better," the Puerto Rican soldier said, looking around at the other troops.

Cole assessed the young man. He wasn't as old as several of the veterans, who were cleaning their weapons in a more practiced fashion. However, he spoke English and seemed to have enough natural authority that the others listened to him.

"What's your name?"

"I am Private Vasquez." He paused. "*Mis amigos* call me Cisco."

"Then I reckon we're *amigos* now, Cisco. My friends call me Hillbilly."

Cisco nodded at Cole's rifle with its telescopic sight. Unlike most of the Borinqueneers' weapons, Cole had worked so much oil into the dark metal of the Springfield that it had a dull gleam, like a black snake in the sun. "You have shot many of the enemy with that rifle?"

"I suppose I've killed more than most and not as many as some," Cole said matter-of-factly. "But what matters is, how many are *you* ready to kill? You and the rest of these Borinqueneers, that is?"

Cisco looked grim. "We are not cowards. We will fight, Hillbilly."

"Cisco, I sure as hell hope so."

At the end of the line, they heard the growl of big engines and were surprised to see two tanks moving into position. Cole left Cisco and walked down there to see what was going on.

He spotted a lieutenant standing half in, half out of the turret of the lead tank. "Sir, these boys don't speak English. You want me to have somebody tell them to get out of the road?"

The tank commander shook his head. "Not necessary, soldier. We are coming with you."

A soldier jumped down from the deck of the tank, where he had been riding. He was a big, rugged guy, but instead of a rifle, he was carrying a camera and a notebook. Something about the soldier looked familiar.

"I'll be damned," Cole said. "Is that you, Hardy? Since when did you become a tanker?"

"I'm just along for the ride," Hardy said.

Up in the turret, the lieutenant looked surprised. "You two know each other?"

"I wrote about Cole here back at the Battle of Triangle Hill," Hardy explained. "It turns out that he has quite a record as a sniper, in this war and the last one."

The lieutenant squinted at the flag on the front of Cole's helmet. "That looks like a Confederate flag."

"Sure, Cole here is a hillbilly," Hardy explained. "They make the best snipers, don't you know?"

The lieutenant laughed. "You're the one digging up the facts, so I'll take your word for it," he said. Deep within the tank, the powerful engine revved impatiently. "Let's get this show on the road. I'd like to get wherever we're going before dark."

"Afraid of boogiemen, Lieutenant?"

"Yeah, Chinese ones."

* * *

THE TANKS COULD REV their engines all they wanted, impatient to get rolling, but it was another hour before the task force was ready to move out.

Cole felt heartened by the tanks. What infantryman didn't? It was the same feeling as walking into a dark alley, knowing that the big guy next to you had your back. Also, to some extent, the tanks made up for the Borinqueneers. They were some of the sorriest soldiers that Cole had seen. He had detected a glimmer of fight in their eyes, however. When push came to shove, could they be counted on? Only time would tell. With any luck, he and Sergeant Weber would have at least a day to try to whip them into shape. Cole knew that there was no hope of training a soldier in a day, but you could teach a man the basics of fighting for his life. You might say that survival was a good motivator.

This fight could very well turn out to be a last stand, even if nobody wanted to call it that yet. Last stand sounded better than suicide mission, he reckoned.

Finally, the order came to move out.

"Let's go!" Ballard shouted, walking alongside the column. "We're going to keep up a stiff pace, men. I want us to be at this so-called fort by nightfall."

"So-called fort, sir?"

"If it was built by a bunch of Korean villagers, I'm expecting to find a pile of rocks."

"We'd be halfway there if we hadn't stood around playing grab-ass most of the morning," Cole muttered.

"Well, I wouldn't mind playing grab-ass with her," the kid said quietly, looking in Jang-mi's direction. She was busy talking with the pilot.

"Looks like that flyboy has the same thing in mind. I'd say you're out of luck."

"Not out of luck. Just outranked."

"That's life, kid. Get used to it."

"I guess I'll just have to wait until my next leave in Japan," he said. "The last time I was there, there was this girl who—"

Cole had heard it all before, but he let the kid spin out his story once again. Like most young soldiers, his thoughts alternated between food and women, with a few moments of terror thrown in for good measure.

"What about that girl you've been writing to back home? Did you put that story in your letter?"

The kid blushed. "No, I guess not."

Cole laughed. "That's all right, kid. Hell, there's plenty of married guys doing the same thing and believe me, they don't write home about it."

Cole just hoped that the kid would have a chance to get home again to that girl. He hadn't wanted the kid to be part of this task force, but he had kept his mouth shut when the kid volunteered. The truth was, Cole was glad to have him along.

Quickly, they left the MLR behind, keeping well to the west of Outpost Kelly and the reach of the Chinese mortars now on that hill. Despite the recent monsoon rains that had turned the supply roads to rivers of mud, the open ground they now crossed was rocky enough to provide good footing. They approached the river and could hear it roaring, still in flood stage. He hoped that there would be no need to cross that swirling brown water.

Before the monsoon and the attack on Outpost Kelly, it hadn't been unusual for the soldiers to take turns visiting a sandy beach nearby on a quiet bend of the Imjin River. It was what they had instead of a shower.

"Want to go for a swim?" the kid asked.

"No thanks," Cole said. He didn't much like the water or swimming —not since he had nearly drowned as a boy while setting beaver traps in a mountain stream. Not much frightened Cole, but he had to admit that he was terrified of water.

Jang-mi led the way, serving as their guide. It was clear that she knew this country like the back of her hand. There was no hesitation as she picked her way through the thickets and jumbled rocky outcroppings. Just when another obstacle loomed in their path, she seemed to know just the way around it.

Despite the fairly solid ground, it was slow going, mainly because of the tanks. In point of fact, the massive tanks were intended for mobility across level ground such as the terrain of Europe. The tanks were much less useful in the hills of Korea. Lieutenant Dunbar's command vehicle was designated "Twenty-one" and the second tank was "Twenty-two." Despite the numbering system, Dunbar did not have another twenty tanks at his disposal; it just sounded better than calling them "Tank One" and "Tank Two."

Jang-mi was finding a path that allowed for passage of these steel behemoths. The tank commander had gotten out and was keeping pace with Jang-mi. From time to time, they stopped and conferred about the best way forward. Cole felt reassured that the tank commander knew his business.

Too often, the tanks had no choice but to crash through the thickets of underbrush. It made an awful racket, so Cole prayed that there were no Chinese scouts about. However, the tanks cleared the trail for the men on foot behind them.

Meanwhile, the Borinqueneers lagged behind. Some stumbled and had to be helped by their comrades. In fairness to them, many of these men had light wounds. None of them had eaten a decent meal in two days, which left some of them light-headed on the march. The Borinqueneers did not complain.

Sergeant Weber moved up and down the column, prodding the Borinqueneers to keep moving.

The irony of it all wasn't lost on the kid. "Isn't that something," he said. "We've got an old German sergeant yelling at a bunch of Puerto Ricans, with some help from a hillbilly who talks like he's got a mouthful of cornpone."

"Yeah? You know what we don't need on top of all that? A smartass."

The kid took the hint, zipping his mouth shut as Weber approached.

"They are sorry looking bastards," Weber confided to Cole, pausing to take a long drink from his canteen. "Do you think they will fight or run?"

"For all our sakes, I hope they fight," Cole said.

"One thing for sure, they'll have nowhere to run. There is nothing around here but mountains."

"They may have some gumption in them," Cole said. "When we get to this fort, you and me will have to whip them into shape."

"Can we do it?"

"Sergeant, we ain't got much choice."

"This is true."

Cole and his squad brought up the rear. With the tanks in front and the veterans in the rear, it created a good bookend for the moving column. Also, the squad kept any stragglers from the Borinqueneers from falling behind.

As they pressed deeper into the hills and thickets, Cole grew quieter. He turned his attention to the surrounding landscape, alert for the slightest movement. His eyes tracked swift birds darting through the underbrush and the occasional leaf dancing in the breeze, but he saw no sign of the enemy.

Cole liked just about any landscape in its own way, but he had to admit that there was not much to redeem the endless scrub and hills of their surroundings. While there were patches of mature trees, they were nothing like the soaring stands of oak and maple and hickory in the mountains back home. The scenery was neither welcoming nor majestic. It was just more of the same.

Gradually, they left the Imjin behind and began to climb. The hills pressed closer, steep cliff faces rising nearby and hemming them in.

Jang-mi brought them onto a narrow mountain road that appeared to be the only way through these rough hills. He caught glimpses of her from time to time, leading the column fearlessly, but with her weapon off her shoulder, out in front of her, ready for anything. If they encountered any advance units of the enemy, the Chinese would likely be forced to use this same road, but from the opposite direction.

The shadows grew longer as the daylight faded and the deep hills cut off the lowering sun. Down along the river, the air had still been warm and humid, but now an autumnal chill hung in the air.

After one last, steep push up the road, the troops entered a clearing. Looming over them, Cole had his first glimpse of the massive stone walls of the ancient fort. He could see at once why Jang-mi had chosen this location in hopes of stopping the Chinese advance. Any force using this road to traverse the rough hills would have to pass beneath the walls of the fort. It was a perfect position, both imposing and defensible.

"Butter my backside and call me a biscuit," Cole said, a little awestruck by the fortress walls. "It looks like the Alamo."

Nearby, Lieutenant Ballard appeared just as impressed. He had been expecting a jumble of rocks, but the stone fort looked sturdy, if somewhat weedy and overgrown. "The Koreans call this place Lŏngmo Sanseong, which doesn't exactly roll off the tongue. Cole, you've got the right idea. From now on, we're calling it Outpost Alamo."

CHAPTER SEVENTEEN

HAVING REACHED THE FORT, there was no time to lose. Without recon, it was hard to know with certainty how far the enemy had progressed. The advancing Chinese army might be two day's march from the fort, or just a few hours away. Ballard sent a couple of men to watch the road through the gap, with orders to fire a warning shot if the enemy vanguard was sighted.

Their best hope in keeping those fresh troops from joining the enemy forces already at Outpost Kelly and all along the MLR was to stop them at this narrow gap through the hills.

On the far side of the clearing, the fort looked down upon the road through the gap. In many ways, it was like a fort defending the entrance to a harbor. Anything that attempted to cross the road or the clearing would be under the guns of the fort's defenders.

"How much time do we have?" Ballard asked Jang-mi.

"Maybe one day," she said. "The enemy should be here tomorrow."

"Should be here?" Ballard pressed. "We don't have supplies for more than a few days."

"Tomorrow if we are lucky," she replied. "We can make some preparations. If we are not so lucky, the enemy will be here tonight."

Ballard nodded. "All right, then. I can see we need to get to work.

Sergeant, get those Puerto Ricans busy clearing brush from the top of the fort's walls. I hope they can handle that much, at least. I've got to say that I'm surprised they made it here."

"Yes, sir. Also, I would suggest having a detail build a barricade across the road to the south."

"Sergeant, isn't that the wrong direction? The enemy will be coming from the north."

"Sir, the last thing we want is for them to use the barricade we built as a defensive position. If we block the road on the far side of the clearing, we'll keep them penned in our field of fire from the fort, just where we want them."

Ballard nodded at the logic of it. "Good thinking, Sergeant. Get to it!"

The name that Lieutenant Ballard had given the old fort had made the rounds. Some thought Outpost Alamo had a nice ring to it, while others pointed out that things had not ended well for the Alamo's defenders.

Whatever abilities they may have lacked as soldiers, the Borinqueneers quickly demonstrated that they were not afraid of hard work. Putting their weapons aside, they used everything from bayonets to trenching tools to clear brush from the top of the fortress walls. The debris was tossed to the clearing below. Another detail dragged the brush to build the barricade that the sergeant had suggested. Without any heavy equipment, the men struggled to move logs and even boulders to create a foundation for the barricade.

Cole and the other men of his squad joined the Puerto Ricans in building the barricade. It was back-breaking work and the men were soon soaked with sweat, but the makeshift barricade grew quickly. The barricade did not need to be impregnable. It just needed to slow down the enemy.

Cole saw with satisfaction that this barricade, along with the thick brush ringing the clear, as well as the fortress itself, had the effect of turning the clearing into a corral. If taken by surprise, the lead elements of the Chinese army would be trapped in a killing field. Cole always had liked a good trap, and while this one was bigger than what

he had used to snare rabbits and other game back home, he reckoned
that it would do nicely.

"I have to say, this is the last thing that I thought I'd be doing in
Korea," said Lieutenant Commander Miller, who had joined in
building the barricade. He grunted with the effort of helping to move a
log into place. "They don't exactly prepare you for manual labor in
flight school."

"You could have avoided all this if you hadn't gone and gotten yourself shot down," Cole pointed out.

"What, and miss all the fun?"

"That's not all you would have missed, sir," the kid said, grinning as
he nodded in Jang-mi's direction. She, too, had joined in the effort to
build up the barricade and was some distance away, dragging a load of
brush that had been tossed down from high above.

"You've got me there, soldier. I didn't know it was that obvious."

"Just be sure to invite us to the wedding, sir."

"All right, all right." The pilot laughed good-naturedly. "But that's
enough of that. Let's get this barricade built. Like Jang-mi said, we
might have less time than we hoped."

As soon as he said it, they all glanced nervously at the road, half-
expecting to be greeted by the sight of hundreds of enemy troops
marching toward them. So far, the road remained empty. But for how
long?

Cole paused to take a long drink from his canteen, studying the
fortress walls as he did so. Although the Puerto Ricans were clearing
brush from the top, most of the foliage had not been growing for long.
According to Jang-mi, the villagers gathered here from time to time to
tend the ancient stone fortress, and that included clearing the walls of
the weeds and small trees that inevitably took root. To the nearby
villagers, the fort was sacred in its own way and tending it honored
their people's history and traditions. After all, their ancestors had
surely been among those who fought and died on these walls,
defending their homeland.

Cole felt reassured that they would be defending the fort; he would
not have wanted to attack these walls. The stone walls rose twenty feet
from the surrounding landscape, the giant blocks stacked without

mortar, but fitting one against the other almost seamlessly to create an intimidating stone face. Time and moss had darkened the walls, giving them a brooding appearance. Short of scaling the walls, the only way in or out was a heavy wooden gate. A square watchtower, no more than twenty feet high, with slits for archers, rose from the center of the fortress walls.

The clever builders of the fort had incorporated the landscape itself as part of the defenses. The high fortress wall linked two adjoining cliff faces, curving slightly like a grim smile. One of the cliff faces rose much higher than the fortress wall, like an impregnable citadel. It was easy to imagine that more than one last stand had taken place on that cliff. A lower wall encircled the rest of the hilltop, but the back part of the hill was so steep that it was hard to imagine an enemy even attempting that approach.

From the fortress walls, defenders in ancient times could pelt the road with arrows or stones. They could rush out to attack an enemy attempting passage through the gap.

The current defenders could do a lot more than shoot arrows at the enemy. In addition to their rifles, mortars, and machine guns, Task Force Ballard had two tanks.

Of course, it was impossible to get the tanks through the fort's gate or to place them on the walls. Instead, the tank commander placed them at the base of the exterior wall, giving the tanks a clear field of fire across the clearing and down the road flowing toward them from the north. When they arrived, the enemy would be met by shells and even machine gun fire from the two tanks.

On the march, Jang-mi had shared some of the history of the fort. As it turned out, the Korean hills were dotted with similar forts. Some were now little more than ruins, but some of the more elaborate fortresses closer to Seoul and other cities had been well-tended and were now tourist attractions during peacetime.

It was hard to know it now, with the Korean people so divided and beleaguered, but they had a proud history. Jang-mi had told them about Jumong, the great warrior king who had founded a kingdom that extended not only across the Korean peninsula, but also deep into China. The nation itself had taken its name from the kingdom of

Goguryeo, the dynasty founded by Jumong that had proudly endured for centuries.

However, the growing wealth and influence of the Koreans in ancient times had attracted enemies and sparked rivalries. From time to time, the Chinese emperors had raised armies and invaded. Then came the Japanese. Ever a warlike people bent on conquest, the Japanese had repeatedly attacked the Koreans.

In times of war, the local villagers had for centuries retreated to fortresses like this. It was a place to halt the enemy or to shelter in place while a more powerful army ransacked the country, and then moved on. The Japanese Empire had finally occupied Korea as a colony in 1900. With the defeat of the Japanese, the influence of China spawned the growth of communism.

Through it all, despite the ravages of armies, and sometimes in victory and sometimes in suffering, the people had endured.

"If these walls could talk, huh?" Miller commented, reaching for Cole's canteen to take a drink. "Do you think this place will do the job?"

"Oh, I reckon it will," Cole drawled. "That fort is solid. I'm more worried about how solid *we* are."

Miller handed back Cole's canteen and clapped him on the shoulder. "No worries there, Hillbilly. From what I understand, that's going to be your job once we get this barricade built. It's up to you to make sure the Puerto Ricans know how to stand and fight."

"Where the hell is Sergeant Weber when you need him?"

"He's finishing up the barricade and setting up the defenses. That leaves you."

Cole grunted, wishing he felt more confident about whipping these former Borinqueneers into shape. He just hoped that he had not been imagining the determination he seen earlier burning in the Borinqueneers' eyes.

He stood up and walked toward them. They were all tired; hell, Cole was tired, but there was precious little time to lose. "Cisco!" he called. "Gather them boys over here. We're gonna learn you all to fight."

Sullenly, the Puerto Rican soldiers assembled in the clearing. They stood quietly, watching Cole expectantly. Some simply glared at him with open hostility. As far as they were concerned, he was just another soldier insulting them and keeping them down. That was fine by Cole —he wanted these men to feel riled up. He wanted them full of piss and vinegar. How else would they ever defeat the enemy?

Cole glared back, taking their measure. One by one, even the angriest of the Borinqueneers looked away. They weren't the first to find his intense, cut-glass eyes to be unsettling.

Meanwhile, Cole considered what to say. He never had been in charge of more than a handful of men in a squad, and even then, he hadn't much liked it. Cole felt content being a lone wolf. It went against his nature to give speeches. But when he finally spoke, his voice rang high and clear in the mountain air.

"Everyone says you're cowards," Cole began. Standing off to one side, Cisco translated like a Spanish echo. When he got to the word *cobardes*, Cole could see the Borinqueneers bristle angrily. He paused, letting that *cobardes* insult sink in. "Here's your chance to prove everybody wrong. You can be brave instead. So what is it gonna be? Are the Borinqueneers cowards or are they brave?"

Cisco posed the question in Spanish. It hung there for a moment, and then the men shouted their reply. "*Valiente!*"

"*Bueno*," Cole said. "Let's get to work."

The first thing that they did was to make sure their weapons were thoroughly cleaned. The cursory cleaning they had done earlier— simply to make sure the rifles were not so caked with mud that they wouldn't function—had not been enough. Again with Cisco translating, he ordered the men to spread out blankets and clean their weapons. Some of the men didn't even know how to dismantle their rifles for cleaning, which showed an utter lack of training. Cole began to appreciate that these men had been tossed into the lion's den without any preparation. There was no way that he could teach them to be soldiers in a few hours, but he would do his best.

He went from man to man, inspecting their work.

The kid came over to help. "If you ask me, what you ought to do is teach them to shoot."

"The first thing to do is get to know all the parts," Cole said. He added with a grin, "Ain't that what you'd do with your girlfriend?"

The kid blushed. "I guess so."

"There you go, then. Getting to know all the parts and how they work is half the fun. A rifle ain't that much different from a woman."

Cole's approach quickly showed its effectiveness as men who had not previously been familiar with their rifles began to handle them with greater ease. He knew that to be good shots, they would need to know their rifles inside and out. That was at least as important as knowing how to aim.

Soon, the cleaning kits were put away and the blankets were stowed. The men waited expectantly, their eyes on Cole.

He was getting ready to teach them how to shoot those rifles when a commotion interrupted them. There had been a warning shout, and someone was pointing toward the forest edge. Cole reached for his rifle, fearing that the enemy had outsmarted them and somehow circled around to attack from an unexpected direction. His heart sank; they were in no way ready for an attack.

"Hold your fire!" Lieutenant Ballard shouted. Jang-mi had appeared at his side, resting her hand on his carbine as if to keep it from being aimed at whoever was lurking in the forest.

"What the hell?" Cole wondered, keeping his rifle ready.

The kid seemed just as puzzled. "Who are they?" he asked.

Cole watched, amazed, as figures began to emerge silently from the forest. They materialized from the shadows as silently as ghosts and entered the clearing at the base of the fortress walls. They carried weapons, but they didn't seem to be attacking.

One thing for sure was that these were not Chinese troops. These were civilians, mostly men and a few women, old and young. None of them wore uniforms.

Jang-mi stepped forward to meet these people and Cole realized that these must be more villagers—if not from her own battered village, than from other settlements dotted across the hills. They had come as allies to help fight the Communist invaders.

"I'll be damned," Cole said.

From across the clearing, he saw Lieutenant Ballard point in his direction as Jang-mi nodded, seemingly in agreement. Soon, Jang-mi gathered the newcomers and led them toward Cole. "Teach them, too," she said.

"They can't understand me."

"I will translate."

Cole nodded. "Join the party," he said.

He looked around at the motley force, Borinqueneers on one side and Korean villagers on the other. The Borinqueneers looked like soldiers, at least. The same could not be said for the villagers, who looked exactly like the peasants they were, right down to their ragged clothing. Some wore only sandals, despite the increasingly cool temperatures in the mountains. But as with the Borinqueneers, Cole saw determination in their faces. These were people who would fight.

"All right," he announced. "Here is what we are gonna do. Kid, you and Cisco run down to the other end of the clearing and set up some targets. Just set up some chunks of wood on rocks and stumps. That'll work just fine."

"You got it," said the kid. He and Cisco trotted off.

When they returned, Cole had his motley assortment of troops line up, facing the targets. At first, he had them go through dry firing, practicing their breathe, aim, fire technique. This was the most basic foundation of marksmanship. Sure, it could be learned in an afternoon —but marksmanship often took months or years to perfect. Once again, he relayed the orders through Cisco and Jang-mi. Along the line, firing pins clicked on empty chambers.

"Make each shot count," he said. "Nothing fancy. Aim dead center."

As the sun began to dip behind the mountain peaks, reminding them all that time was limited, they moved on to live firing. Sergeant Weber came to join them. Walking behind the shooters, he and Cole gave as much instruction to each shooter as they could, having each of their new soldiers fire three rounds each. It was all the ammunition they could spare. In a fight with the Chinese, they would need every round.

Some of the chunks of wood flew ofs the rocks and stumps at the first shots, while others stubbornly refused to be hit no matter how many rounds the Borinqueneers and villagers fired. Cole went around snugging shoulders to rifle butts, raising elbows, and otherwise doing whatever he could to help this motley crew improve their aim. A few more chunks fell.

Weber shook his head. "This is not good."

"Sarge, we both know the enemy will be closer and bigger."

"Chunks of wood do not shoot back."

Cole couldn't argue with that. He would have liked to see the soldiers get more target practice, but they were losing daylight fast. He called an end to the gunfire.

The final lesson needed no explanation. Their shooting lesson over, Cole stood before these makeshift fighters and drew his Bowie knife, raising it high overhead. The cold blade of Damascus steel caught the light of the setting sun. One by one, the fighters drew their own knives and bayonets, holding them high. Cole was letting them know that when the bullets ran out, they would resort to their blades. This would be a fight to the end.

The sun finally slid behind a hill, leaving the clearing and fortress in deep shadow as if a shade had been drawn.

Cisco and Jang-mi shouted orders in their respective languages, dismissing the fighters to find what rest and shelter they could for the night.

Lieutenant Ballard came over. "Are they ready to fight?"

"To be fair, sir, I can't make soldiers out of these people in a few hours," Cole replied. However, Cole had to admit that the Borinqueneers and villagers were far from timid. They had plenty of spirit. He had seen the determination in their faces and in their willingness to learn as much as they could in so short a time. "But maybe that don't matter. They may not be soldiers, but by God, they will fight."

"Let's hope you're right," Ballard said. "We'll find out soon enough."

CHAPTER EIGHTEEN

SEVERAL MILES away from the old fortress of Lǒngmo Sanseong, Major Wu and Deng kept pace with the other Chinese troops hurrying through the hills. Instead of marching in columns, the soldiers had spread out so that the mass of moving men in their grayish uniforms gave the illusion that the thickets themselves were flowing across the landscape.

It always amazed Wu that such large numbers of men could move so quietly. Orders were kept to a minimum and there was no shouting. A few words spoken here and there seemed to be all that were needed. Instead, the officers and non-commissioned officers led by example.

Most of the troops wore light-soled shoes, enabling them to move quietly. However, the thin shoes were not much use against the rocks or the growing cold. Very few of the Chinese soldiers had anything resembling a winter coat and none wore helmets—the Communists lacked enough metal or factories to supply thousands of soldiers with steel helmets.

It was amazing that a force this size had no mechanized vehicles whatsoever, or even any horses or mules to carry supplies. The soldiers themselves served as pack animals, lugging mortar shells and spare food, although there was precious little of that.

No one complained.

Wu felt a swelling of pride for the soldiers around him. They had sacrificed so much and come so far. Surely, they would be rewarded with victory.

"Chairman Mao would be proud," he shouted. "Together, we will crush the enemy in their laziness!"

Several soldiers turned toward him, their eyes wide with alarm. Everyone knew that their success depended upon silence.

"Sir, we must be quiet," a young officer said urgently, glaring at Wu.

"Of course, but it is always good to remind the men of their Communist principles," Wu replied, grinning, although internally he seethed at the lieutenant's rebuke. He decided that when the time was right, he would find this young officer lacking in certain Communist ideals. He might very well find himself in a re-education camp as a result of his outburst. The thought made Wu grin that much more.

Major Wu was not part of the military planning, but as a political officer, he was privy to their objective. This Chinese army would move unseen through the hills and launch a surprise attack on the defensive positions held by the United Nations troops, particularly the United States. If there was any country that was their adversary in this war, it was America. None of the other nations was powerful enough on its own to wage this war. To kill a snake you must cut off the head. If they could strike a blow against the Americans, the victory would serve them well at the negotiating table where lines were being drawn to decide the fate of the Korean Peninsula.

Wu managed to keep silent for most of the march. They moved mostly at night, as Chinese troops always had, forced by necessity to avoid the enemy planes that prowled the skies by daylight. More and more, their own planes had been taking to the sky, but not in numbers great enough to drive away the enemy.

The air war was a bitter reminder that Wu had let the downed American pilot slip through his fingers. What a prize that pilot would have been!

Wu salved his wounded pride by telling himself that it was the American sniper who had ultimately denied him his prize. Wily and

tough, he had arrived just in time to rescue the pilot and those trai-
torous villagers. Wu and Deng had pursued them as far as possible, but
had never caught up.

Now, Wu hoped for a chance to redeem himself in the coming
attack. He commanded a small but effective group of snipers.

He glanced over at Deng, carrying his rifle with its telescopic sight
over one shoulder. Deng was his most reliable and celebrated sniper,
but there were now two others, Liu and Huang. It spoke to Wu's rising
influence that he had been able to obtain two more rifles that shot
accurately, even if these lacked telescopes, as well as two more soldiers
who were good shots.

"Deng, when we reach the enemy line, we will move into position
to make the best use of our sniper rifles," Wu said quietly, having been
chastised already for being too loud. "You will each shoot one hundred
of the enemy."

"I wish to shoot two hundred," said Deng, who had caught on to
the fact that Wu tended to inflate his reports.

"Yes! Even better. Soon enough, we shall put that rifle to work."

"Do you want me to shoot that disrespectful lieutenant for you?"

Wu considered Deng's offer. Maybe the young officer wasn't
destined for a re-education camp, after all. "If he should fall heroically
in battle, this might be for the best."

Deng nodded.

Wu patted Deng on the shoulder and handed him a bottle of rice
wine to keep his spirits up. Loyalty had its rewards.

"I would not mind meeting that American sniper again. You know,
the one with the flag painted on his helmet?"

"We can only hope to be so fortunate," Wu said, his voice carrying.

"Sir? Do you mind? We must be quiet." It was the young lieutenant
again, scowling at Wu.

Wu nodded at him, grinning apologetically. Once the young officer
had moved on, Wu turned to Deng and whispered, "Shoot the American sniper first, but make sure you shoot the lieutenant next."

Deng nodded grimly.

For many miles, they had made their own way through the hills.

But the hills were closing in on them, becoming steeper and more impenetrable. In fact, the army was being funneled toward a gap in the hills, which would be the more direct way of reaching the enemy positions. Closer to daylight, the soldiers began to follow a narrow road through the hills. The officers knew that this concentration of men was under grave threat of attack if seen by enemy planes. They would have to get through the gap and disperse again to use the thickets as cover before the enemy planes began their daylight patrols.

With a few whispered words, the officers urged their men on faster. Wu and his snipers were caught up like sticks swirling in a flooded stream.

All around Wu and Deng, the Chinese army flowed on, moving toward dawn and battle.

* * *

As DARKNESS FELL, the defenders made a cold camp for the night. No fires would be allowed. Their success would depend upon the enemy marching into what was essentially a trap and they couldn't take the chance that the distant light of their fires might give them away. Sentries were strung out along the approach to the fort with orders to fire a warning shot if the enemy was sighted during the night. There was no telling when the enemy would arrive.

Meanwhile, the others tried to get as comfortable as they could.

"I wish we could at least warm up these rations," the kid complained, digging into a cold can of stew and spearing a chunk of potato, which he popped into his mouth and chewed in a desultory fashion. He tugged his jacket tighter. Here in the higher elevations, the nights were chill in the shadow of the fortress wall.

"Enjoy it while you can, kid," Cole said. "It's gonna get right warm around here once the Chinese show up."

"Can we stop them?"

"If we don't stop them, we'll sure as hell slow them down," Cole said.

The kid nodded and forced down another lump of cold potato. "We've got our squad and the two tanks. Those Korean villagers look tough as nails, if you ask me. But do you think those Borinqueneers will hold up?"

"Only time will tell," Cole said. "If they cut and run, we'll be in a world of trouble."

Cole had been in some tight places, and tomorrow promised to be another one. Their ragtag task force was supposed to stop a small army? It seemed a foolish notion, but then again, they had all volunteered for this.

The kid looked out at the darkness, lost in his own thoughts. "Do you think this place is haunted? This fort must have been here for centuries. I'll bet lots of people have died here."

Cole began to lay out the tools to clean his rifle. "I reckon it is haunted. Anyplace this old must have ghosts. But there ain't been a ghost yet to stick a bayonet in your ribs. It's only the living who can do that. We're a lot safer with the ghosts. Get some sleep. You're gonna need it."

"What about you? You can't get that rifle any cleaner."

"Don't worry about me, kid. I'll sleep when I'm dead."

* * *

HARDY WAS SACKING out with the tankers. The remnants of the monsoon clouds had cleared enough to reveal the stars, which wheeled overhead, pinpricks of cold light. There had been rumors that the Soviets or possibly the United States planned to send men into space. Hardy figured there were enough problems in the world that mankind didn't need to worry about space just yet.

A sentry was posted in each tank turret, watching the road. The tank crews were stretched out in foxholes, which was a lot more comfortable than trying to sleep in contorted positions inside the tanks. Given warning, they could be up and at their stations inside of a minute.

"Can we hold back this army?" Hardy asked Lieutenant Dunbar, who lay in his sleeping bag nearby. His tank crews had stretched out on the surrounding ground, but never straying far from the tanks.

"As long as they don't have artillery and they don't rush us, we can give 'em hell all day long if we have to," Dunbar said. "At least, we can until we run out of ammunition. There won't be any resupply out here."

"What happens when you run out of ammunition for the tanks?"

"We'll fight as long as we can, one way or another. You've heard of the Alamo, right? We've been dubbed Outpost Alamo for good reason. It might be like that."

Hardy had brought along a rifle, but he planned to observe the battle and take photographs, rather than fight. Up until a moment ago, Hardy had been excited about the possibility of a great story and photographs for the *Stars and Stripes*. But Dunbar's words and the darkness itself began to sink in. It hadn't occurred to him that there might not be any leaving this place.

The Alamo? Every American had heard the story of the Alamo. And everyone knew that the outnumbered defenders had all died in the end. Even the famous frontiersman, Davy Crockett, had perished.

"I tell you what. If we live through tomorrow, promise that you'll come visit me in Indiana after the war," Hardy said. "I'll buy you a steak dinner."

"You've got yourself a deal."

* * *

NEARBY, the Korean villagers who had come to help defend the fort slept on the ground or ate their own meager meals. Due to the war, their own food was in short supply. They eagerly divided the C rations that Lieutenant Ballard had provided.

Jang-mi did not have so much as a blanket, but had stretched out on the ground near Seo-jun and Chul. She did not know all of the Koreans who had come down out of the hills to fight, but she felt safe near these two, at least. They would defend her, just as she would defend them.

Earlier, she had tried to send Seo-jun away. He was barely more than a boy, and she wished to spare him from certain death. She had no illusions about what would happen once the large enemy force arrived.

Seo-jun seemed too young to understand that this might be his last night on earth.

She was not so old herself, but she had made peace with this life.

The same seemed true of Chul, who was old enough to be her father. He did not talk much, but he seemed content with his fate. His philosophy seemed to be that it was better to die now, then die later. If the Communists won, there might be no safe place in all of Korea for those who loved their freedom.

A bittersweet feeling had seemed to steal over the entire camp, as if the defenders collectively agreed that this might be their last night alive. A few of the Koreans had started singing old folk songs, some funny, some mournful.

Jang-mi was still listening as she started to drift off to sleep, but she jolted upright at the sound of heavy footsteps approaching. These were not the light steps of a Korean. To her delight, it was the American pilot. Against all odds, considering their very different backgrounds, she found herself drawn to the American. Outlined against the stars, he was carrying a folded blanket.

"I thought you might want this," he said. "It's going to be chilly tonight."

"What about you?" she wondered, accepting the blanket gratefully. Neither the cold ground nor her thoughts offered any warmth or comfort.

"You saved my life, remember? The least I can do is offer you a blanket."

"You will be cold. Here," she said, spreading the blanket over her shoulders and lifting a corner to indicate that Lieutenant Commander Miller should join her. A moment later, they were sitting side by side under the blanket. Jang-mi had been in many battles and survived many difficult situations, but she was surprised at the rapid beating of her heart, caused by nothing more than this man's presence.

Suddenly embarrassed at what the others would think of her, she looked around again for Chul and Seo-jun, but saw the older man leading the boy farther away, as if to give Jang-mi and the American their privacy.

"I wish we had more time, Jang-mi," the pilot said. "I would like to get to know you better. All that we have is tonight."

Jang-mi nodded, then tugged the blanket closer across their shoulders, joining them together in mutual warmth. "We have tonight," she agreed.

CHAPTER NINETEEN

ONCE AGAIN, the ancient fortress became a witness to war. The fight began just after dawn, with gunfire from the sentries rousing those who had been able to sleep from what rest they could get. Cole and the others had expected a warning shot or two, but instead, there was suddenly a flurry of sharp rifle cracks. The battle had not started with a trickle, but with a flood.

"Here they come," Cole shouted, mainly for the benefit of the Borinqueneers. Cisco translated the warning into Spanish, although the rifle shots had sent a message that was clear enough. Fortunately, the Puerto Rican soldiers had slept in their positions on top of the fortress wall and were ready for action.

Below, a swarm of Chinese troops appeared out of nowhere, sending the sentries running for cover. Moments before, the road through the mountains had been empty and shrouded in pre-dawn darkness. Now it was packed shoulder to shoulder with hordes of enemy troops clad in their grayish-white uniforms that made them seem ghostly and otherworldly, their rifles bristling.

From the rim of the fortress wall, the defenders had a clear field of fire down onto the road. Aimed at the oncoming enemy, rifles snapped all around Cole, raining a deadly fire upon the Chinese. Taken by surprise, the enemy troops scattered as best they could. However, there wasn't anywhere for them to go. On the one side were the steep cliffs that anchored one end of the fortress wall. And on the other side of the road was a steep drop with a branch of the Imjin river cutting through the valley floor below. The enemy troops were trapped like hogs in a pen, which was just what the defenders had hoped for.

"Pour it on 'em, boys!" Cole shouted, taking aim with his own rifle and dropping a Chinese officer into the dirt. He ran the bolt and fired again. Every soldier they shot now was one that they wouldn't have to fight later.

Cole knew from experience that the enemy would keep coming. The Chinese tossed lives away as carelessly as if they were autumn leaves. It was a tactic that won them battles, but it meant that the Chinese soldiers were only so much cannon fodder.

Cole fired again. And again. He could barely hear the Springfield above the din around him, but he felt the satisfying thump of the recoil against his shoulder.

The one-sided action energized the defenders and a spontaneous cheer went up across their ranks. For the Borinqueneers, this was just the encouragement that they needed. Cole thought that these boys needed to know that they weren't cowards. They needed to know that they could fight. They would need this boost of courage because Cole knew that the fight was just beginning.

It wasn't just the Borinqueneers who were enjoying this shooting gallery. Beneath them, at the foot of the fortress wall, the two tanks opened up on the enemies in the road with devastating results.

The rounds from the tank acted like supersonic bowling balls with the enemy troops being so many bowling pins. Without any solid target, the rounds did not explode immediately, but careened down the road, leaving a path of carnage. Some men were cut in half, while others lost limbs. After a few rounds from the tanks, the surface of the road became slick with gore. When the tank rounds finally struck some rocky outcropping or a tree, they exploded with a final devastating blow. It was enough to make Cole almost feel sorry for the enemy soldiers being cut to pieces.

"It's like a turkey shoot," Cole said to the kid beside him. The kid was also busy firing down at the enemy troops, but had paused to dig more ammunition from a pocket.

"I shot six and then I lost count," the kid said, sounding excited.

"Best to stop counting before you run out of fingers and toes."

Cole wondered how long the element of surprise could last. Clearly, the Chinese had not expected to encounter any resistance in these mountains when the U.N. forces were still many miles away. How long could they hope to turn back the flood of enemy soldiers?

He soon got his answer when the Chinese began to organize and direct fire toward the fortress walls. Bullets began to whine overhead or smack against the stone blocks. A few bullets found their targets, however, and a handful of Borinqueneers went down. Most were hit in the shoulders or shot in the head and killed instantly. All along the fortress walls, shouts for medics rang out.

Back at the Main Line of Resistance, there was at least some hope now that if you were badly wounded that you might be flown out by helicopter to one of the new MASH units. If nothing else, there was at least a field hospital. There were no helicopters all the way out here, however. Carrying the wounded all those miles back would be challenging, to say the least.

The Chinese troops were battle-hardened veterans and the ambush did not leave them dazed for long. The officers began to get the men spread out along the road so that they were no longer such easy targets. The tanks couldn't depress their guns much lower, so that the rounds began to pass over the heads of the enemy. The Chinese took up positions wherever they could behind rocks or clumps of bushes and poured fire at the defenders.

Despite the handful of casualties along the top of the wall, the fire was not very telling at first, but then the Chinese began to bring up their nasty little Soviet-made light machine guns, along with mortars. Here the Chinese had an advantage because the mortars could arch high and rain down upon the walls of the fort. The mortars could even reach into the interior area where the supplies were being kept for the task force. Having traveled light and fast, needing to carry everything on their backs, the task force had only a couple of mortars and a small supply of mortar shells.

The more enemy mortars that were brought into play, the more precarious the defenders' position would become. Down below, the Chinese moved closer to the tanks, which seemed counter-intuitive, but the fact was that it was impossible for the tanks to depress their barrels any lower. Instead, they had to rely on their machine guns for closer targets.

It was lucky for the defenders that the Chinese did not seem to have any artillery, unless it was toward the rear of the column and simply hadn't been brought up yet. If any field artillery was brought into play, the high-explosive rounds would make short work of the fort.

"We need to take out those mortar crews," Cole said, tapping the kid on the shoulder to get his attention. The kid redirected his rifle in that direction. "Make them keep their heads down."

"You got it."

Cole ran at a crouch along the fort wall, searching for Cisco. He hoped to hell that the young Borinqueneer hadn't been hit. It would have meant that they had lost their only communication link with the Spanish-speaking troops. Not only that, but by golly, Cole had come to like that Puerto Rican kid. That boy had gumption.

To Cole's relief, he found Cisco busy with his own rifle, firing down at the enemy. All around Cisco, the other Borinqueneers were doing the same, despite the increasing rate of enemy fire. Tough bastards, he thought, impressed. Still, a growing number of the Puerto Rican troops had been hit, leaving gaps along the wall. The wounded had been dragged behind whatever cover could be found, although there wasn't any safe place on the wall, not with bullets whistling all around them. Everywhere, Cole smelled the familiar odor of gunpowder and more sickeningly, the smell of fresh-spilled blood.

The dead were left where they had fallen. Cole caught sight of a dead Borinqueneer, an older veteran whom he recognized from the march and training. A bullet hole marked the man's cheekbone and his eyes stared sightlessly, never to see his island home again.

Cole jumped down next to Cisco.

"Hey amigo, tell your boys to shoot at the mortar crews," Cole said. "If those goons start lobbing mortar shells up here, they will chew us up good."

Cisco nodded and hurried away to spread the word. Cole knew that they must eliminate the mortar crews if the defenders hoped to hold out for any length of time.

Cole kept going down the length of the wall. The members of his own squad were peppered among the Borinqueneers and the Koreans to set the example. These veteran soldiers resembled the cement holding things together.

The Korean villagers and mountain people held their own, still atop the wall firing down at the Chinese, but several of them had been hit. He looked around for Jang-mi but didn't see her right away. Not among the living, at least.

As fighters defending their country from the invading Chinese, the Koreans had plenty of spirit, but they weren't really soldiers and their weapons were not exactly modern. One youth struggled with a rusted single-shot rifle that had to be laboriously cocked between shots. Glancing at the pitted metal, Cole thought it was a wonder that the old weapon hadn't blown up in his face yet. Cole thrust a discarded carbine into the youth's hands instead.

"Use this!" he shouted. The young Korean nodded grimly.

Fear had gripped some of the Koreans so that they had stopped firing and cowered behind the low walls of the fort, hands over their ears. As a result, their return fire had slackened considerably. Cole stopped to put weapons back into their hands. "You need to fight!" he said. Some nodded and began shooting back at the Chinese, but others could not shake off the grip of fear and dropped the rifles as soon as Cole thrust the weapons at them.

He knew from experience that if the Chinese overran the fort, that they might show some mercy to any captured Americans. American prisoners had value for propaganda purposes. They could be paraded for newsreels and photographs like prize animals at the county fair. Also, captured Americans served as a bargaining chip in the negotiations to end the war. Captured Koreans would be killed outright as traitors, more than likely bayoneted to save bullets. Bleeding out through a bayonet wound in your guts was a slow, painful way to die, but you'd be dead all the same.

That was how the Chinese operated. The Communists were cruel bastards. Any wounded Americans would also be killed because the Chinese couldn't be bothered to care for them. Cole had seen that happen at the Chosin Reservoir. He still had nightmares in which he heard the screams of the wounded GIs being burned alive once the Chinese captured the ambulances.

"Fight!" he shouted desperately at the Koreans, urging them to shoot back. "There ain't no place to hide. It's fight now or die later!"

They couldn't understand Cole's words, but they got the message, hearing the tone of urgency in his voice. Their return fire increased in intensity, scattering the Chinese on the road below.

Finally, he spotted Jang-mi.

She was bent over Chul, who was bleeding heavily from a chest wound. Cole could hear the air sucking in and out of it and knew that the tough old man didn't have long for this world. As Cole approached, Chul pulled Jang-mi's hands away from the rag that she was pressing against the wound. He spoke to her in Korean, which Cole couldn't understand, but he thought that Chul had said something along the lines of, "Don't worry about me. Go on and fight."

Jang-mi nodded, picked up her rifle, and returned to the wall. Chul closed his eyes, sighed contentedly, and died as easily as if he had fallen asleep. It was a better fate than many others this day. Nearby, the boy named Seo-jun looked back at Chul's body, then fired down at the Chinese with a vengeance, despite the tears streaming down his face.

Ballard and old Sergeant Weber were also moving along the wall, encouraging the defenders wherever they could and making sure that everyone had enough ammunition. They moved people to fill the gaps left by casualties. Like Cole, they had seen the danger posed by the mortars and the enemy machine gunners and tried to direct fire before the enemy could take a toll with those devastating weapons.

Jake Miller had chosen to fight alongside Jang-mi and he wielded his rifle awkwardly. One thing for sure, the flyboy was no infantry soldier. But Cole couldn't deny that the pilot appeared full of fight.

He turned to Cole, "Look at that. We've almost got them on the run."

"Almost," Cole replied, although he was thinking that wasn't about to happen.

"What I wouldn't give right now for a Corsair that I could fly in here and drop a bomb on their heads and give them little strafing for good measure," Miller said.

"If you know who to call about that, now would be a good time," Cole said.

"Do prayers count?" Miller just laughed, shook his head, and fired his rifle. No Corsairs appeared and no reinforcements. There was just this motley crew of defenders, their numbers diminishing by the minute as the Chinese fire took its toll.

The fight had only been going on for a few minutes, but already it felt like a lifetime. Cole had found that to be the case with most battles.

A fight never lasted as long as you thought, but every minute of a battled stretched on like some terrifying nightmare that you couldn't wake from.

Jang-mi was doing her best to rally the Koreans, so Cole ran back in the direction of the Borinqueneers. He found that they had settled in for a bitter fight, crouching behind the low wall that served as the fort's parapet or among the rocks where time and storms had scattered sections of the wall—helped by a few Chinese mortar rounds. The smell of sweating men and blood and cordite hung over the whole area. Some of the men were wounded, but they had patched themselves back up and gotten back into the fight. Cisco seemed to be everywhere at once, reassuring the others or running to get more ammunition.

Cole saw the grim determination on all of their faces and grunted to himself in satisfaction. The officers who had pegged these boys as cowards after the debacle at Outpost Kelly was just plain wrong. Hell, even he had been wrong about the Borinqueneers. He understood now that their orders during the fight on Outpost Kelly had just gotten confused by the language barrier. Here at the fortress, these Puerto Ricans were fighting like wildcats.

The kid was fighting alongside them. Running at a crouch, Cole jumped down beside him.

"Where have you been?" the kid asked.

"Oh, I strolled down to the corner store for the paper and a pack of smokes."

The kid grinned. "I'd believe that if you could read and if you smoked."

"You got a point there," Cole said.

"Next time, pick me up a soda pop."

"Hell, I'll do better than that, kid. If we survive this, I'll buy you a beer."

CHAPTER TWENTY

DOWN BELOW ON THE ROAD, Major Wu and Deng had been among those caught by total surprise when the walls of what appeared to be an abandoned fortress suddenly erupted in fire. One moment they had been trudging along shoulder-to-shoulder with their fellow Communists, and the next thing they knew, soldiers were running for cover or collapsing into the dirt.

"Take cover!" Wu shouted as the carnage began. He heard bullets *thwacking* into the bodies of the soldiers around him. "We are under attack!"

"Sir, this way!"

Deng grabbed Wu by the shoulder and pulled him closer to the rock wall they were passing. At least it offered some cover. On the far side of the road, there was nowhere to go, but only a sheer drop. In the confusion on the crowded mountain road, some of the men had been pushed off the edge and fallen to their deaths, screaming in terror. Something passed by with a tremendous *whoosh*, leaving shattered men in its wake. Wu realized that it was a tank round. Down the road, the tank round hit something and exploded, wreaking more havoc.

Wu felt no fear, but only anger. Had the imperialists tricked them? He wondered why their scouts had not noticed the defenses here, but the scouts had barely been able to stay ahead as the entire army rushed ahead almost at a trot, trying to cover a bit more distance before full daylight and the threat of enemy aircraft.

Besides, he could see how the defenders had been cleverly hidden. Even the tanks were covered in brush to camouflage them. Looking closer, he could see a barricade down the road that their troops must cross in order to proceed. It would take some effort to clear the barrier. Meanwhile, the defenders would be shooting at them the whole time. Wu could see that the trap had been set carefully. It was more than he would have given the slow-witted Americans credit for.

Of course, Wu was a political officer who did not command any troops other than his little band of snipers that he had assembled for propaganda purposes. However, he was satisfied that the officers had a clear grasp of the situation that the army was in.

Shouting orders, the officers had sent a team of men forward, toward the barricade in an effort to clear the way. As it turned out, this was nothing more than a suicide mission and those men quickly fell under the heavy enemy fire. One moment, they had been running down the road and the next, they dropped as if cut down by a scythe. Wu blinked, a little stunned by the sight. Undeterred, the officers simply sent more men to die and they would keep doing it until that barricade was gone.

He could see the young lieutenant who had chastised Wu earlier for being too loud. The officer stood amid the chaos like a rock, trying to direct the confused soldiers.

Wu drew his pistol and pointed it at the lieutenant, just a few yards away. Then he thought better of it. Even Wu realized that there was no point in satisfying his petty need for revenge when the entire column fought for survival.

As for himself, Wu was not about to stand by and do nothing. Normally, Chinese political offers took up stations as a kind of rear guard to shoot any man who retreated or shirked his duty. There was no need for that now.

"Come with me," Wu said to Deng. "We are not doing any good here, but we must put our snipers to use."

Wu had quickly gotten the lay of the land at the ambush site.

Between the clearing and the road, there was nowhere for his snipers to set up. There was only one option that he could see.

He looked at Deng. "What do you think?" he asked.

Deng's practiced eyes took in the surroundings. Like Wu, he had seen the cliff rising above them. It wasn't so steep that a man could not climb it, but it would be challenging. "Sir, we need to get up there. If we can get high enough, we may even be able to shoot down at the fort."

Wu nodded. It was exactly what he had been thinking, that the cliff was their best option to do some good during this battle. The cliff face was enough of an obstacle to prevent the bulk of the troops from climbing it and flanking the fort, but a handful of men could manage it. Besides, the road had become a blood-soaked charnel house. Staying here meant certain death. "Gather the other snipers."

Wu started up the steep slope, leading Deng and the two other snipers. The young officer yelled something at them as if thinking that they were fleeing, but Wu told him to go to hell.

Wu climbed. The steep slope required digging in with his knees, along with his hands and his elbows, fighting for every inch of progress up the cliff face. But he was undeterred even as his fancy uniform became covered in dirt and torn from briers.

Deng was more agile and soon passed him, reaching the top of the cliff. The last few feet of the climb were the most frightening because the top of the cliff curled out like a surly bottom lip. Wu struggled, his feet touching nothing but thin air, well aware that if he slipped he would tumble all the way to the road below. His stomach lurched at the notion. Wu felt himself starting to slip backwards and dug his knees frantically into the dirt and shale.

Finally, a hand reached down from above. Gratefully, he grasped Deng's hand and allowed himself to be pulled up. Wu stayed on all fours for a full minute, catching his breath after the climb. The other two snipers pulled themselves up behind Wu, with Deng helping them up those last few feet of the lip.

With a sense of satisfaction, Wu saw that their efforts had been worthwhile. They had reached an ideal position. From the top of this cliff, they could look down and see the wall of the old fortress below.

The sheer cliff face that dropped to the bastion itself was a barrier that prevented a flanking attack by an enemy. In the long-ago days of bow and arrow and spear, achieving this hill would have meant little because those ancient weapons would not have had the range to reach the defenders on top of the fortress wall. However, the defenders were easily within rifle range.

"Spread out," Wu said, although the order was unnecessary because Deng and the other two men knew their business and were already finding vantage points from which to shoot.

Deng crouched behind a boulder that provided cover and also a stable surface on which to rest his rifle. Wu was only armed with his pistol and he cursed himself for not thinking to bring a rifle, even though he wasn't much of a shot. The pistol was more or less useless at this range. However, Wu had brought along his prized binoculars, almost as scarce as telescopic sights in the Chinese army, which still seemed to have one foot in the 19th century in terms of equipment production. These were German binoculars, a relic of the last war in Europe. Putting the binoculars to his eyes, Wu went to work looking for targets.

Not needing to wait for the major, the three snipers opened fire and immediately had a telling effect on the defenders along the top of the wall. The Chinese in the road below also fired at the old fort wall. With Wu's snipers now in play, bullets were coming at the defenders from two directions. Did they even notice the snipers? Not right away. Too much heavy fire poured at them from the large numbers of troops in the road below, along with the occasional mortar and bursts of machine-gun fire. None of the defenders seemed to notice the snipers' deadly toll.

"Aim for the officers," Wu said, using his binoculars to scan the parapet for the most vital targets. He was surprised that there were not many defenders, after all—certainly no more than a platoon. It amazed Wu that they were holding the mountain pass against a much larger number. The Chinese force was comprised of an entire battalion, with hundreds of fighters.

Wu and his snipers alone could put a dent in the relatively small number of enemy troops. On the bastion below, Wu spotted a tall

American giving orders. He shouted at Deng and directed his attention toward the officer. "There! Shoot that officer!"

Deng's rifle fired and the officer crumpled. Smiling with satisfaction, Wu moved his binoculars along the fort wall, looking for additional targets. He was close enough that he could pick out individual characteristics of the defenders. He was surprised to see several Korean civilians. Traitors! Their time would come. But for now, it was the U.S. soldiers that the snipers must reap.

Although their faces were not detailed at this range, to his surprise, a man turned toward him as if sensing Wu and the snipers. From the hilltop, he saw that this soldier had a flag painted on his helmet. With a start, Wu realized this was the American sniper who had caused him so much grief. Finally, Wu would be able to eliminate him for good, which would be quite satisfying. But to do so, he wanted his best sniper to take the shot so that the opportunity would not be wasted.

He crept over to where Deng fired from behind his rock and tapped him on the shoulder. Deng had been about to fire and looked unhappily at the major, who had interrupted his shot, but knew better than to say anything. Wu pointed down at the fort.

"Toward the middle of that bastion is a sniper. The one with the flag on his helmet. Do you see him now through your scope?" When Deng nodded, Wu said excitedly, "You must shoot him. Shoot him!"

Deng pressed his eye tight against the rifle scope and lined up his sights on the man that Wu was pointing at. His calloused finger squeezed the trigger.

* * *

COLE SUDDENLY FLINCHED, both of them ducking low as a bullet from the road ricocheted off the remains of the parapet in front of them.

Beside him, the kid's expression turned to surprise. "I'm hit," he said. "Holy cow, that hurts."

Then his eyes rolled back in his head, and he collapsed among the rocks of the shattered parapets.

It didn't make sense that the kid had been hit by a ricochet, which had zinged off in another direction. Stunned, Cole realized that the bullet had not been fired from the road. It had come from behind them. Desperately, he looked around, caught a glimpse of something on the hilltop that anchored the western end of the fort. Somehow, an enemy sniper had gotten up there.

"Hang in there, kid," Cole said, hurrying to drag the young soldier behind a pile of rocks. There wasn't much cover, not with fire coming at them from below and now from a sniper on the hilltop. Another shot rang out, and another defender fell. Then another shot. Cole realized that there was more than one shooter on that hilltop.

The kid had passed out from the initial shock, but had reopened his eyes. He groaned.

"How bad am I hit?" the kid asked. He seemed to want to say more, but no sound came out when his lips moved.

"I've seen worse," Cole lied. "Save your breath, OK? You hang in there."

"Oh, sweet Jesus, it hurts."

Cole knew it was bad if the kid invoked the savior's name in anything other than a prayer. Looking around, he shouted, "Medic!"

After a minute that seemed to stretch on forever, a medic ran toward them and slid behind cover like he was sliding into third base. "The lieutenant is hit bad," he said reaching into his kit for morphine. "Sergeant Weber too, but the old bastard is too tough to quit."

Cole nodded. The medic could patch up the kid's wounds. But it would be up to Cole to eliminate this new problem created by the snipers. They had been outfoxed and outflanked. Those snipers up on the hilltop would shoot the defenders to pieces.

Desperately, he looked around and saw the watchtower standing in the middle of the fortress wall. It had already been hit by mortar fire, the roof shattered and the soldiers there killed. But it still stood and it was the only structure on the wall that would offer Cole the height he needed to be able to shoot back effectively at those snipers. All along the parapet, bullet strikes raised puffs of dust. If he made it as far as that watchtower, it would be a miracle.

Cole took a deep breath and ran.

CHAPTER TWENTY-ONE

A BULLET PLUCKED at Cole's sleeve, but he didn't stop running. A burst from a machine gun cut the air, tracers inches from his eyes. If he stopped now, he was a dead man.

Cole reached the watchtower and ducked inside, a bullet smacking the stone beside the doorway as he did so. Fragments of stone stung his cheek as he threw himself into the dark interior.

Dang, that last shot was close.

It was hard to say if it had been a random bullet or if he had been targeted by those snipers on the hilltop. If they had already picked him out as a target and seen him enter the watchtower, he would need to make extra sure that he kept his head down.

Considering that the best way to stay alive as a sniper was to make sure that nobody noticed you, he already had a big strike against him.

The interior of the watchtower was a jumble of rubble, having taken a couple of glancing mortar hits. One more round, and it looked as if the whole place might come down.

He noticed a couple of bodies among the stones and debris. They were Koreans who had planned to use the tower as a vantage point. A couple of old-fashioned rifles were still gripped in their hands. Cole checked them for any signs of life, then shook his head. Instead of a vantage point, the tower had proven to be a death trap. Cole knew that he might be pushing his luck if he thought that he could do any better.

A ladder gave access through a wooden floor to a loft, its walls featuring narrow arrow slits instead of windows. It didn't look as if the Koreans had made it up here before they had been taken out. The only sign of recent occupation was evidenced by the thick layer of bat droppings covering the floor.

Cole crept to one of the slits and looked down at the road below. There were a great many Chinese bodies, but the enemy had gotten organized after the initial carnage. At one end of the clearing, a work detail was struggling frantically to remove the barrier blocking the road. The far edge of the road ended at the cliff, but more soldiers had found whatever cover they could and now poured fire up at the fortress walls.

As Cole watched, the tanks let loose with a couple of rounds, one of which whistled over the heads of the Chinese. It hadn't been aimed low enough. However, the second round struck the base of the cliff rising beside the road, detonating with telling effect on the troops trying to hug the cliff face for shelter.

How long can we hold out? he asked himself. It wasn't a question that he could answer. They had every advantage from a defensive standpoint, but they were severely outnumbered.

He crawled around to the arrow slits in the wall facing the hilltop occupied by the snipers. This was the hill that anchored the western wall of the fort. From up there, those snipers had a clear shot at anything that moved along the parapet. He kicked himself for not seeing the danger earlier and making sure that they had some men up there. Then again, who could have expected the enemy to make their way up there?

Glancing at the steep hillside, he had to give the Chinese credit. It had taken some brass balls to climb that cliff in the middle of a battle.

Beneath him, Cole heard footsteps as someone picked their way across the rubble. The ladder shook and creaked as someone put their weight on it.

Cole reached for one of the grenades on his belt. He was prepared to toss one down the ladder to take care of any unwanted company. As far as he knew, no Chinese had scaled the wall yet, but he wasn't taking any chances.

"Anybody up here?" somebody shouted.

Cole relaxed his grip on the grenade.

A moment later, Lieutenant Commander Jake Miller's head popped into the loft.

"Dammit, I almost dropped a grenade on your head."

"Bet that would've smarted."

"What are you doing up here, anyway? I thought you were with Jang-mi, keeping an eye on her?"

"Believe me, Jang-mi doesn't need any help from me to fight the Chinese. Not after they killed Chul."

Cole nodded. He knew all about the motivating qualities of revenge. Some said that revenge flowed through the mountain folks back home like blood in their veins or cold water in a mountain stream.

Right now, Cole didn't feel that sense of revenge. Instead, he felt an old sense of helplessness.

Briefly, he thought about the kid, lying wounded behind the parapet. Cole wasn't sure how badly he'd been hit. He had left the kid in the hands of God and the medic, which was all that he could do on the battlefield.

Cole should have felt that sense of burning revenge now, but instead, he felt curiously hollow. The Chinese had gotten up there on that hilltop and outsmarted him. They had shot the kid, along with Lieutenant Ballard and maybe even Sergeant Weber, from the sounds of it.

He was supposed to be a sniper—the best in Korea, some claimed. And yet, he hadn't been able to do a damn thing to keep his unit from being shot to hell.

He leaned the Springfield against the wall and put his face in his hands, feeling suddenly overwhelmed.

Lieutenant Commander Miller looked at him curiously. "You all right?"

Cole snorted. "What do you think? We're getting chewed to pieces.

Now there's a nest of snipers up on that hill. They even shot the kid. Aside from all that, I'm just dandy, sir. How about you?"

The grounded pilot climbed the rest of the way into the loft, dragging himself onto the piles of guano.

"What's all this stuff?"

"Bat shit."

The officer looked alarmed. "Can't you catch rabies from bats?"

"Sir, I'd be a lot more worried about catching a bullet right about now."

"I came up here to see if I could help."

"Where's your rifle? You can't hit much from here with a pistol."

The pilot patted a deep pocket. "I brought my binoculars. You need a spotter, don't you?"

"It might be too late," Cole said. "I don't know how much longer we can hold out."

The pilot crawled toward Cole, making a face as he moved through the dark-colored guano. "Listen to me, Hillbilly. You know what I'm good at? Flying an airplane."

"Good to know. You got one of them in your pocket, too?"

"Don't I wish. But right now there's a shortage of airplanes around here. You know what your good at? Shooting. Everybody says what a good shot you are."

"Easy to say and hard to do."

"I've seen you in action, Cole. Don't sell yourself short."

"If you say so."

The pilot pointed. "You see all those people fighting down there? They are desperate, Cole. But some of them saw you heading in here with your rifle and you know what, it gave them some hope. They know you are a tough, mean son of a bitch. You scare them a little, maybe more than a little. They're not like you, Cole. If anyone can change how things are going in this fight, it's you and your rifle."

"I'm sure glad they all think that," Cole said bitterly. "Makes it all sound real easy, like I can make the world change all because I pick up a rifle."

Lieutenant Commander Miller shook his head. "Be honest with yourself, Cole. Deep down, you know it's true. Things *do* change when you start shooting. Now, pick up that rifle, you goddamn hillbilly. That's an order. I am an officer, in case you've forgotten."

Cole studied the rifle propped against the wall, but didn't yet reach for it. Against the backdrop of the dusty old stone walls, the battered stock had seen better days and the well-oiled metal of the action and the barrel were concealed by camouflage wrappings.

"You still got them binoculars handy?"

"Right here."

"Good. In that case, you can help me shoot these bastards."

* * *

ON THE HILLTOP, Wu was busy searching for new targets using his vintage German binoculars. He wanted to make sure that his snipers eliminated the officers and non-commissioned officers in order to leave the enemy without leadership.

"You missed your last shot!" Wu complained, grinning at Deng with a broad smile. Deng had been aiming at the American sniper, who had moved at the last second, causing the shot to go wide. The sniper had then scrambled for cover. If the sniper had not known they were on the hill, then he did now.

Deng nodded warily. He knew that with Wu, a smile often meant the opposite of showing pleasure. "The range is very long, sir."

"You are a sniper! Do what you are trained to do. If not, I will give that rifle to someone else."

"Yes, sir. I will do better," Deng said through gritted teeth. He took a deep breath to calm himself. Anger would not do him any good if he wanted to hit his next target and satisfy the major.

"Shoot them!" Wu snapped.

While Deng turned his attention back to the rifle, Wu glassed the fortress wall below. The defenders were still putting up a strong fight, managing to stall the battalion. This must not be allowed, he thought. The longer that the Chinese force remained exposed in the open without moving into its hiding place for the day, the more likely it became that they might be attacked from the air. The delay also gave the Americans more time to reinforce the main line that the Chinese were determined to push back.

Wu and his snipers must do their part to sack this fortress, sooner rather than later, and they were in a perfect position to do just that.

Through the binoculars, he saw an American soldier carrying a rifle with a telescopic sight scramble into the watchtower in the center of the fortress wall. It was the American sniper again! Would they ever be rid of that man?

Wu directed Deng to shoot at the sniper, but the enemy soldier scrambled behind cover like the rat that he was, leaving Deng's bullet to strike the now-empty wall where the sniper's head had been a moment ago.

"Shoot him through the arrow slits."

Deng did not answer, but squeezed off another round. Debris flew from the edge of the opening. They were so intent on the sniper that, too late, they saw another man scramble into the tower.

Deng fired again. This time, Deng's shot seemed to go right into the narrow window.

Wu imagined the bullet bounce around inside there like beads in a baby's rattle.

Wu smiled.

* * *

THROUGH THE SCOPE, Cole studied the hilltop occupied by the enemy. He spotted the man-made geometry of a rifle barrel, clearly standing out against the rough-hewn landscape. He was a little surprised that the rifle wasn't wrapped in some sort of cloth in order to camouflage it, as his own rifle was. Anything that broke up the outline of your rifle or your body helped a sniper to blend into his surroundings. A small bit of camouflage went a long way toward hiding him from the enemy— and keeping him alive.

For the enemy sniper, the failure to disguise his rifle was about to become a fatal mistake.

Cole moved the crosshairs slowly up the length of the barrel until they settled on the head of the shooter, which was the only part of the enemy sniper visible.

Nearby, Miller was glassing the hill with the binoculars.

"Maybe you're right," Miller said. "That's a long way to shoot. Nobody can hit anything that small at that distance."

Cole didn't reply. His universe had shrunk down to the circle of magnification that he could see through the scope. In the vastness of the Korean landscape, it was only this circle three feet wide that mattered.

Now, he did what came so naturally to him. He let out a breath. His shooter's mind did a million subtle calculations, purely by instinct.

He nudged the crosshairs to the left and held high.

Never mind that a bullet smacked into the wall nearby. Never mind that a mortar shell arced over the wall and exploded in the supply area below.

As if in a trance, Cole ignored the deadly chaos and carnage around him. Gently, his finger took up tension on the trigger.

The rifle fired, sending a spiraling bullet from the watchtower to the hilltop in the same span of time in which a butterfly's wings might beat once, twice.

Through the binoculars, Miller saw the spray of blood as the top of the Chinese sniper's head flew off.

"A little high," Cole muttered.

"Holy shit," Miller replied, his voice tinged with awe, and maybe a little fear of the man next to him. It was one thing to engage in a dogfight and shoot down an enemy plane. There was even an element of single combat to a dogfight that went back to the days of knights errant. But what Cole had just done ... this was killing. The brutality of it shocked him.

"Look around and find the others," Cole said, working the bolt of his rifle. The spent brass casing spun away and clattered into the guano. "In case you ain't noticed, it's them or us."

Miller did as suggested, searching the hilltop with the binoculars, which had a much broader field of view than the rifle scope. To his surprise, he spotted something. "How do I let you know where to look?"

"Just like in the air," Cole said. "Pretend it's a clock face."

"Two o'clock," Miller said.

Cole shifted his rifle and saw the other sniper now. Again, the man didn't seem to know enough to wrap the barrel of his rifle, but he was well hidden. All that Cole could see was a splash of face and a single eye.

He put the crosshairs on the eye and fired.

The enemy sniper slumped, his rifle clattering among the rocks.

"One shot. Holy moly. I can't believe it," Miller said. "You nailed him."

But the dragon still had claws. A bullet tore through one of the narrow arrow slits and ricocheted around the inside of the loft. Miller ducked, as if that would do any good.

Cole's eyes had never left his scope. He was looking for something, anything, that might give away the enemy sniper's position. The bastard was dug in good. He was well aware of Cole's hiding place. But Cole had yet to figure out where the enemy sniper was hiding.

Down below, one of the medics trying to help a wounded Borinqueneer suddenly slumped over. He was behind a solid section of the parapet, sheltering him from enemy fire coming from the road. The bullet could only have come from the hilltop.

The sniper up there knew his business. Considering the distance, he was also a damn good shot. He had Cole pinned down in the watchtower, and he was still managing to pick off the defenders.

"There's still another sniper up there," Cole said. "The only reason we ain't seen him yet is because he's smarter than the others."

Cole decided that he'd had enough. There was no time for patience in the middle of a battle. "Sir, I'm about to do something foolish."

"What do you mean?"

"Sometimes, the best way to bait a trap is to act the fool. That sniper could keep me pinned down all day and we ain't got time for that." Cole nodded toward the gap in the wall made by a mortar round. "I'm going to stand in front of that big hole and see if I can lure him out. Short of that, maybe I can see where he's shooting from if I'm standing up."

Cole started to get up, but Miller dragged him back down. "No, you don't. I'm not letting you do that and get yourself shot."

"Sir—"

"Shut up and give me your helmet," he said. The pilot was still wearing the bush hat. Reluctantly, Cole traded, then watched as the pilot made his way to the gap and crouched beside it, ready to expose himself to the enemy's view. "Ready?"

Still on the rifle, Cole grunted.

The pilot stood up and stepped in front of the gap. He raised the binoculars to study the hilltop. Nothing happened. "How long—"

A bullet snapped past his head and he dove for cover before the sniper could fire again.

"I saw him through the binoculars," Miller exclaimed excitedly. "There was a muzzle flash right at—"

"Twelve o'clock," Cole said. "Now, give me back my helmet."

"Wait, you're not going to stand in that gap, are you?"

"Hell no, I ain't as dumb as you," Cole said. "The helmet is for good luck."

Cole settled the helmet with its Confederate flag back on his head. He touched the flag with his trigger finger, then pressed his eye back to the scope. He held the sight picture he had seen earlier in his mind's eye.

He could not see the sniper, but he knew where he was.

He already had a good sense of the range from the other shots that he had put on the two other enemy snipers. He put the crosshairs right where he wanted them, started to squeeze the trigger.

Another shot hit the watchtower, but Cole hadn't even seen the muzzle flash.

"I didn't see him," Miller said, binoculars still on the hilltop through one of the arrow slits. "There's nothing to shoot at up there."

Cole didn't respond. He was too focused on a spot back in the rocks that seemed like it didn't belong. Maybe it was a shadow, or maybe it was the enemy sniper.

Miller was telling him again that there wasn't any target, but Cole wasn't listening. What he might have told the lieutenant commander was that instinct is what we have when the facts fail us.

He fired.

* * *

Wu watched through the binoculars as the arrogant sniper had displayed himself through the gap in the wall. It had been the same sniper with the flag on his helmet. Deng's shot at him had just missed.

"You missed!" Wu pointed out. For once, he was not smiling.

"Yes," Deng said through gritted teeth as Wu pointed out the obvious. "I will not miss again."

Wu gazed through the binoculars, but the sniper was no longer there. "You won't get another chance like that."

Deng fired again, this time raising a puff of dust near one of the arrow slits. Surely, the enemy sniper was watching them through one of these.

"You missed again," Wu said.

Major Wu had just turned to further chastise Deng when the bullet came in and hit Deng square in the forehead. The neat hole appeared just beneath the brim of Deng's *ushanka* cap.

Wu ducked, his heart hammering. The other two snipers that the enemy had claimed had been forward of this position. Deng and Wu had set themselves farther back, well hidden in the rocks. He could see the watchtower below, but it seemed impossible for the sniper in the watchtower to see them.

However, Deng now lay slumped over the rifle, his eyes bugging out from the force of the impact.

The bullet had come out of nowhere and killed Deng. Wu was incredulous. He looked at Deng's dead form in disbelief. How was this even possible? The American sniper had killed not just Deng, but Liu and Huang, both capable snipers in their own right.

In a fit of rage, Wu reached for the rifle and began to wrest it from Deng's dead hands. It would now be up to him to return fire and eliminate this enemy for once and for all.

Keeping low and out of sight behind the boulder, Wu fumbled with the unfamiliar weapon. Was it even loaded? He wasn't sure how to check. How was the scope sighted in? Would he hold low, high, or right on the target? He realized that he had never been schooled in the actual use of this rifle.

As these questions swirled around Wu's mind, he came to the realization that perhaps he was not the best man for this job. He was a political officer; he was not a sniper.

But then, a deeper emotion began to take hold. For the first time, a frisson of fear went through Wu. The American sniper had managed to kill Deng, who had been tough and competent, seemingly unstoppable. Wu had been stingy with his praise of Deng, but the man had been highly capable. If he had fallen, would Wu be next?

Not if he could help it.

Wu slung the valuable rifle across his back. Deng's rifle with its telescopic sight was hard to come by. It would be up to him later to find a man who could put the rifle to good use.

He crawled toward the edge of the steep slope leading back down to the road. One good thing was that he was out of view of the sniper. But getting off this hilltop wasn't going to be easy. First, he had to work his way around the jutting lip at the top of the cliff, his feet dangling beneath him and his heart hammering. Finally, his legs dropped low enough so that his boots touched the steep slope.

He soon found that climbing up had been easier than climbing down. It was hard to see past his feet, so that he was moving blindly down the hill. His boots slipped every few feet on the loose patches of dirt and shale so that he nearly began tumbling backwards down the slope to certain death. His head swam, made dizzy by the height, and he feared that he was going to lose his balance. This wasn't going to work.

He got himself turned around and readjusted the rifle so that it was slung across his front. In a way, this was worse, because he could see how far he would fall if he began to tumble. However, he had more control over his descent.

Using his hands to slow himself, ignoring the fact that they were being scraped raw, Wu slithered on his backside all the way to the bottom of the cliff.

Although there were many dead, he saw that the attack against the fort was now far more organized. The return fire from the defenders had slackened, thanks in part to Wu's snipers before they had been killed. Even the guns of the tanks had fallen silent, although they still spit machine-gun fire like hissing, cornered iron dragons.

Wu grinned, pleased to see that the tide of battle was turning in their favor.

CHAPTER TWENTY-TWO

As COLE and Lieutenant Commander Miller climbed down from the watchtower, it was becoming more evident that the battle for the fortress had reached a turning point. Below, Chinese soldiers swarmed across the road in coordinated attacks. Some troops focused on dismantling the barricade, while others crept closer to the walls of the fort itself, firing all the way.

On the fortress wall, with so many wounded, there were fewer defenders now to shoot back. Those who could still fight were having to scavenge ammunition from the dead and wounded. Whoever had called this place the Alamo wasn't far wrong.

"We can't hold out much longer," Cole said.

"Should we pull out? I guess that's up to Lieutenant Ballard."

Cole shook his head. "Ballard is badly wounded, along with Sergeant Weber. They've both been dosed with morphine. Lieutenant Dunbar is down in his tank, which means he's got his hands full. You know what? That makes you the ranking officer up here on the wall."

"Ranking officer? Hell, I'm the *only* officer still standing," Miller said. "But I've got to say, I feel a lot more at home in the cockpit."

Cole nodded, appreciating the officer's honesty, and decided to offer some advice. Most officers did not want to hear anything from enlisted men, but by the pilot's own admission, he was in a different situation. "Sir, we might have called this place the Alamo, but it doesn't have to end the same way," Cole said. "We've held the Chinese off for as long as we could. I hope they put that time to good use back at HQ and brought up some reinforcements."

"You're not talking about surrendering, I hope."

"Hell no, sir. I'm talking about living to fight another day."

"Good. I like the sound of that. Anyhow, I'll be damned if I'll surrender to the Communists and get paraded around for their cameras like a monkey in the zoo."

"You would be the lucky one, sir. The Chinese won't take many prisoners. They never do. They'll kill all of the wounded, maybe the Borinqueneers because they don't look like proper Americans or even speak any English, and they will definitely slaughter the Koreans."

"Those bastards would kill Jang-mi and all the rest?" Lieutenant Commander Miller looked stricken by the thought of the fate that might befall Jang-mi and Seo-jun, not to mention the other villagers. "We can't let that happen."

"We've done our part," Cole said. "Our orders were to fight a delaying action, not stop a whole battalion. I reckon we have delayed them all that we can."

"I hope it's enough."

"If we leave now, there's a chance that we can get out ahead of the Chinese, especially if we have a rear guard to hold them off. We can come out on the other side of the barrier, which the Chinese still have to cross."

"We'll need to gather the wounded and make stretchers for those who can't walk. We'll leave anything else we can't carry, except for weapons."

"What about those two tanks?" Cole asked.

"What about them?"

"I have an idea for how we can put them to use."

"I'm all ears."

Cole explained his plan, and Miller nodded.

"All right, let's move out," Lieutenant Commander Miller said. "That's an order."

* * *

AT THE FOOT of the fortress wall, the two tanks and their crews fought for their lives. The Chinese were throwing everything they had at the tanks, intent on revenge after the tanks had wreaked so much carnage on the road.

"Our gun is useless, sir," the gunner reported. "We can't depress the barrel low enough to hit these bastards."

"I know, I know," Lieutenant Dunbar said impatiently. He was well aware that the tanks were in trouble. "Fire in short bursts to hold them off and preserve our ammunition," Dunbar said to the crew of tank Twenty-one, then relayed the same message to the crew of tank Twenty-two.

Private Hardy was crammed into a corner of the tank, trying to keep out of the way—which wasn't easy in such a tight space. He could hear enemy rounds of small arms fire hammering insistently on the armor plating of the tank. Without thinking about what he was doing, Hardy put his hands over his ears as if hoping that he could squeeze out those sounds.

"We're low on ammo, Lieutenant," came the reply from tank Twenty-two, crackling over the radio. With the other tank just a short distance away, the note of fear in the other tanker's voice registered clearly.

"Short bursts," Dunbar repeated.

He knew that there was no hope of resupply. When they were out of ammo for the machine guns, that was it. Once the Chinese swarmed the tanks, it would all be over. Sure, they could button up and hold out for a while, but for what purpose?

They would just be caught inside like sardines in a can. The thought brought up an unhelpful image of a spinster aunt, peeling open a can of sardines to feed to her many cats. Dunbar shuddered at the memory of the sharp smell of fish and those nasty, mewling cats. Those enemy hordes weren't much different, waiting to claw them to pieces.

If nothing else, the Chinese could pour gasoline onto the tank and set it on fire. If the burning gas didn't seep into whatever chinks it could find in the armor, then the flames would slowly suck all the oxygen out of the tank. Dunbar had seen the aftermath of this approach more than once.

He wanted a better ending for his tank crews, but he was at a loss.

"Sir?" The gunner was asking him something.

"What?" Dunbar snapped.

"We're almost out of ammo for the fifty."

"That's just great."

"What are we supposed to do, sir?"

He noticed the others looking at him, a little surprised. He knew that they had always been able to count on him for solutions or to get them out of a jam. But Dunbar was finally out of answers.

He reached down and drew his sidearm, then jacked a round into the chamber. The sound was so loud in the confines of the tank that it made Hardy jump.

"Listen, fellas, I won't tell anybody how this ends for him, but I know how it ends for me. When the time comes, I'm not going to be burned alive inside this tank, and I'm sure as hell not going to surrender." He held up the pistol. "If any of you feel the same way, let me know. I'll shoot myself last."

The inside of the tank grew quiet as the crew considered the dreadful decision that they must make in the next few minutes.

That's when the radio crackled, breaking the silence.

"This is Lieutenant Commander Miller, up here on the Alamo," came the voice. The pilot sounded almost cheerful.

Dunbar grabbed the radio. "Miller? Where's Lieutenant Ballard?"

"Wounded. Listen, we are pulling out."

Dunbar might have argued that he was the ranking Army officer and it wasn't a pilot's decision to make. But the way he saw it, the time had come either to retreat or die in their tanks. With the enemy pressing in around them, he wondered if it wasn't already too late for options.

"We'll have to abandon the tanks," he said. "I hate to do it, but they will only slow us down. Anyhow, we don't have enough gas to make it back."

"You're right about leaving the tanks, but we've got an idea for that," Miller said, then explained his plan.

Lieutenant Dunbar nodded, then signed off. For the first time in hours, something like a grin crossed his grim features. He gave the order to fire up the engines one last time.

The tank crew had overhead the order to retreat, but it was easier said than done. There was the best part of an enemy battalion shooting at them. With the barricade across the road, the tanks were as boxed in as the Chinese battalion. Even a tank would be hard-pressed to smash through that mess.

"Where to, sir?" the driver asked, clearly puzzled.

"If we could do it, I'd have you drive us back to Seoul," Dunbar said. "Short of that, I'd say we've got enough gas for one last fight."

As it turned out, the tanks didn't have far to go. With engines roaring, they charged across the clearing toward the road. The troops in front of them scattered, being no match for several tons of churning steel.

Individual soldiers came at them with Bangalore torpedoes, heading for the tracks in hopes of disabling the tanks. The tanks' machine guns picked off the attackers they could see, but others ran at them from their blind flanks, ready with their destructive stick grenades.

A rifle fired from the fortress wall, dropping one attacker with each shot. It was Cole, giving the tanks a clear path toward the road.

"Slow it down!" Lieutenant Dunbar barked, worried that their momentum was going to carry them over the cliff on the far side of the road. The tank did not have the precision handling of a sports car. "If we go over the edge, that's it!"

The engine slowed, and they were joined by tank Twenty-two.

"Easy does it. I'll bet nobody has ever parallel-parked in a tank before."

Maneuvering carefully in the tight space between the fort and the road, the two tanks positioned themselves end to end, nosing into the piled logs and brush to add their tons of armored steel to the barrier across the road.

The lieutenant ordered everybody out and the crews of both tanks fled through the hatches. Fortunately for them, their sudden maneuver had caused the enemy fire to slacken enough that they all managed to get off the tanks and on the other side of the barrier without anyone being hit.

Like the captain of a sinking ship, Dunbar was the last man out. However, he still had one last task. Taking a jerry can of gasoline, he tipped it over to flood the inside of the tank. From the top of the tank, the sheer face of the cliff was just below. When he glanced that way at the yawning space, the gasoline fumes and vertigo made him feel dizzy.

He shook his head to clear it. He wasn't done yet.

Bullets whistled overhead as he pulled the pin on a grenade and dropped it down the hatch of his tank.

"Sorry about this, old girl," he muttered. "Fire in the hole."

A gout of flame erupted through the hatch and the tank shuddered. He ran over to the other tank to pour gasoline and drop a grenade down its hatch as well.

The tanks were now burning madly, so that at any moment the ammunition inside was going to blow sky high.

Dunbar figured that he would scramble over the barrier, but the piles of brambles caught at his uniform like barbed wire, and jagged branches gouged at him no matter which way he crept. No wonder the barrier had been so effective in holding back the enemy. Finally, he landed in a scratched heap on the other side.

"Remind me not to do that again," he said.

Nearby, the surviving defenders were joining the tank crew on the road. They had used the back way out to escape the fort. Dunbar shook his head at the sight of so many wounded. Many were wounded in the shoulders or arms and could still walk. The worst of the wounded were on makeshift stretchers and carrying them was a back-breaking task that was going to delay the retreat. Nobody even considered leaving them, because that meant certain death at the hands of the enemy.

The barrier and the furiously burning tanks would slow down the Chinese, but for how long?

* * *

COLE TOOK a drink of water from his canteen, having much the same thoughts as the tank commander. There were a lot of walking wounded and a handful of stretchers. He considered all the long miles back to the MLR, much of it through rough country. The barrier would hold back such a determined enemy for only so long.

He nodded, having made up his mind.

He looked around for the kid. If he had been wounded at the front line, he would have been sent to an aid station at the very least. But out here, when every man was needed, the medic had patched him up and given him a tiny dose of morphine that dulled the pain but kept him in action.

"Kid, get me a spare rifle from one of the wounded," Cole said. "Make sure it's loaded and has some extra clips. Then put it by that log there."

"What do you need the rifle for, Hillbilly? You've already got your sniper rifle."

"Just do it, kid. We ain't got much time."

Of course, the kid figured out what they were for. The painkillers hadn't addled his mind that much, at least. "We're going to fight them off, aren't we? They can only come across the barrier in small groups, so we'll have a chance to pick them off. We can hold them off for a while, at least until everybody else gets away."

"Ain't no *we* about it, kid. You go on with the rest. I'm going to stay right here."

"What are you talking about? I can't leave you here alone. You can't face all those Chinese by yourself—"

Cole interrupted him. "I've already made up my mind and there's no changing it."

"No, you can't—"

Cole held out his hand in a gesture meant to end further argument. "Maybe I'll come out the other side of this and maybe I won't. Either way, it's been good knowing you, kid. You ever get to Gashey's Creek, look up Norma Jean Elwood for me, will you? Tell her how much I appreciated those letters and that none of any of this was her fault. I've made my own choices in this world, and that's a fact."

With tears on his cheeks, the kid shook Cole's hand.

"Go on. Catch up with the others." Cole nodded toward the barrier, where the massed enemy could be seen on the other side of the flames, looking for a way through. "Now is the time to git while the gittin' is good."

Once the kid had left, Cole turned his attention to the defenses at hand. He knew that he couldn't hold the Chinese off forever. There were simply too many of them. But he could hold them off for long enough that what remained of the task force could have a chance of escaping.

On the other side of the barrier, the enemy was making every effort to get past the obstruction. It didn't seem to matter that the tanks were burning. Soldiers were sacrificed to pull away logs or flaming brush, even if it meant catching on fire themselves. Bit by bit, one log and stone at a time, the barrier was being dismantled. When that happened, the enemy would come pouring through.

Cole picked up the M-1 and started shooting through the flames at the figures on the other side. The licking fire made the figures seem devilish and inhuman, like demons from the underworld. Cole fired again and again, his bullets adding to the misery on that side of the barrier. He reloaded and fired until the magazine was empty.

An hour went by as the enemy worked to tear down the barrier and Cole shot at them. Now and then, someone shot back, but the bullets went wide. Despite his efforts, the barrier slowly came apart. The tanks were burning themselves out, leaving smoldering skeletons that the Chinese soldiers clambered onto—never mind that the metal was still so hot that the soles of their thin rubber shoes melted. They were urged forward by their commanders and their political officers, which meant that there was no choice but to go forward.

"Come on, you sons of bitches," Cole muttered, taking aim as soldiers began to get through, first in ones and twos. Cole picked them off. He had wanted the semiautomatic M-1 for just this reason because he could drop soldiers as fast as he could pull the trigger.

A small group charged across and Cole put down the rifle when it clicked on an empty chamber, then pulled the pin on a grenade and threw it. That held back the enemy for a little while, at least.

Another group charged, and Cole threw another grenade. He still had one more grenade to go.

Cole reached for his rifle, picking up the Springfield this time. His rate of fire was slower, but he liked the feel of the familiar stock in his hands. Better to die with an old friend, he supposed.

He put the rifle to his shoulder and fired, dropping another soldier.

But now, more and more soldiers streamed through the barrier, gathering in the road in front of Cole. They were led by a political officer who looked as if he had been through the wringer, his once-fancy uniform now torn and dirty. Cole thought that the Chinese officer had the same frantic energy as a mean little banty rooster.

Across the road, the two men locked eyes and a jolt of recognition passed between them. Cole could see that this was the officer who had terrorized the village and tried to capture the downed pilot. This was also the officer who had been on the hilltop, directing the snipers shooting down at the parapet.

The son of a bitch seemed to know Cole, too—he was smiling at Cole with a wolfish grin.

"*Nín!*" the Chinese officer shouted.

"You," Cole muttered back.

Cole tried to pick him off, but somehow, the officer always managed to keep a buffer of soldiers in front of him. The mass of soldiers grew, fanning out down the road and pressing toward Cole, forcing him closer to the edge of the cliff beyond the road.

He kept shooting. More Chinese swarmed onto the road now, his bullets barely making a dent in their numbers. A few bullets whistled around Cole, then stopped. To his surprise, the Chinese officer seemed to be ordering the men not to shoot.

Cole didn't plan on returning the favor. He fired at a man no more than a dozen feet away who looked ready to rush him.

Cole realized that the Chinese weren't trying to shoot him anymore. There were at least twenty rifles pointed at him, but nobody was shooting. They intended to capture him.

Cole remembered what Lieutenant Commander Miller had said about the Chinese wanting to put prisoners on parade like animals in a zoo.

"Like hell you will," Cole said. For good measure, he shot another enemy. The faces of the soldiers looked terrified, knowing that they might be next, but they held their fire. They were more scared of the officer than they were of Cole.

Cole was down to his last clip. He fired several more times, but the Chinese just stepped over the bodies of the dead and tightened the circle around him, trapping Cole against the cliff.

Finally, he had one bullet left. Not sure what else to do, Cole lowered the rifle muzzle but kept the Springfield pressed to his shoulder.

The officer stepped forward, still wearing that broad grin. He held his hand out toward Cole, indicating that he should hand over his rifle.

Cole looked past the officer at the grim Chinese faces encircling him. He edged backwards, trying to put as much space between them as possible, but there was no place left for Cole to go. He was at the edge of the cliff. He looked over his shoulder at the yawning emptiness. He saw treetops, boulders, the glimmer of water far below.

Pretty as a picture postcard, he thought.

"You surrender," the Chinese officer said in passable English, gesturing again for Cole to hand over his rifle.

If he made any effort to raise his rifle now, he would be riddled with bullets—or those soldiers would rush him and capture him once he had shot down one last soldier.

Damn, but he hated to give up when he still had one bullet left.

The officer watched him expectantly, still smiling. "*Tóuxiáng!* You surrender!" he repeated more insistently.

"You can go to hell," Cole said.

With his back to the void, there was nowhere else to go. He wasn't sure what he was going to do next until he did it.

Cole stepped off the cliff.

The Chinese watched in amazement, too stunned to react. For an instant, Cole appeared to defy gravity and hung in the air. It was just enough time to raise the rifle and shoot that banty rooster of an officer through the head.

Then Cole fell.

CHAPTER TWENTY-THREE

WHAT REMAINED of Task Force Ballard began its retreat toward the Jamestown Line, abandoning the fortress. They had accomplished their mission, which was to delay the advancing Chinese troops. Vastly outnumbered, they'd never had a chance of stopping the enemy.

Battered and bloody, the survivors hurried down the mountain road. The wounded who were able to do so limped along, often supported by a buddy's shoulder. Several other wounded had to be carried on stretchers by the more able-bodied. No one still living had been left behind. As for the dead, well, they were beyond caring. Although it was normally a matter of pride to bring back the dead, that was not possible without vehicles.

There was no panic or fear in anyone's eyes, however. The look in their eyes was one of defiance, indicating that they had done all that they could, and now the only option was retreat.

"Where's Cole?" Lieutenant Commander Miller asked the kid, looking around for the sniper. "I haven't seen him. I figured that if anyone knew where to find him, it would be you."

The kid just shook his head. "You know that hillbilly. Cole is stubborn as a mule. He stayed behind to hold back the Chinese at the barrier, to try and buy us some time."

"By himself! That's crazy." The officer turned and started to walk toward the rear of the line as if he was seriously contemplating going back and fetching Cole, but the kid reached out and grabbed him by the arm to stop him.

"Sorry, sir. I know you are an officer and I shouldn't do that. But there's no point in going back now. If anybody could take on the enemy single-handedly, it was Cole. But let's face it, sir. He's gone now. We need you to take charge and get us back."

Miller stared at the road behind them. Smoke still stretched into the sky, but they had made enough progress that the fort and barricade were out of sight, more than a mile away. "How old are you?"

"Nineteen, sir."

"You're pretty smart for nineteen, kid. I guess you're right," Miller said. "Between me and Lieutenant Dunbar and his tank crews, I suppose we can keep this column moving. It can't be any harder than flying a plane, anyway."

"Yes, sir."

Miller looked behind them one last time and shook his head. "That goddamn hillbilly. If we make it back in one piece, it's because of him."

But the task force wasn't out of the woods yet. Cole was just one man, and there remained hundreds of Chinese soldiers coming up fast behind them.

"We need to pick up the pace," Miller said. "Spread the word. Double-time!"

When they had marched up this road the day before, it had been in tight-knit groups. For the most part, the Korean villagers had not mingled with the Borinqueneers or the veterans of the rifle squad. Now, everyone was mixed together, helping each other where they could. A wounded Borinqueneer limped along with the help of a Korean guerilla. Two soldiers from Ballard's original squad carried a stretcher with a wounded Korean. Before, there had been language barriers between them. Now, none of that seemed to matter. They were united in one purpose.

Cisco moved among the Borinqueneers, helping where to could to urge them along or tend to the wounded.

"*Aqui!*" someone shouted, and Cisco ran to help a man whose bandages had come undone. Quickly, he worked to staunch the fresh flow of blood as the soldier winced in pain. He urged the soldier to hold the fresh bandage in place and keep moving. They had no time to bind the wound properly. Cisco shook his head. What this soldier needed was rest, fresh water, and something to eat, but there wasn't time for much else. To stop now meant certain death at the hands of the enemy.

"Move it!" Miller shouted, the urgent tone of his voice needing no translation for those who didn't speak English.

Behind them, maybe not more than a mile away, the Chinese soldiers were coming after them. They couldn't see any sign of them yet, but there was no doubting that the enemy was in pursuit all the same. The enemy was not encumbered by their own wounded, which they had left behind to die.

If the enemy caught up to the remains of the battered task force, nobody would reach the line.

"How much farther do you think we've got to go?" Miller asked the tank officer, who was helping to keep everyone moving along as rapidly as possible.

"At least five miles," he replied.

"We're not gonna make it that far before they catch us," Miller said.

"That's what I'm thinking," Dunbar agreed.

"Any ideas?"

"I'll take my men and form a rear guard." He grinned bitterly. "It won't be the same as a tank, but at least we can hold them off for a while if the enemy catches up to us."

Miller agreed to the plan and the tank officer assembled his men, who moved to the back of the column. They would keep moving, but fall back to fight if the need arose.

Unfortunately, even that small measure had cost them precious time. Some of the tankers had been carrying the wounded and had to shift their burdens to others, which required some organization.

Time was something that the retreating task force didn't have.

"Here they come!" the kid shouted.

Looking behind them, they could see the vanguard of the enemy, approaching at a trot. There were only a handful of soldiers, but it was clear that their intent was to catch the task force. They were like hounds chasing rabbits. The road went around a bend, and the vanguard in the distance was temporarily lost from sight.

Weapons that had been slung over shoulders were put back into hands. Fresh rounds were jacked into chambers by grim-faced soldiers. They all knew that this would be a fight to the end this time.

"What's that?" someone shouted.

"I hope to hell those belong to us and it's not more of the damn Chinese!"

Miller looked up. He had heard it, too; the unmistakable sound of aircraft. He counted three planes. The planes were coming in low, settling in above the road. To his relief, he recognized them as United States planes.

One of the Corsairs waggled its wings at the task force, where the soldiers waved their arms wildly. Then the planes swept toward the north and the pursuing Chinese troops. Explosions and machine-gun fire from the planes marched up the road toward the enemy.

"Give 'em hell, boys!" Miller shouted. He ached to be back in the cockpit himself, but for now, all that mattered was getting these survivors back to the line. He ran to help a wounded soldier who had stumbled, dragging the man's arm across his own shoulders. "Let's go!"

* * *

TWO HOURS LATER, thanks to the intervention of the planes, the task force survivors reached the Jamestown Line. As they entered the barricades and trenches, some collapsed as if they had just finished running a race. In a sense they had—they had managed to outrun the enemy.

More reinforcements had been brought up to the line, and with the air cover and added artillery, they braced themselves for a Chinese attack. What had been a thin line of defense was now much more solid, ready to repel the enemy.

By then, the enemy had lost all element of surprise. The Chinese troops were battered from the battle at the fort and then from having been caught out in the open by the planes. When the attack against the main line came, it had no more effect than a wave crashing on the shore in all its brief fury, only to quickly recede into the sea. There was no second wave.

All along the MLR, the defenders held their breath and kept their weapons close, but the Chinese had retreated to dig into the hills and lick their wounds. The Jamestown Line had held.

* * *

ONCE AGAIN, Don Hardy was at a borrowed typewriter the next morning, trying to put into words the experiences of the last few days. The *Stars and Stripes* published straightforward battlefield accounts. There wasn't any space in the newspaper's pages for philosophical matters or what the editors like to call navel-gazing. Just why had the battle been fought or what had been won? Those questions would not be addressed in *Stars and Stripes*.

Laboring that morning at the grimy keys, Hardy could not know that thirty years later, as a more seasoned writer, he would win the Pulitzer Prize for a history of the Korean War. But for now, he was still finding his way around the battered keyboard, struggling to put the images in his head into words. He paused just long enough to take a swig from a mug of bitter coffee balanced on the board set across two crates that served as his desk.

Like everyone else who had survived the last stand by the task force at the fort, he was exhausted. He would have loved nothing more than to crawl into a tent somewhere and sleep. However, he needed to get this story out. His typed pages would need to be delivered by Jeep to the *Stars and Stripes* editors and the sooner he sent them on their way, the better.

Already, his writing had changed considerably since coming to Korea as a budding journalist. His early articles had been filled with literary allusions and even a few poetic descriptions that were sneaked in, an echo of his many college literature classes.

The sights and sounds of war had cured him of that urge. For example, what place did a couplet from Wordsworth have in the mud and blood of Korea?

. . .

*A*ND THEN MY *heart with pleasure fills,*
  And dances with the daffodils.

HARDY SHOOK HIS HEAD. His article contained nothing flowery or
poetic. Just the cold, hard facts, like what it felt like to turn to your
buddy and see that he was dead with a Chinese bullet through him.

Still, it made him a little sad to turn his back on Wordsworth and
all the rest. Maybe all the fighting now was so that there would be a
place for poetry in the future.

A clerk approached, wielding a dented coffee pot.

"More joe?"

Hardy nodded. "Got anything stronger?"

The clerk looked around, then surreptitiously went to a bag,
produced a flask, and poured a dose into Hardy's mug.

"The colonel would have my ass if he saw that, but I figure you
deserve it." He shook his head. "It's amazing what you guys did."

"It's the Battle of Thermopylae in the Korean mountains, is what
it is."

"Not sure I know about that battle, but if you say so." The clerk
added another splash of whiskey to Hardy's mug.

"Thermopylae was where a group of Spartan soldiers held off an
entire army at a mountain pass, thus saving Greece from invasion."

"When was that? Back in forty-two?" the clerk asked, thinking that
Hardy was referring to a battle from the last war, when the Germans
had attacked Greece.

"More like 480 B.C.," Hardy said. He took a gulp of the bourbon-
laced coffee, a combination that somehow amplified the worst qualities
of both beverages. He choked it down and nodded his thanks to the
clerk, then turned his attention back to the typewriter.

"You're talking about ancient times. Guess that's why I never heard
of it. Hell, nobody around here can remember what happened last
week, let alone two thousand years ago."

Ignoring the clerk, Hardy kept typing. He was getting better at writing quickly and clearly, having been whipped into shape by the beady-eyed military editors with their sharp pencils. Scarcely an adjective survived their attention. Hardy described the last stand in hard detail, including the heroism of the Puerto Rican troops. Nobody would question their courage now. Their earlier failures had been forgotten and threats of court martial had quietly been swept under the rug. Every last one of the Borinqueneers was a hero now.

There was no word yet on the fate of the sniper, Caje Cole, who had stayed behind to single-handedly hold back the enemy so that the task force could retreat. He wrote what happened, then shook his head. The account seemed unbelievable as he wrote it, but anyone who had ever been caught in the gaze of Cole's cold gray eyes wouldn't doubt it for a minute. If Cole didn't deserve a posthumous Medal of Honor, he didn't know who did.

For all the heroism that had taken place at the fort, however, Hardy couldn't help the sense that this was just one more meaningless battle in a meaningless war.

The Chinese kept pushing, but it was clear that they had their problems as well. The Chinese were poorly supplied and heavily bombed. Their losses were atrocious. How much longer could they continue this war?

Meanwhile, men on both sides continued to fight and die. The civilian population in the war zone continued to suffer.

Eventually, the fighting would end and a truce would be declared at the negotiating table in Panmunjom. The Chinese had kept up the pressure, attacking wherever they could, in what was essentially a land grab. When the negotiating stopped and an agreement was reached, nobody could expect the communists to withdraw from any of the territory they held. The enemy's strategy would prove to be effective.

"At least we held them off," the clerk announced. To his credit, he had left the command post and done his duty with rifle and bayonet in the line until the threat of being overrun by the enemy had passed.

"Don't worry, whatever we held, they'll be sure to give away at the negotiating table," Hardy said.

Hardy had seen the maps; the Jamestown Line was ten miles north of the 38th Parallel that was being discussed as the new boundary. He hated to see hundreds of square miles that they had fought for simply handed over to the Communists.

Hardy's fears would prove to come true. The Korean Peninsula would be divided along the 38th Parallel to create two countries: a Communist state north of the boundary and a Democracy to the south. No one yet had a crystal ball to see that the free people of South Korea would grow to become one of the world's great economies, while shortages and famine continued for decades in the north.

By the time the war was over, at least three million people would have died, many of the dead being civilians slaughtered on both sides. Adding to the butcher's bill, more than thirty thousand young American men had perished in the hills and valleys, along with more than one hundred thousand young South Korean soldiers, fighting for their freedom. The Korean Peninsula was soaked in blood from one end to the other.

All that was a story that was yet to be told. The final chapter had yet to be written. For now, Hardy struggled to tell what had happened at the fort, how a small task force had held off a Chinese battalion and possibly saved the entire Jamestown Line from crumbling. In the end, they had not fought for anyone but each other.

He typed the last word, gathered the pages, and ran to find a Jeep that would carry the news of what had happened at Outpost Alamo.

CHAPTER TWENTY-FOUR

COLE AWOKE to a world of hurt.

His heard hurt. He had crusted blood in his eyes. A big gash in his side. And he could barely move his right leg.

But it could have been worse. He hadn't expected to wake up at all.

Stepping off the cliff like that had been his way of turning the tables on the enemy and denying them the satisfaction of capturing him. He saw it as his final act of defiance in the face of defeat.

Or so he had thought. Because now here he was at the bottom of the cliff. Bloody and broken, but breathing.

There didn't seem to be any Chinese around, so he was thankful for that much. They must have thought he was dead.

Cole would have thought the same thing. He looked up, wondering how in hell he had survived. It was a good one hundred and fifty feet, maybe two hundred, to the top of that cliff. But it wasn't a straight drop. A big clump of trees grew about halfway up, jutting from a ledge, and another cluster of trees grew at the bottom.

If he had fallen straight down, he would have been flatter than a pancake. But he was lying under those trees at the bottom of the cliff.

"I'll be damned," he muttered.

He sort of recalled having hit those trees on the way down and they had slowed him down. He didn't remember anything after that. However, the trees at the bottom must have cushioned his fall like a big ol' feather bed. *Yeah, right.* More like how the ball felt after getting hit by the bat.

Cole lay flat on his back, his arms and legs flung out. He supposed that he looked like a picture he had once seen in a church book of a fallen angel, cast out of heaven for his sins and forced to live as a demon in the mortal world. He groaned and tried to roll over, but it took him a couple of attempts. Once he had managed to sit up, he took stock of his situation.

Aside from the blood in his eyes, his head seemed intact. At least he was thinking more or less clearly. A tree limb had speared him good in the side, laying him open clean down to the ribs, cracking a couple in the process. A little lower, and he would have been skewered in the guts. Still, it hurt like hell to breathe.

He could live with that. However, it was his leg that worried him the most. His right leg was fine. But the left leg twisted off at a funny angle. He had suffered broken bones twice as a boy, and they had been painful in their own way, a deep ache. His leg looked fairly shattered and he could hardly feel it, like it wasn't even part of him.

He'd have to deal with that soon, and he wasn't looking forward to it.

His rifle was long gone, surely lost in the fall, and out of bullets, anyhow. He was glad that he had saved the last one for that Chinese officer and put a rifle slug through his skull. No regrets about that.

Pistol? Gone. Somehow, he still had a grenade strapped to him. He ought to have used that up on the cliff. If things got too bad, he felt reassured that he could just blow himself up.

He also had his Bowie knife, which was the only tool he needed to survive. He drew it from the sheath and admired the mottled Damascus steel blade with its razor-sharp edge. He felt a sense of gratitude to his old friend Hollis Baily, who had made it in his workshop. Maybe one day, Cole would get to be as good at making knives. But first, he had to get the hell out of this valley and back to the American lines or he would be permanently missing in action.

First, he had to deal with his leg.

"This is gonna hurt some," he said aloud, just in case the fates were listening and decided to take pity on him.

Dragging himself around some more, he found some sturdy sticks. He then dragged himself to a pile of rocks and rearranged them enough to wedge his ankle between them. He had to admit that he felt sick to his stomach noticing that his left foot was pointing in an unnatural direction.

He sat up, took hold of his leg like it was a chunk of cordwood, counted to three, and twisted.

Birds flew out of the trees overhead when he screamed.

The pain made beads of sweat stand out on his forehead, but at least now, his foot was facing in the right direction.

Using strips cut from his uniform shirt, he bound the sticks against his leg to make a splint. Using a much longer stick, he was able to get back on his feet.

It hurt like hell. He couldn't exactly walk, but he could hobble.

Back home in the mountains, he had known people hurt just as bad in a farm accident, or at the sawmill, or even falling off the barn roof that they had been trying to fix. The hospital was a long ways off and getting there—and paying for it—had been beyond the ability of many country people in the Great Depression. Surviving a terrible accident wasn't always a blessing because it meant a lingering death with maybe some moonshine to dull the pain. Better to fall and break your neck than suffer.

He knew that by tomorrow morning that he would likely have a fever. If he didn't get help by then, he would probably die, too weak to move—infection finishing off what the fall had not. The Army doctors could fix him up—if he could get there in time.

"Ain't time to give up yet," he told himself, and started his slow, painful hobble toward the stream he had seen from the top of the cliff.

Cole hadn't seen any maps and he didn't know the name of this stream or this valley, but he knew the simple truth of water, which was that small streams flowed into bigger streams, which flowed into rivers. Along the banks of a river, there would be help.

He soon reached the running water. The sound of it gave him

solace, for running water meant life. He knew this stream would flow into the Imjin River, which in turn flowed past the Army outpost.

Of course, there might be more than a few Chinese between here and there, but he tried not to worry about that yet.

The water was still muddy from all the monsoon rains, but he didn't care. His canteen was gone, so with great effort, Cole got down on his belly and drank his fill like some wild animal at a watering hole. He sucked in gulps of the gritty water through blood lips, thinking that he had never tasted anything so good.

A little while later, he realized that he needed to urinate. He was not reassured to see his red-tinged flow spattering on the sand. The blood surely meant he had internal injuries. He'd thought that maybe he had a day to find help, but maybe he'd been wrong about that. Maybe he had a few hours.

He trudged along the bank of the stream, which ran swiftly, perhaps ten feet across. Rocks and brambles lined the far shore, but he was lucky to have the sandy side where the going was easier.

He found comfort in the sound of running water against the backdrop of utter quiet. There was something mysterious in the babbling of water, as if it spoke a message he couldn't quite hear. Then again, maybe he was already getting delirious if he was listening for the stream to tell him something.

The stream did remind him of being a boy back home in the mountains, running his trapline. Back then, would he ever have thought that he would be limping along a stream in Korea? Not likely. He'd never even heard of the place.

Cole wondered if he ever would get home again. He wouldn't have minded wandering that stream again. He wouldn't have minded seeing Norma Jean Elwood, either. But he supposed that this remote valley in Korea was as good a place to die as any.

He pushed the thought from his mind. *You ain't dead yet.*

Although the fight at the fort had started at dawn, the shadows already stretched long and the sun was sinking toward the mountaintops. The day seemed too short, but he was missing a big chunk of it. He must have been knocked out longer than he realized.

He pressed on as long as he could, but as it grew darker, he knew that he would have to stop for the night. He had no light of any kind, and if he stumbled and fell in the dark, he wasn't sure that he would have the energy to get back up.

He was also getting cold. And hungry. If he was going to do something about those two things, the time to do it was while he still had some daylight. Whatever food and matches he'd had in his pockets had been ripped away in the fall, so he would have to try something else.

Cole kept going until he found a wide, sandy bend in the stream where the waterway deepened and slowed, the current moving like a smooth brown muscle. Slowly, painstakingly, he gathered what he needed for a fire. First, he needed tinder. He found something that resembled milkweed and gathered the feathery tufts. Then he found bone-dry kindling that was buried deep in a pile of flood drift.

Using the walking stick for support, he managed to lower himself to his knees. Clearing a space in the sand, he built a fire lay that resembled an Indian teepee—bigger sticks on the outside, with a heart of fine shavings and the weed tuft. His hands shook, whether from cold or weakness he couldn't say.

There was no shortage of flint, and he held a sharp-edged piece in one hand and struck the stone with the spine of his knife.

It took a couple of tries, but he got some sparks. They skewed away and winked out, but he directed them the next time at the heart of tuft and shavings. Finally, a spark landed and lit the tuft. He blew gently, and the smoking ember turned into a tiny flame. The fire spread and grew, catching on the outer layers of the teepee. He felt welcome warmth on his face.

He knew that it was something of a risk, having a fire out here in Indian country. But if he didn't have a fire, the risk was that during the cool of night in his condition, he might die of exposure. Besides, there was no telling what critters might be prowling the night. Wolves and even tigers had once roamed these mountains before being wiped out by Japanese hunters decades before. These predators were supposedly gone now, but there were stories about a few surviving in the more remote places. Wouldn't that be a hell of a thing now, to get eaten by a tiger?

With the small fire going, he turned his attention to filling his empty belly. He had not eaten since the night before and getting this far down the bank of the stream had taken all his energy.

He had no rifle, not that he had seen any game, anyway. There wasn't any time to trap.

However, there would be fish in that deep water in the stream. He just didn't have a fishing pole, hooks, or any bait.

Cole considered his options. What he did have was a hand grenade.

As a boy, he remembered how he had once gone with his pa and some friends to the river. They had climbed into a leaky old skiff that the men had trouble rowing in the current. It hadn't helped that the men had been about half-drunk, or maybe mostly drunk, which wasn't unusual for his pa. These drunken fishermen had gotten hold of a few sticks of dynamite, which was popular then for the removal of stumps and large rocks from farm fields.

"We are gonna do us some hillbilly fishin'," his pa announced. "Best cover your ears, boy."

Cole did as he was told, then watched as his father lit a stick of dynamite and tossed it far out into the river.

The resulting explosion had sent a wave that nearly swamped the boat. Cole had found himself more excited than terrified. The men whooped. And then, in their drunken fashion, they had paddled the boat around to scoop up the stunned fish on the surface of the river.

"Time for some hillbilly fishin'," Cole said.

He pulled the pin on the grenade and tossed it into the deep water, then threw himself down in the sand.

The grenade lifted a geyser of water several feet in the air and shattered the stillness of the valley. He hoped to hell that the Chinese hadn't heard that.

He saw a couple of fish on the surface, just as he had hoped, but the fish began to drift away on the current. Cole realized that he had miscalculated. How would he get at these fish in his condition?

But as luck would have it, the blast had tossed one fish onto the bank nearby. Not fully stunned, the fish flopped around in an effort to get back into the water. Cole pounced on it, his ribs screaming in protest as he did so.

Soon, scaled and gutted, he had the fish on a stick over the fire. He didn't know what kind of fish it was, maybe something like a Korean small-mouth bass, but it smelled delicious. He could barely wait for it to finish roasting, and he then picked the bones clean and threw them into the stream along with the offal so as not to attract any critters.

He stretched out on the sand next to the fire, letting it be his guardian. The stars burned overhead. They had been there before him and would still be there long after he was gone. The question was, would he be going tonight?

Cole didn't fall asleep so much as he passed out.

He awoke a few hours later in the gray light of dawn. The fire had burned down to coals and he felt cold. His whole body ached and he felt feverish. But the pain felt good in a way because it meant that he was still alive.

With an effort, he managed to get back to his feet.

Covering the first twenty feet that morning took him half an hour. He was that stiff.

"Gonna have to pick up the pace," he told himself.

It was easier said than done, and mostly he was dragging his hurt leg, but the next twenty feet took considerably less time to cover. He kept going.

By the time he reached the Imjin River, the sun was high overhead. There wasn't any sign yet of the U.S. forces. He might still have miles to go following the riverbank before he came to any friendly forces— assuming that he didn't run into the Chinese first. Helpless as he was, they would make short work of him.

Also, he saw that he had a logistical problem. He needed to cross the stream. He was on the eastern shore, which meant that the stream itself blocked him from following the Imjin downriver.

Slowly, Cole waded into the stream. He hated water, having almost drowned as a boy during a trapping mishap. The water was deeper here where the stream emptied into the river, and he took his time, fighting against the tug of the current. If he went under, that would be that. He didn't have the strength or agility to do anything like swim. He cursed himself for not crossing the stream earlier, where it had been shallow, but he hadn't always been in his right mind.

When he finally reached the opposite bank, he had to crawl out and rest for a while. When he lifted his head, the sun had traveled some distance and he was shivering. He realized that he must have passed out again.

"Better get moving, you dumb hillbilly," he urged himself. He doubted that he would survive a second night out here at the mercy of the elements and animals, so he pushed on.

It was just getting dark when he saw the bridge ahead, then trucks and soldiers. To his relief, they were Americans. In fact, this was the same bridge that the tanks under Lieutenant Dunbar had protected during the monsoon flood by blasting debris out of the river.

He tried to call out to the soldiers, but his voice was a croak. He had no choice but to keep hobbling. The sentry on duty at the bridge clearly saw him, but ignored him. Then Cole realized that the man thought the ragged, bloody figure holding himself up with a stick was a Korean peasant.

"Go away, you damn gook," the soldier said. "No civilians across the bridge. No ticky, no laundry, get it? Now, beat it!"

Cole kept shambling forward, his voice a rusty rasp in his parched throat. "American," was all that he got out.

"Yeah, I'm American," the soldier said, annoyed. He took a step toward the figure on the road and raised his rifle butt, intending to teach the peasant a lesson. Then he halted and stared, wide-eyed, as he recognized that the ragged figure wore a torn U.S. uniform and had an American face, though bloodied and bruised.

The sentry hurried to help him, shouting for a medic.

"Holy cow, buddy," the sentry said, getting an arm around Cole to support him. "What happened to you?"

"I fell," Cole said.

For Cole, the fighting was over. A medic helped him into a Jeep and rushed him to the aid station. Early the next morning, when there was enough light to fly, choppers arrived to airlift him and other wounded to a MASH Unit. It would be the start of a painful recovery and a long journey from Korea to Japan to the United States, but Caje Cole was finally on his way home.

NOTE TO READERS

This novel was inspired by several unconnected events from the Korean War that came together here for the story. In the late stages of the war, the conflict entered the stalemate phase described by historian Max Hastings. Instead of fighting back and forth, the two opposing sides were now facing each other across a wide and fluid front. Communist forces still probed and attacked in an effort to gain as much territory as possible for when the negotiations of a truce finally reached a conclusion. Meanwhile, many fought and died as the "peace talks" dragged on.

Outpost Kelly was one of the places where that fighting took place. The background for the battle comes from *Outpost Kelly: A Tanker's Story*, an engaging memoir by Jack R. Siewert. The story of the 65th Infantry Borinqueneers that resulted in actual court-martial charges comes from the fight over a different hill, which has been combined here with events at Outpost Kelly just to streamline things. There's no doubt that the Borinqueneers faced many obstacles in terms of training, language barriers, and 1950s prejudice.

The last stand at Outpost Alamo draws upon several separate incidents but is itself fictitious. Interestingly enough, there really are many ancient mountain fortressses throughout Korea, which has such a fascinating history. Finally, it's worth noting that the dogfight against MiGs imagined here was inspired by several accounts. Thank you as always for reading.

—D.H.

ABOUT THE AUTHOR

David Healey lives in Maryland where he worked as a journalist for more than twenty years. He is a member of the International Thriller Writers and a contributing editor to The Big Thrill magazine. Visit him online at:

www.davidhealeyauthor.com

or

www.facebook.com/david.healey.books

Thank you for reading! If you enjoyed the story, please consider leaving a review on Amazon.com.

Made in the USA
Columbia, SC
15 September 2023

22946458R00133